TIM HARTWELL
Open Your Heart Trilogy
(Books 1-3)

Aeneas Middleton

TIM HARTWELL: Open Your Heart Trilogy (Books 1-3)

Tim Hartwell - Open Your Heart Trilogy is a work of fiction. The characters and events portrayed in this book are fictitious. Any similarity to real person, living or dead, is coincidental and not intended by the author.

Copyright © 2014 by Aeneas Middleton

All Rights Reserved. Under the U.S. Copyright Act of 1976, no part of this publication may be reproduced, distributed, or transmitted in any form or by any means, or stored in a database or retrieval system, without the prior written permission of the publisher.

Royal Middleton publishing
Baltimore, MD
royalmiddletonpublishing@gmail.com

ISBN-13: 978-0692261026
ISBN-10: 0692261028

Library of Congress Control Number: 2014913177

Middleton, Aeneas, 1980-
Tim Hartwell - Open Your Heart Trilogy:
by Aeneas Middleton
-
1st Edition | Open Your Heart Trilogy
Books One-Three (Bk. 1-3)
Copyedited by Ruth Goodman

Printed in the United States of America

Cover and book design by Aeneas Middleton

1 2 3 4 5 6 7 8 9 10 11

Mary doesn't care since the robe belonged to her mother, Lilly.

The robe with the Coat of Hartwell, the red shield on the bottom pocket, always reminds Mary of where she came from.

Mary places a kettle on the burner to make some char. "So tell me, why are you still up?"

"I couldn't sleep," says Tim, beginning to pick up steam as he talks. "I've been having these weird dreams about fantasy places—places that are so beautiful it feels like I'm actually there."

"Fantasy? Well, tell me what happens exactly," says Mary, pulling back a lock of her hair.

"I am in a dark place, not like any other. It has a spinning dial that makes a clicking sound. That's all I can remember," Tim answers, wiping sweat from his forehead.

He looks over to an hourglass, flips it over, and watches the sand flow down for a second. Mary notices he is trying to move away from the subject, as if she doesn't believe him.

"When I was younger, I had a similar dream about the spinning dial," says Mary. "I was about your age, and I went to your grandmother's house and asked her the same question." The tea kettle begins to whistle with a high pitch.

Mary takes the kettle from the

TIM HARTWELL: Open Your Heart Trilogy (Books 1-3)

TIM HARTWELL series
(Tim Hartwell Ennealogy)

Tim Hartwell - Open Your Heart Trilogy
(Part One) Includes:

Tim Hartwell and The Magical Galon of Wales (Book One)

Tim Hartwell and The Brutus of Troy (Book Two)

Tim Hartwell and The Death of Ages (Book Three)

*Tim Hartwell - Trust Your Heart Trilogy
(Part Two) Includes:

Tim Hartwell and The Death of Ages (Book Four)

*Tim Hartwell and The Wizards of Windsor (Book Five)

*TBA (Book Six)

*Tim Hartwell - Find Your Heart Trilogy
(Part Two) Includes:

TBA (Book Seven)

TBA (Book Eight)

TBA (Book Nine)

[*Coming soon]

TIM HARTWELL: Open Your Heart Trilogy (Books 1-3)

TIM HARTWELL
and the Magical Galon of Wales

Volume 1 (Pg. 5 - 233)

TIM HARTWELL
and the Brutus of Troy

Volume 2 (Pg. 237 - 467)

TIM HARTWELL
and the Death of Ages

Volume 3 (Pg. 468 - 729)

TIM HARTWELL: Open Your Heart Trilogy (Books 1-3)

Volume 1

- Original Copyright Information -

Copyright © 2010 by Aeneas Middleton

ISBN-13: 978-0615549217
ISBN-10: 0615549217

Library of Congress Control Number: 2011917864

Book One (Bk. 1)

TIM HARTWELL: Open Your Heart Trilogy (Books 1-3)

Contents

7   The Night Unfolds

62   Strafford's Proposition

104   Fight Near The Cicketts

123   Jump Over World's End

146   Accident on Crackwell Street

181   The Last Galon

196   Rise of Truth

219   Training Inside Massif

The Night Unfolds

The moon is shining over Carmarthen Bay in Tenby, Pembrokeshire, which is one of the most beautiful places in all of Wales. In Welsh, "Tenby" means "little fortress of the fish." The thirteenth century buildings, covered in pastel colors, flow all the way down Crackwell Street to the Esplanade. Tourists are walking through the town, and some are still walking past Tudor Merchant's house on Quay

Hill. Couples are screaming with joy as they walk back to the Belgrave Hotel on the Esplanade.

Across this seaside town, a young boy is sitting on the balcony with his legs through the metal fence. The boy happens to be Tim Hartwell, and he can't sleep because tomorrow is the last day of school before summer vacation. Not too far from where he is sitting, his mother is knocked out after a long day of work selling fish along the harbour and making honest pay.

Tim stands up so he can get a better look at the boats pulling into the docks below. He has always liked boats—the way they move and glide across the water. Sometimes, Tim turns his face to the sky with his eyes closed and listens to the water as it hits the shore and pulls away in the dark night.

Opening his eyes, Tim sticks his head out of the window, rubs his toes together, and knocks the sand from between his toes. Tim is completely out of it. He helped his mother fish earlier in the day. He now remembers his father, Humphrey Hartwell, who never really loved him that much.

Humphrey moved to America before Tim was one year old. Humphrey became a squire, got married, and had more kids. After Humphrey moved, Tim never heard from his father again. Humphrey was an intelligent, middle-age man with oversized feet.

The clicking of a vintage clock catches Tim off guard.

There are sounds of firecrackers, just up St. John's Hill on the edge of Norton. Another melody rises in the distance from a cream yacht with blue highlights.

A group of people is sailing on North Beach near Goscar Rock. Their singing wakes Tim's mother, Mary Hartwell, who was sleeping inside the apartment.

She calls to Tim in a loud tone, sounding like her late grandmother, Lilly Hartwell, who lived in Wolf's Castle for ninety-two years.

Mrs. Hartwell spent most of her life helping her mother sell clothes.

They worked long hours in the markets during Wolf's Castle festival week, which happens every year in the city.

Mary keeps vintage photos of her mother and her father, Benjamin Hartwell. She walks into the living room with a few of the photos. They are her good luck charms. She loves her family unconditionally.

Mary carries with her pictures of the sea. Pictures of ocean currents decorate every wall in the apartment.

A vase of flowers sits atop the nonworking fireplace. Mary picks up a couple of tulip petals that had fallen to the floor.

Heading into the kitchen, Mary grabs two white teacups from the cabinet above her. She opens the refrigerator and pulls out some cheese, along with laver bread and grilled tomatoes. She hands some Welsh bacon and laver bread to Tim. As he grabs a napkin, Mary tries to figure out why he is still up past eleven o'clock.

"What are you doing up so late, Timothy?" Mary asks.

Tim shrugs nonchalantly. He knows she only calls him Timothy when she's curious. "Everyone calls me Tim at school, Mam." Mary smiles, chuckling for a bit as she grabs her glasses from the desk near the head counter.

She reaches for her old robe, which is hanging on one of the kitchen chairs. One of the sleeves is torn, but stove and pours two cups of tea. Tim scratches his arm and asks more questions.

"What, what, did you say?" Tim whispers to the thoughts in his head.

"Have you ever heard about the Seven Wonders of Wales?" Mary asks. "Yes, I've heard of them. I just don't know the detailed history about them," Tim replies while eating his laver bread and taking sips of his tea. He looks worried as he waits for Mary to reply.

"Well, are you up for it?" Mary pauses as she drinks some of her tea.

Tim remains quiet as Mary starts to explain the story her mother used to read to her all the time.

"One night, I had a dream

exactly like yours. Lilly explained to me that I was dreaming about some of the old tales of the House of Hartwell.

"My parents shared with me that the Seven Wonders of Wales are actually magical locations to find the Spinning Heart. All of our descendants' secrets are in this book. Some of our family members were even beheaded for speaking about the use and knowledge of magic.

"In order to protect our families' magic, we left clues down the generations at each of the Wonders to find the location of the Spinning Heart. It's a special, magical locking system. Only a Hartwell who bears a Galon key can break the lock.

"Your grandmother, Lilly, was always too scared. I always thought it was a bloody joke until she gave me one of the Galons," Mary reminisces.

"She gave the key to me on my eleventh birthday and told me all keys have special powers. Then I started having these weird dreams about the Spinning Heart. It has a circular lock, along with some of the best craftsmanship." Mary looks at Tim, losing focus for a bit.

She walks over to the kitchen cabinet. She pulls a cloth from a sugar canister on the shelf, opens the cloth inside, and reveals a key.

"This is a Galon key," Mary says as she points the key toward Tim. "I found it at the first Wonder of Wales.

"It's from the waterfall of Pistyll Rhaefr, discovered by one of Lilly's great-great- grandmothers. It took her twenty years to find it. A Galon is very special, so treat it with respect and honor."

Mary dangles the Galon key, which is attached to a gold braided necklace, in front of Tim's face.

Tim opens his eyes as wide as the moon shining at night.

Mary places the Galon on Tim's palm and walks into her bedroom to sleep once more, as if they didn't even have a heart-to-heart. Mary utters a few words as she ruffles the pillows in her bedroom.

"Don't stay up too much longer. You do have school tomorrow. By the way, say hello to Owen," Mary says as she readies for sleep.

Tim watches the Galon on the golden necklace as it swings and twirls before his eyes. The beauty of the key reminds him of a medieval key, except that the handle is engraved with the Coat of Hartwell.

"Keys? Magic book? I have to find out more about this," Tim whispers to himself. Tim gets up, turns off the kitchen light, and heads into his room. He puts the necklace holding the Galon around his neck. He plugs in his nightlight and picks up one of the many maps that are on the floor. Turning on his bed lamp, he glances over a map of Snowdonia and the mountain elevations.

After a while, he turns off the lamp and falls silently asleep. Hours later, the wind around Tenby begins to pick up. The clouds cover the moon at times as they glide through the beautiful night sky.

The Galon around Tim's neck becomes illuminated with white light. The light begins to move toward the ceiling, short-circuiting the nightlight in the room. The mysterious light moves down the wall and through some wooden dolls, made by a local man, Mr. Brackenbury.

The light continues down the

leg of a dresser and moves back up the bed, floating above the key, and disappears into the air.

One of the ink pens on the dresser begins floating over to a large map of Tenby and the outer regions, which is stuck above Tim's bed.

The pen begins marking an "X" over a region on the map, then continues to move across the room back onto the dresser. As the pen flops onto the dresser, a small figure appears in the mirror above it.

Behold, the twins, Verlock and Alfred! They are wyverns, made from an "amazing personality" spell from the Book of Hartwell. Their eyes glow in the dark, and their noses and ears resemble those of cats. Alfred notices that Tim is wearing the Galon key. Verlock, being playful, grabs a small orange basketball laying on the floor next to a Michael Jordan poster.

A few words from Verlock make the basketball fly into the air toward the plastic hoop on the back of Tim's bedroom door.

Alfred jumps into the air, trying to block the ball from entering the goal.

Verlock notices that Alfred is trying to stop him from getting his two points. Verlock zips to the ball, and his hand guides the ball toward the hoop for the slam dunk.

"SLAM!"

Mrs. Hartwell bursts through the

door, turns on the light, and throws a few dirty clothes in Tim's hamper. A mother is always working on a few more duties. Mary closes the door and heads back to sleep.

Verlock and Alfred slide down the wall, as thin as pancakes. Both are in agony, as they puff back out.

"Ouch, that hurt," Alfred yells with a high-pitched tone.

"That door is completely hatstand," says a still-woozy Verlock, adding some humor to the situation.

"Do you think he is brave enough to find all the Galon keys? He doesn't look like the one to me," says Verlock, wiping his eyes, still wedi blino.

"He just might be, if he's

completely hatstand," says Alfred, mocking Verlock.

"Look at these dabs on the window. Mary needs to clean these things," says Verlock, looking around the room and pointing to the glass.

"Will you stop that!" Verlock says, rubbing his growling stomach.

"Do I need to keep a hairy eye on you, eh?" Alfred acts miserable as they both leap out of the window, gliding through the air into the starry night.

Minutes later, the magic of the Galon key freezes the night in time. Not a sound can be heard in Tenby. No birds are flying in the sky. No tourists are still up singing. There is complete silence.

Streaks of light are shooting from the loopholes on Palmerston Fort on St. Catherine's Island. Another set of white flashes streaks around the back of the building. Seconds later, red light starts flashing from the gun platform near the cartridge hoist to the gatterns.

The town is silently asleep, controlled by the Galon key. Out of nowhere a tall, dark figure standing two-and-a-half meters appears on the beach. The power of the Galon has released Stratford Hartwell from imprisonment. Here is a man who had turned into a raging beast. Hartwell is an outcast of the House for killing women and children with his magic.

The stench from his body fills the sky. His breath is as heavy as a brown bear. His oversized shoulders are filled with excitement.

Stratford can feel the power of the Galon within the walls of Tenby. He begins to stand up in the water, stretch his arms in the air, and muster his first words after being dormant.

"I have awoke. Who has touched the Galon? Who is trying to find the Book of Hartwell?" Rubbing his hands together, Stratford slides through the water.

His eyes, filled with rage, shine in the night. His face is hidden with a permanent shadow. Stratford raises his nose in the air, moving toward Castle

Sands. As he reaches St. Julian's Street, he begins sniffing the air once more, trying to feel out the exact location of the Galon.

He continues up St. Julian's, which turns into High Street. Two light flashes stop him in his path where High Street and Crackwell Street meet.

Verlock and Alfred, the Galon protectors, jump in front of Stratford.

"Wotcha! If it isn't Stratford. Where do you think you're going?" Verlock demands as he and Alfred hold Stratford in a magical field.

"Get out of my way!" Stratford says with a huge attitude. "You won't be able to protect the Galons forever. I will get my revenge." Stratford's anger is beginning to show.

"You should know by now that you cannot stop any Hartwell descendent with only one Galon, so get lost. You are forbidden here," says Alfred, pointing toward the harbour and demanding Stratford to leave.

"I will get my revenge. I will be waiting. I will destroy you along with the carrier of the Galon," Stratford says before disappearing down the street and leaving a trail of disgusting scent behind.

"Would you look at that," says Alfred. "He is truly out of control. No matter what, he must follow the rules. We must protect this Hartwell descendant, for I fear this time,

Stratford will try to deceive us once again." Alfred is worried about how angry Stratford looked.

Verlock and Alfred then fly into the dark sky. The power of the Galon lifts, and all of nature's sounds begin to pour back into town. Birds begin chirping, as sunrise is just a few hours away.

The buildings are lit with a dark orange glow within the dark night. A boat passes by Goscar Rock, heading into the harbour. A few fishermen begin walking out of their houses, setting up their boats before the early catch of the day.

As the sun rises, birds begin singing and flying across the rooftops of

Tenby. North Beach becomes packed with tourists. Families pack in the pubs for an early beer.

The Haydn Miller, a Tamar-class, passes the Tenby Lifeboat Station. Even the St. Mary's Church bells ring at o'clock, waking Tim from his sleep.

Tim looks around his room, searching for his school uniform and some of his books for school. Mary is already out fishing with her three-man crew. She left cheese, laver bread, and slices of pork on the table for Tim to eat. Picking up some of the food, Tim rushes out the door to catch the bus for school.

Tim notices that his senses are much clearer than before. He pulls the key out from under his shirt, pulling his senses together.

The school bus is getting ready to pull off without him. Mr. Carter, the school bus driver, stops for Tim to get on.

As the bus heads down St. Johns Hill, making a right onto Heywood Lane, Tim sits quietly in his seat, looking out the window. Owen Anholt, his best friend and classmate, is running behind the bus, wailing for the driver to stop. Mr. Carter stops and begins blabbering about his route schedule.

Tim sticks his head out the window while Owen approaches the bus door.

"Owen, you almost missed us,"

Tim says, sticking his head back in the window as Owen walks down the aisle of the school bus.

"Tell me about it. I missed my breakfast too," says Owen, plopping onto his seat next to Tim. Unfortunately, the school's bully, Victor Drury, smacks the back of Owen's head, making a popping sound. All of the kids on the bus start laughing. Mr. Carter turns around, yelling at Victor for stepping out of line.

"Victor, just for that, I am going to inform the principal and your parents about your bad behavior. Do you understand?" Mr. Carter screams.

"Yes, sir." Red-headed Victor leans back in his seat, crosses his arms, and puffs out his pink, freckled cheeks.

Owen picks up his books from the aisle and sits next to Tim.

"Why does he always pick on me?" Owen pouts, wiping the dirt off his pants and beginning to calm down.

"Victor picks on everyone. He has always been like that," Tim replies.

"Everyone knows he tries to bully people," says Nicholas, a kid who lives on Upper Park Road.

Owen notices the golden necklace around Tim's neck. "What's that gold?" he asks, reaching for it. Tim sticks his hand out, blocking him. "I was just trying to touch it . . . ," Owen replies.

"My mother gave me this, and it's very important to me, that's all,"

Tim explains, trying not to hurt Owen's feelings.

"Okay, don't get all wacky on me now. Did you do your math for Mr. Patrick's class?" Owen asks.

"It was a little hard, but I got it. I just can't wait until school is out. What are you doing this summer?" asks Tim, leaning back in his seat.

"Well, father wants me to help him paint the house again. This morning, he was trying to figure out what color he wants it to be," says Owen while eating a candy bar that was in his pocket.

"That should be fun. Mam and I are going to be working extra hours at the harbour. I heard it will be raining sometime tomorrow," says Tim, looking out the window as they approach Greenhill School on Heywood Lane.

As the school bus pulls into the drop-off area, lots of kids pour into the front entrance of Greenhill. Some of them are dropped off by parents.

Tim looks back at Owen and raises his hand in the air. "I will catch you later, Owen. See you during lunch." Tim rushes in, heading down the hallway for English class.

His instructor, Mrs. Helen Forster, is standing outside of the door, waiting for her students to arrive for class. She looks toward Tim as he walks in the doorway, greeting her with a kind smile and then placing his stuff on his desk.

Mrs. Forster begins handing

out her final for the year. Some of the students look at each other with amazement. Their faces are glued to the test, looking at how much harder it is than they thought it would be.

Tim glances at the test, pondering how much he needs to pass it. Without hesitation, he picks up his pencil and begins reading some of the questions. One of the students, Zoe Beckham, smiles at Tim and then concentrates on her test as well.

Morgana Evans is one of the smartest students in class. Her hazel eyes and brunette hair have drafted her as the most popular girl in school, without breaking a nail.

"Tim and Morgana, keep your

eyes on your own paper," Mrs. Forster alerts them. You wouldn't want me to think you are cheating now, would you?" she asks as she organizes paperwork at her desk.

"No, Mrs. Forster," Tim and Morgana answer in unison, almost by mistake.

A few minutes later, the Galon key begins to glow under Tim's shirt. He puts his hand over his chest, covering the Galon.

Small lights appear, which seem to outline all of the multiple-choice answers on the test. Tim glances down at the test and cannot believe it.

No one else can see the magic. His pencil moves, circling all of the correct answers that are illuminated. Tim is in disbelief, knowing the Galon is involved. His face shows that he doesn't mind having this type of magical power, however.

Tim waits for twenty-five minutes and hands in his test. Everyone looks up, wondering how he finished his test so fast.

Mrs. Forster looks at Tim with a slight grin, knowing that she caught him talking earlier. "Tim, are you sure that you answered all of the answers correctly?

Tim says hesitantly, "Well, I studied pretty hard last night."

Mrs. Forster squints her eyes at Tim, looks down toward the paper, and nods her head.

"Well, you may head to breakfast, if you like. Enjoy your weekend, Tim," says Mrs. Forster, her mood changing drastically.

Tim glances back at Morgana and winks as he walks out the doorway and heads to the cafeteria. En route, he runs into his science teacher, Mr. Oxley, who always wears a long white jacket and slim metallic reading glasses.

Mr. Oxley started balding last year, so he brushes his hair for about an hour every day before he comes to work.

Mr. Oxley always wears his graduation ring on his right hand to represent his accomplishment. Most of the faculty think he's a little crazy.

"Hello, Tim. Are you ready for your summer?" asks Mr. Oxley, holding his folders in his hand.

"Yes, I cannot wait. Are we doing anything special in your class today?" Tim asks while changing the subject.

"That will be my little science secret, so be prepared . . . ," says Mr. Oxley, pausing for a moment.

Tim puts one thumb up and continues to walk toward the entrance of the cafeteria. Small groups of kids are sitting down, eating breakfast already.

A couple of teachers are drinking coffee, talking about the weather. Tim walks over to the food area and grabs some dry frosted cereal, a small bowl of oatmeal, a small glass of milk, and a small glass of orange juice. Tim is still a growing boy who needs to feed his appetite. The cashier, Mr. Parsons, sticks out his hand and asks for Tim's menu card. Mr. Parsons has always been short, ever since he was a kid. He keeps a larger bar stool in the trunk of his small car, which allows him to use the register without stretching.

Some of the kids call him "Little Bach," teasing him about his height as his Birkenstock shoes dangle from his feet.

"Okay, that'll be four pounds," says Mr. Parsons, looking down at Tim's tray of food, swiping Tim's menu card into the system, then handing the card back to him. Mr. Parsons picks up his Tenby Observer, a weekly newspaper, and continues to read.

Tim looks around the cafeteria for a place to sit, then notices Owen and Owen's cousin, Hurt Palmer, eating in the cafeteria.

Hurt is Greenhill's star rugby player, leading them to the Championship of Pembrokeshire. He's also the most popular boy in school. Most of the girls think he looks like James Dean.

Hurt and Owen both enjoy their big family reunion every summer on North Beach.

"Hello, Tim. How was your first test?" Hurt asks as he spins the rugby ball on his finger and tosses it in the air.

"Pretty easy, I say," Tim responds with confidence as he rubs the Galon under his shirt. He sits down, almost spilling his oatmeal. Tim quickly readjusts and catches himself before he looses balance.

Owen begins to cheer loudly as he looses more points on some portable video game player.

Some of the art teachers in the group across the room interrupt them, asking them to keep it down.

"Keep your voices down, you three," says Mr. Berry while looking back. The teachers then begin to talk about some of their favorite TV shows.

The rest of the kids at Greenhill

start pouring into the cafeteria, making lots of noise, happy that their tests are done. Some of the kids, including Owen and Hurt, don't start their tests until the class after breakfast.

"Looks like they will have to tell everyone to be quiet. Ha!"

"Maybe not," says Tim.

Every boy in the cafeteria gets quiet when a girl walks in. Hurt begins falling in love and taps Owen on the shoulder.

"Would you look at that!" Hurt says, wiping his hair back, trying to make some type of impression.

"That's Zoe Beckham. Wow, would you look at her." Owen's mouth hangs open. He yanks his shirt, acting like it is getting hot in the cafeteria.

"She doesn't even have a boyfriend?" Owen asks Hurt, drinking the rest of his juice with much disbelief.

Zoe glances over toward them and smiles as she whips her hair back.

"She wouldn't be interested in us, but maybe Hurt," Tim says, adding some humor.

"Really? She's never said anything to me before," Hurt says, thinking he has a shot.

As all of them laugh, Hurt crushes an orange juice box on his tray, then tosses the crushed box into the trash from afar. Then Hurt continues to talk to Owen and Tim about rugby.

Tim looks out of the window and

suddenly hears voices from across the cafeteria.

"Good shot!" one of the voices says, as Tim continues to listen to Hurt.

"Hello, there." Tim hears the same voice again, so he turns to look around the cafeteria. Owen and Hurt are still talking, but Tim is still looking over his shoulder. He is certain he heard voices trying to speak to him.

"Did you hear that?" Tim asks Hurt and Owen. They both look with blank stares; they didn't hear a thing. Hurt begins talking to Owen about how Shane Williams is one the best wingers in all Welsh rugby and around the world.

Tim hears the voices once more, which makes him get really suspicious.

"Hello, there. We see you are a bearer of the Galon key." Both Verlock and Alfred express some enthusiasm but stay hidden. Their voices sound like they are speaking directly in Tim's ear.

Hurt and Owen start leaving for class. Tim stays inside of the cafeteria, wondering where these voices are sprouting from.

"You're getting warmer . . . ," Alfred yells. Tim walks slowly over to a table, trying not to get the attention of any of the teachers still in the cafeteria.

Tim reaches over to where he suspects the voices are coming from and lifts the tablecloth, slides under the table, and drops the cloth behind him.

He notices two small figures looking at him from underneath the table. Taking a few deep breaths, he immediately begins to ask questions.

"Who are you?" Tim asks anxiously.

"Who are we?" Alfred replies, putting his right hand up, granting him the power of the first Galon key.

"Silurian!" says Verlock and Alfred, speaking the magical spell.

In a flash, the magic power of the Galon illuminates all three of them, sending their bodies magically across Wales, right below the Pistyll Rhaeadr waterfall in Powys, Wales. One of the Seven Wonders of Wales is right in front of him.

"Holy cow, how did you do that?" Tim can feel the cold mist from the waterfall.

Local residents and tourist who were taking pictures of this famous location appear to be frozen in time. Verlock throws a small rock that skips across the water, bouncing left to right, up and down into the water.

Alfred waves his hand toward Tim, getting his attention. Alfred gets in his granting stance and holds one of his hands out.

"Silurian!" Verlock says, his voice carrying through the air. He looks at Tim as the sky begins to change to night, with a single spotlight of sunshine over Tim's body. They both continue to read the spells:

"Your gifts are the ability to stop time, magical powers to heal others with your mind. No one can take the Galon from around your neck. Now you can run as fast as a lion. Furthermore, inside this Wonder lies also the seventh Galon."

Tim's body is covered in streams of light, almost godlike, as the Galon lights up the skies once more. He notices a small metal object floating out of the Pistyll Rhaeadr waterfall. Another Galon glides in the air and lands gracefully in his hand. His eyes focus on a chiseled, titanium-colored key. As Tim turns the key over, rubbing his fingers along its edge, Alfred begins to speak about the next step.

"You must not travel to Snowdon, to the Devil's Kitchen."

Tim wonders why he received the seventh Galon instead of the second. They both summon the stairwell of travel, located at each of the Seven Wonders of Wales. Verlock straightens, warning Tim before he heads into the parallel world of Snowdonia. He floats right in front of Tim as he explains what he must do to run to the Devil's Kitchen.

During this time, he must run across the Devil's Appendix in one minute, which will take him there.

"We must warn you about a man named Stratford. He is the creator of this parallel world of Snowdonia. Going through the stairwell of travel gets you to both sides, from reality here to Stratford's ruling area.

"Later in your journey, you will find out more about him. It's the reason you have to play his Selwyn's Chancer game, a very constructed spell."

Tim walks under the waterfall and puts his hand under the path of the water. Feeling the water pressure, he asks Alfred and Verlock how he gets there.

Alfred points his finger and creates a doorway to the stairwell of travel on the left side of the waterfall.

"Run safely, my boy, run safely," says Verlock, giving Tim some words of confidence.

Verlock and Alfred disappear. Tim steps into the entrance heading into a world of the unknown as the light consumes his body. Night goes to day and time unfreezes. Everything is back to normal as people continue to take pictures, unaware of what happened.

Tim's body moves faster than the speed of light through the stairwell of travel. He feels like he's just woken up from a dream. As he slowly opens his eyes, he notices that he is standing in the field of Cwm Idwal. Before he can grasp the situation, a loud roar fills the sky. The terrifying voice of Stratford is coming his way. Tim begins to run toward the Llyn Idwal lake. The Galon illuminates and shoots a beam of light, blasting toward the location he must go to get home.

Tim notices a dark gorge, the Devil's Kitchen, to be exact. His Galon illuminates the area around him.

Stratford's howling strikes again, but even closer—approximately 914 meters away. The ground begins to shake, almost as if a huge prehistoric beast were raging toward him.

Around the edge of the lake, a dark beast stands 45 meters away. Sweat is dripping from its face, and it is growling with anger.

Tim begins to run faster up the hill, noticing the doorway home just a few meters away. Stratford begins to howl, his breath, a ferocious smell. He leaps toward Tim, trying to get him before he escapes back to Tenby.

The Galon's power opens the door as Tim desperately jumps toward the stairwell of travel. Its doorway is filled with pure light.

Stratford's claw just misses Tim's shoe as Tim escapes through the doorway, which slams loudly behind him.

Tim looks up and notices that he is inside the maintenance and service closet at Greenhill School.

He begins breathing heavily, looking at his watch. His eyebrows raise, for he is five minutes late for his next class.

Tim grabs some of the paper towels on the shelf and wipes his head. He then books down the hallway toward his classroom, hoping he makes it inside without his math teacher getting mad.

As Tim reaches the classroom door, he looks through the window of the door, accidently opening the door, making a large screeching sound. Owen and the rest of the class give him a blank stare—especially his teacher, Mr. Patrick, who is displeased to see him so late.

"I will excuse you for being late, only because it's Friday," says Mr. Patrick in a stern voice. Tim nods his head and takes his seat next to Owen.

Tim, still in shock from the previous

events, is puzzled, wondering about the connection between Stratford and the Galon keys.

Victor, the school bully, shoots a paper plane that hits Tim on the side of the head. Mr. Patrick raises his hand toward Victor, telling him he will have detention after school for his disruptive behavior.

Mr. Patrick tells everyone to get their number 2 pencils, and then says, "Are you ready for your test? There will be no talking during the exam. If anyone has any questions, feel free to come up to my desk. Will someone volunteer to pass out the exam folders?"

"I will, Mr. Patrick," Tim replies, walking toward the teacher's desk.

He notices a small bruise on his hand, which he received as he was climbing the sharp rocks in Cwm Idwal.

Using the Galon, Tim heals the bruise in a flash. He passes out all of the tests and sits down so he can get started. When he pulls out the math exam, all of the answers, including the essays, are filled in with his own handwriting.

Tim doesn't find this amusing, understanding now that the joke is on him.

"Something is very different. Why am I so ready to use the Galon? I can answer these questions myself," Tim whispers to himself.

"This must be too good to be

true," he says in a low tone, but loud enough for Mr. Patrick to remind him that there is no talking in class. Tim nods his head, reaches in his pocket, and notices the seventh Galon is missing. Leaning over his desk, Tim notices that he has dropped it on the floor next to Victor.

Victor notices the Galon and starts to lean to pick it up, but Tim zips faster than the eye can see. He picks up the key and returns to his seat and begins taking his test again. By the time Victor reaches down, the Galon key isn't there. Shocked and amazed, Victor whips his head around, looking for where the key went. As he looks up. Mr. Patrick gives Victor the look to get back to work. Meanwhile, Mr. Patrick sits back in his chair, playing a knight and armor video game on his new computer tablet.

After a while, most of the class members finish their exams. Tim walks over to Mr. Patrick's desk and hands him his exam, which Mr. Patrick grabs with his left hand while reaching to press the pause button on his tablet. As he does, Mr. Patrick knocks the cup of hot coffee onto his briefcase.

Mr. Patrick jumps up and wipes off his soaked documents. He cleans up the rest of the coffee and waves for Tim to leave.

Owen signals Tim before he leaves, telling him to meet him in the library after class. Tim shakes his head up and down.

Mr. Patrick quickly gets off the computer to look through some of the paperwork on his desk while everyone in class continues to finish.

TIM HARTWELL: Open Your Heart Trilogy (Books 1-3)

Stratford's Proposition

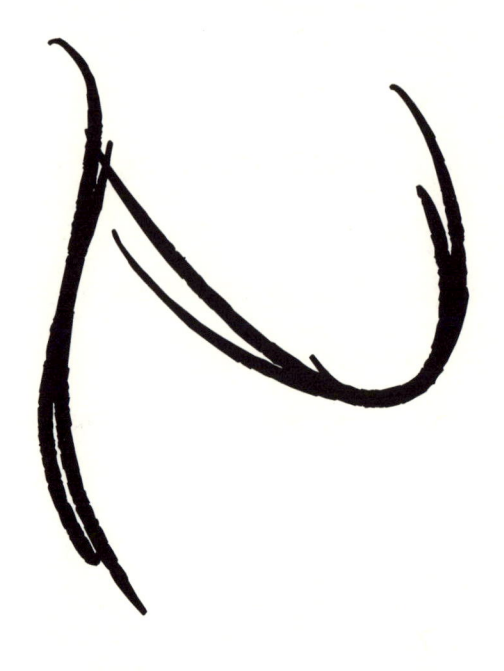

Outside in the hall, Tim looks at huge posters for the rugby match that read "Greenhill School vs. Rhydywaun School."

The laboratory is right across the

hall, so he stops there for a minute to splash some water on his face.

He uses both hands to put his head down on the sink. Tim closes his eyes, just for a second, and reopens them to turn on the sink water, but realizes he is not in the laboratory anymore.

Tim is standing in a dark room, under Stratford's Proposition spell—a counter spell for any Hartwell descendant on the path to the Spinning Heart. The Proposition spell has designed a classroom with Stratford, disguised as Mr. Patrick. It has also enabled Stratford to transform into any human being that a Hartwell descendant comes in contact with, in the real world or in his own parallel world.

"It's just part of the game," Stratford says, speaking in Mr. Patrick's voice.

"Why are you looking at me like that? Are you having second thoughts?" Stratford chuckles with amusement.

"Well, don't look like an unhappy lad," he continues. "Remember, you are the one who put on the Galon." Stratford tries to act sneaky while taking off Mr. Patrick's glasses, whose prescription is way too strong. "I guess I do not need those contraptions," he adds.

Tim sits down in a chair and

begins to hear things crawling inside the storage built on the large desk.

"No, you don't want to go in there. That's only if you don't answer three questions correctly," Stratford says, taunting him.

"Three? That's all? Why do all bad guys always give you three chances?" Tim says, laughing with confidence.

Stratford stands up, holding both exams that Tim had turned in to his math and English teachers earlier.

"Did you cheat on these tests? Answer me!" says Stratford, using a dark tone. "You will be expelled. I didn't know you were a cheater, Tim." Stratford slams the tests down on the desk.

As Tim tries to move, he notices that his leg is shackled to the desk.

"Are you trying to go somewhere? Those Galons will not work here, dear boy!" Stratford shouts with laughter.

"Where am I?" Tim says with a not-so-confident attitude.

"Welcome to my game, made up with many spells that I have designed over the years," says Stratford.

"Welcome to the game of all games. Yes, here . . . in this very room. You have to answer all of the questions over again. The Galons' power will not be able to help you." Stratford smiles from ear to ear.

"If you answer all of them correctly, you will be able to leave.

My Proposition spell will make you stay here for an eternity unless you answer those questions correctly."

Stratford walks back to Mr. Patrick's desk, pulling up his pants, showing his white socks with green stripes.

"Get on with it." Stratford smiles again, waiting for Tim to screw up. "Oh, yeah. Keep an eye on the clock up there, Timmy. You have ten minutes."

"What on earth?" Tim looks down at the test, which appears to be written on thirteenth century paper.

Tim scratches his head, trying to figure out what to do next. Before he can think too long, he looks up at Stratford, who is in the form of a bulky, muscular beast wearing a long white shirt, black tie, and custom-made trousers.

Now Tim knows this is the same beast from the Devil's Kitchen.

Stratford raises his three fingers on his left paw. On his right, he grips his human hand, playing Mr. Patrick's video game. Stratford's Proposition spell controls the look of everything Stratford sees.

He laughs at Tim, knowing that he is in total control. "You can't cheat your way out of this one, Tim Hartwell, for I have perfected Selwyn's Chancer, my dear boy." Stratford's features morph into Mr. Patrick's exact facial features.

"This is the first time I have ever been awakened to see the seeker of the Book of Hartwell. A little boy," Stratford says, then whispers to himself. "Usually, they are female."

Stratford pauses a moment, continuing his normal formula for the Proposition spell.

"I pity you, so I can feel you are something different when the sun sets. Clearly, you will never get out of my counter spell. Did I say counter?" says Stratford, sounding confident.

"You will never get out of my lovely **Ugly as = M spell**," Tim responds with a nasty tone, feeling the pressure.

The first Galon stops time, without his control. Stratford is frozen in his seat, looking at the computer screen.

Two small figures emerge through the wall on the right—Verlock and Alfred—who also underestimate the magical power Tim brings to the Galon keys.

Verlock floats over desk and sits right on top. Rubbing his hands, he burps about the next plan and acts casual. Verlock and Alfred are excited to see some new action under the Proposition spell.

"We cannot tell you how to escape, but we can tell you to follow your heart," says Alfred. "Listen to the seventh Galon. Remember, each key has its own powers." Alfred taps on Verlock and once again, they disappear into thin air.

Then a faint voice asks Tim for help. The voice is coming from under his shirt. He places the seventh Galon on the table so he can hear the woman's voice more clearly.

"Hello, Tim. I am Eleanor Hartwell, mother of Lilly, your great-grandmother. I am the guiding voice of the seventh Galon, created to protect the Hartwell family and to help you unlock the Spinning Heart. I am also here to protect you from Verlock and Alfred.

"I know the answer you are looking for. It's a trick question. All you have to do is not take the test. Place it on the table and tell him you give up.

The downfall to Stratford's counter spell is that he can only convince you in his world. You have the choice to leave. His Selwyn's Chancer is not as strong, since you are a boy." Eleanor pauses and thinks of Mary.

"Don't worry, Tim. Walk out the door and you will return to your world, your time." Eleanor's words give him more confidence. Tim stands and walks toward the doorway.

"Good luck, Tim," says Eleanor, reassuring him that he will be okay, even knowing that his journey will be surrounded by danger.

Stratford is still frozen in Mr. Patrick's body as Tim walks through the stairwell of travel, which leads him back to Greenhill School's library. Stratford is knocked out in one of the aisles, and no one can see him. Tim is perfectly placed back in his reality.

A few students are playing on the computers toward the back of the library. Mrs. Watcliff is using her scanner on the side of the books as she stacks them on the shelf. Each book's spine is perfectly matched with the edge of the shelf. She is always a perfectionist.

Owen is using one of the computers in the back of the library, which is where Tim is waking up—an uncommon side effect of traveling through the stairwell of travel.

Tim dusts himself off, brushes his hand across his hair, and notices that he has a fresh haircut. Walking right behind Owen, he scares his friend to the point where Owen screams out in fright.

"Holy Tenby!" says Owen, jumping out of his seat and falling down. "You came out of nowhere. You nearly scared me half to death."

Tim picks up Owen's books that had fallen onto the floor. Owen had been looking up some information on the computer. He now unleashes some of the ideas he had researched before Tim showed up.

"There's an old saying, Tim. I am surprised Hurt hasn't told you about this." Owen points to the light coming from Tim's shirt. "Hey, what is that?"

"Oh, nothing. Just a magic trick, that's all," says Tim, playing it off while he covers the small light from both Galons.

Tim leans back in his chair and notices the computer screen scanning rapidly with all types of pictures from all over Wales. The screen stops on a picture of the Great Tower, which is at the St. Giles Parish Church.

"It's one of the Seven Wonders of Wales. So, what about it?" asks Owen, pulling sweets out of his trousers, knowing that it's against library rules.

Tim places his hand on his chin for a second. "I have to get there," he says, starting to come up with a plan.

"St. Giles, all the way in Wrexham?

Are you winding me up?" says Owen, giving Tim a surprised expression.

"Of course not, Owen. I just have to figure this out," says Tim, stretching out his words.

The first Galon, using his thought process, takes Tim to Wrexham in the flash of a second. He opens his eyes into another dark blue, dark night sky. The moon is parked right behind the Great Tower.

Tim begins walking past the iron gates and sees the words "Go In Peace, Sin No More" inscribed below a cross as he moves quickly along the bushes to the back of the church. Walking into the back door, he hears someone in the distance singing opera. Walking into the nave, Tim begins strolling around, amazed at the art inside the St. Giles Parish Church. His eyes pan the walls, falling in love with the array of colors, which are coming inside the church like it's daylight outside.

Sixteen different angels appear out of nowhere and begin playing the melodies of harmony with their instruments, floating high near the camber beam ceiling. Multicolored light starts to mix with other streams of light, swirling through the stained glass. The Rudhall bells begin ringing loudly, and the sound fills the church with its sequence before it begins to slow and fade.

Tim lifts his head, noticing more

sound coming from the stained glass. Above, five male figures appear side-by-side in the glass. The fourth male knight begins moving his lips, singing a simple melody.

Alfred begins speaking to the left as he morphs into the stained glass with the second knight with golden armor.

Verlock morphs into the glass with the fourth male knight on the right, who is decorated with red and blue armor. Tim interrupts Verlock and Alfred, who are talking.

"Hey, what is going on? Why am I all the way in Wrexham?" says Tim, demanding a detailed reason.

"Answers, answers . . . They always want answers," says Alfred in his usual snobby tone.

"Not this one," says Verlock, speaking the truth.

"I thought you guys were the protectors of the keys," says Tim. "And aren't you supposed to be protecting me? Stratford nearly set me up in Snowdonia. What is going on?" Tim looks toward Verlock and Alfred, pointing his finger at them.

"We can't tell you everything now. Come on, cheer up," says Alfred with a callous tone. "We gave you the seventh Galon, which led you to the next phase of your quest. For, as you see, the St. Giles is one of the Seven Wonder of Wales." Alfred turns his head to look around the church.

"We must follow the rules," he continues. "Even better, we can tell you that the next Galon you must seek is within these very walls. So you want a hint? Here's your hint. Besides, patience is a virtue. We haven't been up for ages, so we would love to have a little fun once in a while."

Alfred zips his lips as soon as Verlock looks at him.

"You think this is fun?" says Tim. "Have you seen the size of Stratford, especially when he is chasing you?" Tim cuts their fun and games short.

"Believe us, you need our help," says. "No matter what you might think, there is a bigger issue. There's more than you know. So just look for the fourth Galon. Believe in us, Tim, and you will find the Book of Hartwell."

Tim begins to look around the church for clues that will lead him to the next Galon. Trusting them only for now, Verlock and Alfred move out of the stained glass and follow Tim as he looks for the next Galon key.

One of the sixteen angels somehow appears and dangles a tiny string one meter from the floor. A shiny object tied to the bottom of the angel's body gives off more light, right near the camber beam ceiling.

"His journey back to reality will be much harder this time," Verlock whispers to his twin.

"Will you pay attention!" says

Alfred, covering Verlock's mouth so he can get a better look at the situation.

Tim walks over to the key, which is different from the first and seventh keys he already earned.

The fourth Galon has a shield handle on the body of the key. The shield is marked with the Coat of Hartwell, which has four feathers, two up and two down, and a circle with a black key shape in the center of it.

Verlock and Alfred hover over Tim, pointing out the next stairwell of travel he must pass through.

"Good luck, Tim. We wish you well," says Alfred.

"Hey, Tim. You didn't ask about your new magic!" says Verlock.

"Will you shut up?" says Alfred. "You are telling him what to do, you imbecile." Alfred slaps Verlock with his white glove that he magically makes appear.

"He's completely hatstand!" says Verlock, looking at Tim as Verlock points one of his fingers toward Alfred.

Tim begins to laugh out loud while Alfred shakes his head with modest disgust.

"What magic?" says Tim, who was starting to look upset at the both of them.

"Magic? He didn't say 'magic,' he said 'hour, look at the hour'," Alfred says, eyes bright with a smile from ear to ear and looking very suspicious.

Verlock and Alfred start backing up, since they haven't been one hundred percent honest.

"Are you telling me you are sending me to get messed up?" asks Tim. "I knew I could only trust you guys for a second."

Tim walks over to Verlock and Alfred like a lion in the jungle. The twins shrink to the floor, the size of mice, with both hands over their mouths.

"Tell me now, you little twerps," says Tim, name calling. "Okay, okay, just don't hurt us," Alfred says in a cowardly tone, backing up.

They both puff out to their normal size. Verlock raises his right hand, snapping his fingers. All three of them magically appear back in time on a beautiful night in 97 AD—right inside a Roman military amphitheatre in Caerleon with grassy tops and flame torches burning slowly as the torches release white smoke into the air. They are in the Roman legionary barracks in Britain. Tim begins panning his head left to right. The stars shine above as he looks straight ahead at a glass-shaped figure hovering with light, sparkling with beauty.

"What is that?" Tim shouts loudly.

"Go and find out," says Verlock, tapping on his shoulder.

Tim hops down from the barracks, goes over to this mysterious nomenon, and stops in front of the light.

"This is the magical source of the fourth Galon," says Verlock

"Make doors within doors. And If you are ever caught by Stratford, you can escape. You also have the magic to see as far as the landscape."

Alfred took over, getting a little jealous of his twin brother.

"Will you shut up? Let me do the talking from now on," Alfred shouts with a mean tone. "I am the eldest. You just stand there and be quiet."

"Now, where was I?" he says.

"Why isn't this one like the others?" Tim says as he looks at the light going inside the body of the fourth Galon. He puts the key with its necklace around his neck with the other two keys.

Verlock wraps up the conversation before they leave again. "We have been talking way too much. Let's go, Alfred."

They both snap their fingers, which leads Tim back to Wrexham, standing in front of a wooden door inside St. Giles Church. Reaching for the door knob, he opens the door and enters the stairwell of travel.

He arrives back in present-day Snowdonia, standing on the A5 road inside the Glyderau Range. He glances at his watch, noticing that the time is frozen on twelve forty-five p.m.

Eleanor begins speaking from the seventh Galon again. She tries to guide Tim back home the best way she can.

"One destination that even us Hartwell's couldn't tell each other was to never let any male descendant know about the Book of Hartwell," she says. "The keys, everything. For he would be the descendant to finally open the Spinning Heart and find the true power of the Book of Hartwell over a period of time. It began writing itself, adding more pages. The mastermind, Ellington Hartwell, thought hard, for the book was originally designed for a woman to read. But Ellington was always undecided on which Hartwell would have complete control of the House."

A loud, familiar roar comes from afar, distracting both of them. Tim looks up and notices a head the size of a large dragon right above him. The mouth zips down toward him, slamming on the ground like an earthquake, covering Tim in complete blackness.

Nine lights start glowing in the darkness. The inside of the mouth of the beast is the size of a huge cave. The keys around his neck begin floating in the air.

Colors that Tim has never seen before begin streaming out, almost in rhythm, down into the throat of the

Alynn dragon.

Guarded by the Diablo Arches, with their flat-shaped heads, arms made of bows, and fingers made of burning arrows. Streaks of red light are coming out of their eyes. All of them stay under the control of Amelia, Stratford's wife. As she grows older, he keeps her enslaved for her powers as a witch; her Spanish dragon is more of a prize to him. He used the Transporlyn spell to keep her from aging, double-crossing her mind so she loves him forever without hesitation.

Inside the Alynn dragon, they all pass through the gates of Amelia's Chamber, made from rock that shines like metal.

Strong winds pour through the fortress walls as some of the guards walk out to get Tim. Walking toward the entrance, he looks down at the rocky floor, which turns into a glass floor with fire traveling beneath it. The Alynn's heart is right below the glass as well, smothered in lava as it beats like a drum.

Tim glances right as he begins walking up the flight of steps that leads to the fortress. His vision focuses on a castle, just like the one on St. Catherine's Island, with enormous black sheets of purple crystal as walls. A huge panther named Sylkin roars as it guards the front of this castle. Its eyes glow as it prowls back and forth and finally lies down with its tail whipping back and forth.

One of the Diablo Arches catches Tim being nosey and pulls his arm toward the entrance. Tim resists, and everything freezes around him. The Diablo Arches are frozen, which gives Tim enough time to pan across the fortress to the other castle and pass the Sylkin through the crystal glass into the holding area with his vision ability.

Tim focuses on a book sitting on top of a mantle. He tries to get a better look at the words, when a large wolf-like hand with hairy fingers and razor-sharp nails grabs his face, right before Tim can make out the title of the book.

"Do not test my patience," says Stratford. "Even if it hurts me, I will show you discipline."

Stratford claps his hands together using a counter measure against the first Galon's power, which makes time normal again. Before Tim can think, he realizes that he is sitting at a long dinner table.

Stratford changes his appearance to human form; he is wearing luxurious clothes and a gold ring. He orders servants to bring in tons of delicious food.

"Are you of age to drink?" Stratford asks as some roasted pork and other food arrives.

Tim sits silently, not moving because he thinks the food may be poisoned. Stratford stands up with his right hand on his dagger, which is clipped to his black belt. He points to some of the art and style that flows throughout the interior of the dining hall, filled with gold and precious jewels.

"Eat something, Tim. If I wanted you to be dead, you would be. I'm no barbarian. I only believe in getting what a man wants, when he wants it."

Stratford begins eating some of the fire-cooked pork on his plate. Tim looks at him from the other side of the table and begins to eat some of his own food as he pokes his chest out. Tim begins to drink some of the wine in his huge glass, letting go for a moment. His words slice the air, guarded by disbelief and motivation. One day he will be controller of all the Houses around the world—especially the Houses that keep themselves hidden to survive through the ages.

The food is some of the best Tim has ever had. The Alynn dragon takes a deep breath. The wind flows through the lungs, into the belly, where Amelia's Chamber thrives. The vocal pattern shocks the entire fortress. It's not a damaging sound, but almost a deep humming sound—deep and ridged, which usually means the dragon is resting somewhere high in the mountains, hidden in the clouds.

"Tomorrow will be your day of choice, so do me a favor and sleep well."

Right before Stratford reaches the top of the steps, he snaps his fingers, making Tim disappear, only to reappear in one of the guest rooms inside Amelia's chamber fortress. Tim's cup is full of water. He is dressed in new plush pajamas, and he notices the riches in each room. The chambers are filled with luxury. The bed is coated with silk blankets, the burgundy floors have gold-trimmed carpet, and lion-face markings are embroidered on the center of every major accessory in the guest room. Tim jumps on the bed and relaxes for a little while.

A cool breeze floats through the room, making the crystals on the golden chandelier refract. The light turns from white to red, flashing inside the room. Amelia morphs into a female human shape. Her arms stretch over the mirror, far on the other side of the room, appearing right in front of Tim with her blue eyes and brunette hair.

"Surprised to see a woman five hundred years old?" she asks. "Don't worry, I won't bite."

Amelia speaks with her old spirit, which is beautiful on the outside with the power to read the future, resurrected through a spell to keep Stratford ahead of the game. Over time, he fell in love with Amelia, so he informed her about the Book of Hartwell. She keeps him informed on what she knows, but in escaping, she hopes one day she will grasp the power of the book for herself. Maybe she can get her hands on the Galon keys as well.

She floats through the room, turning herself into mist, unseen by Tim. His senses cannot pick up her presence. Smoke drags from behind. She begins placing her fingers gently along the vintage piano.

Stratford, back on the other side of the fortress, looks at his crystal-framed vertical mirror mounted on the wall. He stares at the reflection of his beast image. The only reason he is looking human at many points is due to Amelia. That is one of the true reasons he loves her.

His ears pick up a piano melody

of Amelia singing on the other side of the fortress. Closing his eyes, he magically appears in the guest room.

Tim is still lying on the bed with his eyes closed and feet crossed. Stratford reaches right outside the door, remaining invisible to the naked eye, and waits next to the door. His right hand grips the door, silently waiting for Amelia to speak about the future. His eyes are shaped like a panther's; his mouth waters for new details. His Selwyn's Chancer spell is unpredictable with Amelia. The chance of glory, she lets her words free, keeping her eyes closed. The piano is playing itself. Every note is played with perfection, never missing a beat.

TIM HARTWELL: Open Your Heart Trilogy (Books 1-3)

"A Hartwell son will travel one day,
The Spinning Heart unlocks a key.
The greatest treasure a boy can see,
his magic hands, avoid the sea."

All three Galon keys illuminate. Stratford glances at Amelia, wondering why she stopped singing. The room's large window smashes, sending glass flying into the room, totally avoiding Tim. Most of the glass heads in Amelia's direction. Glass cuts into the piano, cutting the wood into many pieces; the glass even sticks into the door where Stratford's head is resting. Amelia makes herself untouchable. Before she walks through the wall, she utters, "This is your fight, love," and lets out a small laugh.

A gigantic wyvern wing smashes through the room. Tim is still asleep, for the melody of Amelia hasn't worn off yet. Stratford, in disbelief, walks over to the edge of the room overlooking the inside of the Alynn inner structure. The Diablo Arches begin shooting their arrows towards Verlock and Alfred, who have transformed themselves into two huge, vicious wyvern.

Both Verlock and Alfred pull Tim out of the fortress and place him inside a large brown cage on Verlock's back. The Galons have power over them, and their eyes are charged with electrical current. Both of them roar as they turn around and grab Sylkin, who is already in the air jumping toward them with his razor-sharp paws. Alfred's giant fist smashes the top of the panther's neck as Verlock cracks Sylkin's leg. The panther wails in pain. The twins' magical power to protect the Galons is unmatched. They can appear in both worlds without the stairwell of travel.

Stratford screams at the top of his lungs. "Verlock and Alfred, I should've known." He stands there, using his hands to project his voice. "I will find my way out of Selwyn's Chancer."

At the same time, Verlock and Alfred grab Tim and disappear into thin air. Silence fills the room. Amelia appears right next to Stratford, whispering something into his ear.

Stratford grins once as he grabs her waist. They both begin dancing, waiting for another time to strike. Classical music springs from the piano, even though the entire body of the piano is damaged. Stratford and Amelia hold hands, dancing slowly out the room with much anticipation, thinking about how they each get what they both can get for themselves out of the situation.

TIM HARTWELL: Open Your Heart Trilogy (Books 1-3)

Fight Near The Clicketts

A flash in the sky shoots toward Greenhill School. Thunder strikes through the sky to the ground.

Tim opens his eyes and finds himself sitting next to Owen at the exact same time, back in the library—the same moment when Owen said the same words he said at school earlier.

"Are you winding me up?" Owen asks Tim while he continues to eat some chips out of his bag. Owen stands up, knocking over the entire bookrack. Tim quickly helps Owen pick up the books when one particular book catches his attention. Suddenly, the school bell rings for the next class. Owen rushes out of the library, followed by Tim.

"Go ahead, I will check it in on Monday. Just remember to bring it back," says Mrs. Watcliff.

Tim nods his head as he cuts the corner, bumping Owen and trying to scare him.

"I almost scared you, right out of your britches," Owen laughs. Tim rubs the Galons under his shirt.

As the two boys make their way to class, Mr. Oxley, the science teacher, turns on the projector with his remote. Mr. Oxley clears his throat to begin.

"Science is something special to all of us. This is your biggest grade of the class. You have one hour to finish all of the questions, which are multiple choice. After you are done, you may head down to the Clicketts for the rugby match." Mr. Oxley looks around the class, looking for some help.

"Cambria, will you pass out the test for me?"

"Yes, Mr. Oxley," she replies with a soft voice, keeping her face covered with her long black hair. Cambria's father, Gywn Wallace, moved to Tenby with his wife, Gloria. They both work at the harbour, selling goods. During the winter, they vacation in West Wales and ride horses in the countryside.

Cambria looks at Tim, running his fingers through his hair. Everyone in class is working on their test, concentrating on each question. Nine minutes have passed, and most of the students look nervous. Mr. Oxley wants them to work hard for their grade while learning everything they can about science. He moves to water his small plants in the window sill.

Without warning, the seventh Galon begins to speak to Tim. Eleanor informs him of what he needs to pay attention to.

"Remember, Stratford can take the form of anyone you come in contact with, so stay focused and remember who you are talking to," Eleanor whispers as she casts a spell that speeds up time.

Tim looks around the classroom at the other students, who appear to be in fast-forward. Eleanor makes another flash, which sends Tim under the bleachers at the Clicketts.

Most of the students and faculty are above him in the bleachers, cheering loudly. Tim looks down at his new clothes, for he is wearing a blue Greenhill rugby jersey, black shorts, and blue calf socks.

Eleanor begins to speak from the

Galon again, but her voice is muffled from the jersey. Tim pulls the seventh Galon from under his shirt while the fans chant Hurt's name as he scores a record-breaking try. The announcer goes crazy over the talented Greenhill School player.

As the crowd calms down, Eleanor says, "Be careful, Tim. Your magic power from the keys is growing in such a way that you could lose control of your emotions. Even your toughest decisions haven't been made yet. Stratford will be back, for his Selwyn's Chancer is stronger than you know. He won't be gone for long, so keep your eyes open."

Owen, who was searching for

Tim, finds him under the bleachers.

"Are you crazy, Tim? What are you doing back here, huh? The match is going on right now. We have to get back to the bench now!"

Owen tries to move things along. Both of them begin walking from underneath the bleachers toward the side of the scrum, near the home team bench. Their rugby coach, Mr. Smith, hasn't realized they have walked up yet; he is tied up with the action of the match.

Both Owen and Tim sit on the bench and watch the match continue.

"Holy Tenby," Owen says about his cousin, Hurt, who is running within his own twenty-two. Even Tim wonders how Hurt is able to break out of tackles the way he does. Hurt, quick on his feet, jumps over #13 Broderick Haul, who is the best second-row player on the Rhydywaun team.

The Rhydywaun coach, Mr. Davis, knows very well that Hurt is talented, so he yells over to his prop, #8, Michael Evans, to tackle Hurt before he scores the winning try of the match.

Michael runs around and dives forward, stretching his arms for the big tackle. Hurt is leaping at the same time, and Michael grabs one of his legs in the air. Hurt tucks the ball under his arms for protection as he falls down near the goalpost. His shoulder smashes into the pole, but he lands safely, scoring a tying try.

The entire Greenhill team jumps up, cheering loudly. The crowd on the bleachers chant, not knowing that their star player is badly injured.

Hurt starts twisting and turning on the ground. The referee blows the whistle for Coach Smith to check out his player. Smith orders everyone to give Hurt some breathing room. Coach Smith raises his hand in the air for the school trainer to run over. A representative from the Pembrokeshire District Junior Rugby Association is scouting Hurt. His name is Christian Jones, who has shown up to see what all the talk is about concerning the Greenhill School star player.

The crowd in the bleachers, along with members of the opposite team and family members, wait patiently to see if Hurt is okay.

With a few thoughts racing through his mind, Tim uses the Galon to freeze time. Both teams and all of the people in the bleachers are frozen stiff. Tim wraps his fingers around the first Galon with the intention to heal Hurt.

Verlock and Alfred appear out of the sky, descending in front of Tim as he bends down to aid Hurt.

"Don't do it!" Alfred yells at the top of his lungs.

"Let time go its natural course, Tim," Verlock adds.

"Why can't I help him?" says

Tim, removing the first Galon key from around his neck. He reaches down, not paying attention to the twins.

Verlock grabs Tim's wrist, stopping him. "He's completely hatstand!" Verlock says, looking at Alfred as Tim pulls his arm away.

Alfred looks at Hurt's body, frozen in a position of agony. "He really does look hurt, doesn't he?" says Alfred, sneaking in a joke as they look at the way Hurt's body is positioned.

"The more you use the Galon in reality, Stratford will become stronger over time. We told you that," says Alfred. "Please leave things the way they are supposed to be in your world. There are many reasons why this must be."

Alfred begins judging Tim's motives while Eleanor projects her words of wisdom as well.

"Listen to them wisely," she says. "You have a chance to unlock the secrets in our families' book."

Tim's emotions overrun the situation. He places the first Galon on Hurt's body, healing him instantly. A split second after that, the sky turns dark as night. Everyone in the crowd and on both teams magically disappears. Verlock and Alfred know that Tim is playing with fire. Verlock takes a protective stance, knowing that Stratford is up to something. Near the opposite side of the field, thunder strikes throughout the sky. Alfred sticks his nose in the air, smelling the unbearable stench of Stratford's body.

Red lights begin to sparkle in the sky when a comet falls out of the clouds toward the field, creating a gigantic explosion that sends dirt and debris flying. Dust fills the air, thicker than volcano ash. Stratford howls as he climbs out of the huge crater he forms from landing on the field. Without hesitation, he takes control of the situation.

"What do we have here?" Stratford's feet sink into the ground as he steps near Tim and the twins. Pointing his hands toward Verlock and

Alfred, Stratford says, "He will have to play my Selwyn's Chancer no matter what you imbeciles try to come up with. The journey to the Spinning Heart will not be easy.

"Mary was ambitious in giving a boy descendant a Galon key," Stratford adds as the dust begins to clear. He then begins to lay out his next plan.

"You will have to play another game in the town of Llangollen," Stratford laughs. Amelia's eyes illuminate and fade, catching them off guard, for she has been watching the entire time. Amelia begins to spin in a tornado-like motion, which makes Stratford and her vanish, turning everything back to normal. There is Rayleigh scattering across the daytime sky.

The sun is beaming toward the Clicketts; Tim is caught off guard by the transformation of events. The crowd in the stands notices that Hurt is perfectly fine and is standing in front of Tim.

"Tim, I was in pain, but somehow my shoulder is fixed," says Hurt. "I am not sure what happened, but I feel better than ever."

Coach Smith, who believes Hurt just got the wind knocked out of him, asks Tim to kick a drop goal when he gets in during the next conversion.

Tim's mother, Mary, who had a dental appointment, finally arrives at the match. She arrives just in time to catch her son getting his first minutes in the match. As Greenhill kicks off, one of the Rhydywaun players drops the ball out of bounds. Greenhill begins a lineup with only fifty seconds left in the match. As a scrum occurs, both teams wrestle to get position. Hurt digs out the ball and tosses it back to Tim for him to kick a drop goal.

Broderick races back as fast as he can to block the kick, but Tim smashes the ball with his foot, just before Broderick gets a chance to block him. The ball sails through the air and begins to float as if in slow motion. It slowly rotates over the crossbar, right between the uprights, as the clock buzzer goes off. Greenhill fans begin cheering as they win the match against Rhydywaun, 16-13.

Owen and the rest of the team run toward Tim and Hurt with excitement. Members of the loosing team shake their heads with disappointment. Some of them are not happy to be in the lineup to shake hands after the defeat. Tim's intuition makes him look up, catching Broderick, the last player to shake his hand before they leave for the buses.

Tim glances into his eyes, which have the same glare as Stratford's. It is the look of insanity and power. Stratford has total control of Broderick's mind.

The contact with him, shaking hands, is all he needed to control Broderick. Tim, out of the corner of his eye, notices his mother looking at him. Her lips are moving slowly as he tries to read them. Tim can only decode some of what Mary is saying.

"Jump to the left with all your might," she whispers. Tim turns around and sees Broderick, who is throwing a water bottle toward him. The water pours out of the bottle and becomes bigger as it gets closer to him. The water widens like a small wave from the River Dee, covering his sight. Tim attempts to dodge out of the way but is engulfed by the huge amount of water that leads Tim's body into the stairwell of travel without using a door—an idea Stratford has perfected over time to manipulate Selwyn's Chancer.

Jump Over World's End

Night brings out the shadows on the horizon. The sound of the River Dee soothes Tim's ears. Looking over the edge, he notices the current thrusting its way underneath the Llangollen bridge. The moon has parked itself over the railway station, glaring over the entire town of Llangollen. His senses pick up a presence nearby; Tim scans the brick houses and notices two small figures flying past the slate roofs ahead of him. The two figures swoop down below the bridge and then fly up onto its edge, parking themselves like birds. Behold, Alfred and Verlock, keeping up as they inform Tim of his task ahead.

"We must warn you of great danger ahead," says Alfred. "This will not be easy. Stratford is waiting for you to reach the Spinning Heart, for he is willing to do anything to get the Book of Hartwell. His bitterness against the House will make him do anything."

They all start walking toward the other end of the bridge, opposite of the railroad station. Verlock points toward a small streak of light that is hovering. Turning gracefully, Tim says in an astonished whisper, "It's another . . ."

Tim pauses for a moment while he walks over to the Galon. Its body is glaring with crystals, which give off streams of light toward Tim's chest. The other three Galon keys rest on his chest.

A necklace appears as he reaches for the Galon's body. His eyes are wide with promising tales of fortune. Verlock and Alfred both smile as Tim slides on the necklace holding his new Galon key. Tim anxiously awaits his gift and closes his eyes before the twins speak.

Alfred's eyes become slim as his twin snaps his fingers, shouting "Silurian" once more. Lights swirl around the bridge as Verlock grants Tim his new magical powers. Alfred speaks in unison

TIM HARTWELL: Open Your Heart Trilogy (Books 1-3)

with Verlock:

"The fifth Galon brings strength,
you may burst through any tree.
May your hands illuminate
blue fire from your fists.
Turning cold, what you see."

Tim opens his eyes to blue flame, which cover his hands with fire swirling around his arms. Verlock parks himself back on the edge of the bridge as he waits for Tim, who is holding his arms in the air, to yell out a magic power. Many thoughts race through Tim's head, leading to one work, constantly pounding in his head.

Tim screams "Firewyn," which

distinguishes the fire around his arms.

"Very well. Use that word wisely to start or finish the sequence of your new heart of flame," says Verlock.

Tim proceeds to the edge of the bridge, right next to Verlock. Alfred follows behind him, looking over the River Dee. His eyes turn to halo blue. He stares at the current below as the water begins to slow. The sound of ice sliding together can be heard. Tim jumps six meters into the sky, landing on one of the rocks in the middle of the river. The water is frozen by the time he lands on the rock. The entire lake is frozen, all the way to the center of Llangollen. He jumps back to the top of the bridge as the water turns back to normal. The town is still sleeping; no one is walking in the streets. The power of the Galon made everyone in town unaware of what is going on.

Alfred clears his throat and points toward the north. He explains that he will have to fight one of Stratford's allies, who is a vicious two-headed monster—part dragon and part lion, dangerous in every way.

"In this stage, killing Cynfor will be the only way to get back home," says Alfred. "Once you do, the stairwell of travel will appear. You are three Galons away from reaching the Spinning Heart. Stratford has designed this stage in Selwyn's Chancer for you to lose, so believe in your heart. We will be watching."

Alfred snaps his fingers, and Tim finds himself on the edge of World's End in Denbighshire in northeast Wales. Tim's feet are right on the edge of the cliff. He jumps back, looking into the distance.

Heading toward Castell Dinas Brân, which used to be controlled by the Kingdom of Powys, Tim walks across the southern wall, keeping guard for his life. Jumping on the mote, he turns westward, looking over the lands. He then turns around and looks through one of the arch-shaped windows of a medieval castle. He senses a weird breeze in the air, which seems to be coming from behind him.

With hesitation, he jumps through the arch gap while the mouth of a monster smashes through, barely missing Tim's agile but strong body.

The monster with two heads sneaks up on Tim as one of the heads blows fire through the air. The fourth Galon sends out light rays that blind the monster enough to let Tim escape through the Eglwyseg Valley. Cynfor stomps on the ground, which feels like an earthquake. Looking back, Tim notices both heads above the trees as they blow more fire toward him, destroying everything in his path.

Tim dashes faster toward World's End. Reaching back to the cliff, he turns around and starts taunting Cynfor.

"You want me, then come and get me. I am not scared anymore. I'm not afraid."

The lion-face head is half of Cynfor; it also has the gift of speaking English. The second head is part of a lost species, which is known for attacking without remorse. The body of the monster sways from left to right as the lion face begins to speak.

"If it isn't Tim Hartwell, the brave son of Mary. You will not reach the Spinning Heart as long as we are breathing. Stop now. Go home and give your key to your future daughter descendant. No boy can live through the emotion and stress of the Galon. We will give you the choice to leave now." The lion face pauses for a moment before continuing.

"Oh, how rude of me. How could I forget to introduce myself? My name is Miniver, and he is Cynhafar. We are the rulers of the House of Cynfor." Miniver's voice is as powerful as the legendary lions from thirteen thousand years ago in London. Miniver continues to lure Tim closer so they can trick him. Miniver's name was given to him for his golden spiky hair.

"So what will it be?" Miniver says, trying to distract Tim by waving his tail and knocking down a few trees in the way.

Tim, keeping his composure, steps closer to the edge. Miniver looks sideways, keeping an eye on Tim's movement.

"You don't plan to jump off the edge, do you? That means Cynhafar's dinner will be flat," Miniver smiles with anticipation, thrusting out his claw while trying to get Tim with a deadly blow.

Tim looks toward Cynhafar's head, which begins to freeze. The weight of Cynhafar's head pulls Miniver's head and the entire body of Cynfor crashing back into the trees.

Tim steps forward a bit, not knowing if they are dead or alive. Miniver's claw smashes out of the ice barrier surrounding their body. His howling fills the sky with a powerful angry toner. Cynhafar begins to roar, spitting fire from its mouth to heat and break the ice around his head. Cynfor stands up, and Tim backs up toward the cliff once more. Miniver begins to speak with hatred flowing through the creature's veins.

Cynhafar spits out a tremendous amount of flame toward Tim. Quick on his feet, Tim screams "Firewyn," which ignites the blue flame and stops the red flame that is coming toward him.

Both of their flames are locked together; Tim tries to keep their fire from pushing him off World's End. Miniver is amazed at the power of Tim. He orders Cynhafar to push harder, and white light begins to grow between each colored flame. Tim freezes Cynhafar's head once more, as it dangles downward. Its head causes Cynfor to fall backward toward the right.

Tim rolls to the left, trying to distract Miniver from getting back into their attack position.

Verlock and Alfred hide behind the trees, making sure their presence isn't felt. "He's completely hatstand," Verlock whispers to Alfred. They both cannot believe that Tim has chosen to stay.

Miniver is growing tired of fooling around, so he uses his tail to whip Tim off his feet, his body landing right off the edge of the cliff. Pieces of rubble begin to fall as Tim finds himself in a crack in the cliff, holding on for dear life.

Miniver begins to chuckle as his head peeks over the edge, looking down at Tim, wondering if Tim has fallen off the edge.

Below, Tim keeps his eye on Cynfor's feet as he moves one foot over the edge of the huge crack. Miniver monster knows what is going on. Tim freezes their foot on the edge of the cliff. At the same time, he uses the power of the fifth Galon and punches as hard as he can, directly under Cynfor's foot. Tim's new strength knocks huge pieces of rock slab from the cliff, and tons of rocks start to fall. Some of the rock that Tim is holding on to starts to break away, so he jumps to the other side of the huge crack, his arms flailing.

Loosing their grip, Cynhafar's mouth spits fire while Miniver screams at the top of his lungs.

They've been tricked, fooled by a young boy. Miniver is ashamed of his defeat. His eyes look down at the trees below. There's silence with every breath. Now they won't be able to get home. Selwyn's Chancer beat them with their own fate. In their minds, Cynfor's body smashes on the rock below, blood going all over the land.

A mushroom explosion creates fire that reaches all the way up to where Tim is standing, because their blood is thicker than heavy crude oil. Tim jumps back from the fire, holding his right hand above his eyes, which covers the fire's glare.

Fire turns into dark grey smoke that finally fades. Sunrise approaches the horizon with golden rays shining through most of the trees. A minor cut over Tim's arm starts to ache. He rubs his hand over the wound twice, healing it in the process.

"His magic has become second nature to him," says Alfred, who is hiding behind the trees with his brother. "I wonder if Ellington ever knew a son of Hartwell would even live through this journey?"

Tim sits on the edge of the cliff, holding all of the Galons in both hands. All of them light up in a difference sequence. Each one turns blue and white, giving off random, high-pitched chimes. Getting himself together, Tim notices a strong smell coming down the cliff. The stench of methane from the dragon's glands fills the air. Out of the blue, Tim begins to see thousands of images from the past. Looking up in the sky, he notices a whirlpool turning into a door of light. The stairwell of travel has shown itself as two different, made of light, which begin to split in two. Both doors are fifty meters off the cliff, hovering over the pathway below. Alfred and Verlock appear next to Tim. Knowing he must reach the stairwell of travel, Tim stands and brushes the dirt off his trousers, remembering what his mother said about jumping to the left. Collecting his thoughts, he walks back toward the trees behind the cliff. Taking a deep breath and trying to figure out the right pacing, Tim dashes forward toward the edge of World's End, moving as fast as lightning. He jumps off the cliff into the sky, heading toward both stairwells of travel in the air. His body enters the left stairwell of travel, moving as fast as a rocket breaking the sound barrier. A huge flash lights the sky as his body enters the doorway.

Verlock and Alfred watch while both doors begin fade into the sky. Alfred walks over to the edge of the cliff, looking down at Cynfor's dead body, and scratches his head.

Stratford and Amelia won't be too happy when they find out that Tim has killed the ruler of the House of Cynfor.

Astonished, Verlock says to Alfred, "He must be the one." The twins then fly into the clouds, disappearing until the next game in Selwyn's Chancer begins.

Night falls once more over World's End. Stratford appears at the bottom of the cliff alongside Amelia. They are stunned by what they see. Stratford rubs his hand along the neck of Cynhafar. Amelia resurrects Miniver's head so he can explain their failure.

"Oh, Miniver, how you have failed us so. Redeem your honor

by telling us what happened," says Amelia.

Miniver, resurrected, opens his eyes, adjusting their lenses and trying to focus. His breath is frail. Whimpering, blood oozes from his mouth as he speaks his last words.

"He . . . he is too strong. His magic is nothing like I have seen before. Beware. I think he can destroy you both." Amelia smiles as she looks over at Stratford in human form, dressed in a brown vest over a white linen shirt with black trousers.

Stratford picks up one of the huge rocks that cracked away from the cliff. He reaches back and throws it toward the field, skipping it along the grass. He turns back toward Miniver and gives him a piece of his mind.

"Is that so, Miniver? You dare warn us about this little boy? We are very aware that only females are allowed to find the Book of Hartwell. You are left with no honor and will get no sympathy from me to return to your lands."

Stratford taps on Miniver's forehead. Miniver begins to beg for his life, but Stratford raises a huge rock slab in the air with his magical power and smashes it over Cynfor's body. Amelia warns Stratford that Miniver can foresee and is capable of predicting the future.

"We must not play with Tim anymore. Kill him now!" says Amelia, walking over to Stratford and trying to convince him to handle the situation. Stratford cuts her off by covering her mouth.

"Silence!" he yells, his voice echoing in the sky then fading away.

Amelia steps back. "We have no idea what this boy can do. If you don't kill him, then I will. The Book of Hartwell is very important to you. I understand you have waited ages to get your hands on this priceless power." Stratford cuts her off once more and explains what she doesn't understand.

"We continue to be patient. The more he uses the power of the Galon, the stronger Selwyn's Chancer will be. I have done this many times over. How do you think the ruler of the House of Cynfor was at my command? We will see, Amelia. Trust me, my love. We can rule the world, their world." Stratford looks down at Cynfor's blood still dripping from Craig y Forwyn at World's End.

Amelia begins to create black smoke, which engulfs them both in the night, since this Hartwell descendant has picked up the magical power easily.

TIM HARTWELL: Open Your Heart Trilogy (Books 1-3)

Accident on Crackwell Street

Waters recede toward the banks the next morning back in Tenby. There is a lot of commotion in the streets, especially above the century wall. Tim's ears pick up several conversations around town. He hears mothers with their baby strollers riding over the cobbled streets. He even hears wine pouring into the glasses of locals who are eating breakfast around the way.

Tim made it through the stairwell of travel at World's End, which landed him back into his own bed as if he never left.

A gannet flies onto the window sill and looks directly at Tim, who is lying in bed. The bird starts flapping its wings, trying to wake Tim. The bird has a long white-and-black-outlined beak and a light brown spot near its head. Its elegant cream feathers and blue eyes are beautiful and catch the sun as it shines through the window.

TIM HARTWELL: Open Your Heart Trilogy (Books 1-3)

Tim is tired. The randomness of his new quest has taken a toll on his body. The first Galon lights up from underneath him. Tim doesn't feel the wing nudging him. Ellington, disguised in the gannet's body, unleashes his words to speak Welsh.

Ellington tries again to wake Tim without disturbing Mary in her master bedroom, who is painting in the break-off area.

"bachgen enwir Tim!"
(A boy named Tim)

Ellington's words send a cool breeze that lifts the cover off of Tim, as he is still wearing his soccer uniform from the rugby match. Ellington begins to speak to himself, almost laughing for not being able to wake Tim from his deep sleep.

"Amser a ddengys"
(Time will tell.)

Tim stretches his arms upward as he walks over to the window, thinking, and then scratches his leg as Ellington begins to lay down some important information. The orange sunrays flow through the room as Ellington begins to speak, his feathers ruffling a bit.

"Tim, you have now collected four Galons. You must now travel to Flintshire. This will be one of the hardest things you will ever do. You must believe in your heart to receive the next Galon. I am the oldest of the House.

"Trust no one, not even Verlock and Alfred," he continues. "They are too under the control of Stratford's Selwyn's Chancer. You should know that by now. There are even a few things you should not reveal to your mother. This will be hard, but remember one thing . . ." Ellington looks out the window to make sure he has not been followed, then continues.

"You must remember that the Galon's magic is binding to your body and mind. When you reach the holy well, the pilgrimage site will show you the path to the red cliffs. Once you find it, bring it to me on Ynys Gwales (Grassholm).

"Beware of Stratford and Amelia, for they both will do anything they can to stop you from reaching me again. I am sure he will be lurking around between Skomer and the mainland." Ellington spreads his long wings and allows his feathers to breathe as one of them falls inside Tim's bedroom.

Tim looks into the blue eyes of the gannet, believing every word Ellington says, for Tim has never had a father figure to guide him. His mind begins to wander as he looks out the window at the water. Tim wants to become better; he wants to be a man, to be there for his mother.

Mary, in the master bedroom, pulls her headphones from her head. She stops painting another ocean landscape, tossing her brush into some water in a plastic cup. She overhears Tim having a conversation with someone in his bedroom. She walks over to Tim's door, which has a poster of Shane Williams diving, scoring a try.

Mary opens the door, only to find Tim reading the book that he rented from the library at Greenhill. Looking toward the right, she notices a gannet flying out of the window. Mary is not puzzled at all. She knows something is going on.

"What are you reading this morning?" Mary asks with a relieved tone. She has never been the type of person to ask a million questions.

"It's a book written by Michael Hudson about the secrets of Wales during the Roman era," says Tim. He opens the middle of the book to a bonus section about Brutus of Troy and his arrival in 1103 BC. Brutus is the supposed founder of London, but in this historical book, he is considered more of a mythological character. There is a picture of Brutus with white feathers sticking out of the top of the helmet, which bears his family crest. The crest has a lion-type character resting on top of a white shield.

Tim looks up; Mary has already walked over to the window and is glancing to the right. Kids are singing the Welsh national anthem in the street. A harp melody is coming from a radio that someone is carrying to provide the soundtrack. The notes are dancing in the wind, filled with positive energy, happy as can be.

"Voices of joy. No worries. I can see that now," Mary whispers to herself as she begins to sing along with the kids outside.

Her voice relieves the stress in the room. She then sits on the edge of Tim's bed, rubbing her hand through his hair as if he were only five years old. Mary is caught off guard by one of her paintbrushes floating in the air. Tim looks at more things in his room as they begin to float in the air, including his school book and pieces of paper from the floor. Mary, taking this as a sign, informs him that she never should have given him the key, She knows she broke the rules of Selwyn's Chancer. She can live with that now. She even regrets helping him before he traveled to Llangollen. But her love of her son explains that Ellington cannot be harmed by Selwyn's Chancer, no matter what. Putting her hair in a ponytail with her fingertips, most of the floating objects in the room go back to their original places.

The Galons, which are on the floor, float over to the map on the wall, all four of them dangling in front of the map like crystals on a chandelier.

"I cannot interfere anymore. Be safe, Tim," says Mary. She walks out of the room as if she knows something is going on. Mary locks the door behind her, leaving Tim alone in his room. He walks over to the map and to the "X" marked over Skokholm Island.

Tim, not wasting any time, jumps into the shower, bathes, then changes his clothes. He puts on a white polo shirt, black trousers, and a royal blue cardigan with the Hartwell coat of arms on the chest.

Alfred and Verlock pop their heads above the window, check in, and then disappear underneath the window.

Tim opens his closet and grabs his Welsh dragon messenger bag, tossing the strap around his neck. Then he grabs all of the Galons, adding them to the necklace around his neck. Putting his finger on his chin, he remembers to grab the Wales map from his wall as well.

Heading for the door, he stops in the kitchen and grabs a few snacks, along with some British pounds he was saving for himself.

Tim waves goodbye to his mother, who is in her bedroom, and runs downstairs to the front entrance. He overhears his mother yelling downstairs, just before he closes the front door.

"Tim, it's Owen. He wants to

know if you want to hang out sometime today," says Mary, while wiping some paint on her apron.

"Will you tell him I will meet up with him later? I think I am on to something. Bye, Mam."

He turns back to the front door and is caught off guard by four girls standing near the entranceway. All of the girls are in nineteenth century Welsh clothing. Their garments are made with Welsh flannel, and they're wearing red petticoats, white apron, knitted stockings, bed gowns with loose sleeves, tall black silk hats, paisley shoulder shawls, and white cotton kerchiefs. The girls' shoes are sparkling, made from glace leather with metal buckles.

Tim stands back for a second as they all look at him and burst into laughter. All of them start running away as they head down White Lion Street across from Norton, right past North Beach. Tim notices an RAF Sea King helicopter flying toward the harbour. He then picks up his bike and flies down Norton until he turns onto High Street. He then goes left on Crackwell Street, which leads to Bridge Street. Tim is going so fast that no one even notices him. He quickly dumps his bike and heads to the viewing area of St. Mary's Church. The RAF helicopter flies closer toward the light boat station and then on toward Caldey Island. In an instant, a loud construction explosion on Crackwell Street rattles loudly. Tim quickly bikes over to the area to see what happened. When he arrives at the scene, he ditches his bike and sees someone's arm sticking out of the metal siding. Painters working on one of the buildings didn't secure the metal wall cage properly, which crashed by accident.

Then a loud explosion goes off near Caldey Island. Tim looks back toward the woman, noticing head trauma. He uses his magic to freeze the metal cage, breaking away the fragments. Tim reaches inside and lifts the metal off of the woman. Then he uses the magic of the first Galon to heal her instantly; her eyes open with a blank stare. Then she looks at a girl named Alice Morgan. The woman's skin and hair are partially covered in blood, even though she is healed. Her sight becomes dazed as locals come toward her, screaming about the danger that occurred. Tim notices a member of one of the medical teams arriving from the lifeboat station to help her.

"Are you okay? My name is Jeffrey Collen, with RNLI. What happened here?" Jeffrey asks Tim as he checks her vital signs. Tim begins to back up a little as more paramedics arrive on the accident scene.

Tim magically transforms himself

into Mr. Collen so he can find out what is going off on the island. He grabs his messenger bag and leaves the rest of his clothes. His radio starts buzzing about the activity on Caldey.

He rushes toward the light boat station, runs inside, then jumps in the back of the lifeboat with the rest of the team.

One of Collen's teammates looks at Tim wearing a new bag over his yellow oversuit gear.

"Hey, Jeff, I didn't know you like those messenger bags. I like the logo on there, brother," the man says as the boat gets louder inside the station.

Tim, unsure of what to say without knowing the man's name, looks at the man's nametag, which says Helmut Collen. He then knows that Helmut must be Jeffrey's brother.

Tim nods his head then follows Helmut's lead by strapping on to the lifeboat.

"Don't forget to put your protective on, buddy," Helmut reminds Tim about his head gear. Tim, still not used to his new body, thanks Helmut when everyone is holding on to the railing.

When the locking mechanism releases, the lifeboat shoots down the ramp, diving into the water with a giant splash.

The rest of the RNLI team disperses to their positions, looking forward as they see the smoke coming from Caldey Island not too far off. Most of the team stares into the distance at the island, wondering if the Coast Guard team stationed there is still alive. The expression on some of the faces of the team members is grim. Many bodies are floating in the water, burned to a crisp. It takes Tim a little while to get used to Jeffrey's body, since Jeffrey is tall and muscular. Tim starts to think about what is real and what is the parallel world of Selwyn's Chancer. The lifeboat reaches the outer banks of Caldey Island.

Seconds later, the environment landscape changes. Rain begins to pour harder than ever. All of the crew members are wondering what is going on. Lightning begins to strike as thunder pounds another bolt from the cumulonimbus clouds above. The waves begin to pick up as they notice an RAF helicopter landing on Caldey. The thunderbolts are larger than anyone on the lifeboat has ever seen.

Helmut, unafraid, pumps his fist for everyone to lock into their positions, to stand strong regardless of the weather.

Fire rises in the air like an explosion on an oil field. Tim grabs his helmet as a large wave knocks against the lifeboat. The entire RNLI team is mentally focused. All of the training has paid off.

They have no fear. These people, some with families, are volunteers. They are there to save lives, no questions asked. Sticking to the fundamentals gets them on the docking station.

Most of the lightning stops. Helmut orders Tim to get into the helicopter, and from there, to take control in the air. Without Tim knowing it, the Galon keys magically appear back around his neck. His heart is bursting with trust in his new family. Tim jumps into the Sea King HAR3 helicopter. The lead pilot uses every bit of the Rolls-Royce Gnome turboshafts. Smoke fills the air; the pilot hand signals Tim to get a gas mask on.

Tim grabs the air mask stationed

above, then looks down at the size of the fire rising toward them. Winds pick up, and then time freezes. Everyone is frozen in the air; even RNLI members in the lifeboat below are frozen.

The helicopter pilot notices a large face appearing out of the fire; the face is almost dragon-like. It begins to move upward, headed right for them. The face in the fire is that of Stratford in his beast form. Stratford roars louder and louder as the face of fire comes toward the helicopter faster than a jet. Tim quickly jumps out the side of the helicopter fifteen meters up. Stratford's face opens as the blaze from his mouth devours the entire helicopter.

A large explosion goes off; the

gas tanks explode without warning. Pieces of metal fly down into the water. Some of the blades zip by, almost hitting Tim's leg when he dives into the water.

Moments later, the body of the Sea King HAR3 crashes into the water, falling into the depths.

Tim, holding his breath, swims toward the surface. At first glance, everything is back to normal. Tim looks at his hand, noticing that he is not Jeffrey anymore. Sunrays blind his eyes. A boat full of people heads full speed to his location. Tim quickly goes back down into the water, avoiding the boat by mere seconds as the propeller almost cuts him to shreds.

A light flashes below, catching Tim's eye. He begins to hear the sound of the Welsh national anthem, muffled by the water. Swimming deeper, his mind tells him that he has found the sixth Galon. The key is surrounded by light flashing toward his chest. It forms a lock and links itself onto the necklace with the other Galons. Then, out of nowhere, his body shuts downs from exhaustion. Just before he faints, Tim feels a pair of arms pulling him out of the water, only to find himself at St. Winefride's Well in North Wales.

The next day, the sky looks like the heavens. Tim wakes up in a private guest house on the back side on Caldey Island. He is wearing black trousers and a white shirt. His messenger bag is laying on the floor next to the bed. Not knowing about his surroundings, he puts his shoes on and runs out the front door into a sunny, beautiful day. He looks around and doesn't see any proof of fire or damage. Selwyn's Chancer has run its course, by Tim using more of his magical power from the Galons. He begins running to the side of the Calvary stuck in the ground. He sees Tenby not too far off on the horizon, along with boats floating in beautiful royal blue water.

Tim heads toward the western part of Caldey Island. The Galons give him the power to leap high, making Tim run faster than the speed of sound and jumping with all of his strength. His body leaps high above the clouds. The Galons illuminate, taking control as he travels across the sea. His body projects toward the island of Skokholm.

He descends from the sky, shooting toward the ground like a lightning strike. Time freezes quickly, and he lands on Skokholm unnoticed. Nature goes back to normal; time goes back to normal.

Tim begins to look for a particular red cliff. He then notices a group of small puffins gathering near one of the cliffs.

His mind drifts for a moment as he looks west to the island of Greenholm. The sun begins to set. The sky turns a darker blue and orange on the horizon. Tim's hunger builds. He pulls out a few snacks that he packed in his messenger bag when he was home. Eating some of the strawberry bars, two puffins approach him, following his every move. Both puffins walk over to one of the cliffs, which appear stained with red on the rock formation.

Something shiny appears out of the rocks below. Tim reaches down and picks up a few glowing Overton yew leaves wrapped around an object. The leaves are still fresh, plucked from the branches within the courtyard of St. Mary's Church, which is another one of the Seven Wonders of Wales.

Tim pulls out a golden key.

Verlock and Alfred begin to speak to him, disguised as the two small puffins he met earlier.

"You've found the third Galon of Hartwell. That is six you have now, my boy. Very good," says Alfred. "Please, sit, as we grant you the new magic"

Verlock yells "Silurian." Energy waves start racing against the ground, coming up from the water and moving along the grass toward Tim.

All of the energy heads toward his feet and attaches itself inside his body. Water from the ocean recedes, and Tim is left with a blank stare.

"What happened to me?" Tim questions.

Verlock replies without hesitation.

"This one will be more special than you know. Jump in the water and find out."

Tim tosses his bag aside and jumps into the sea water. The deeper he goes, the more he finds that he doesn't need air under water. His skin is even resistant to the cold temperature of the deep. He swims faster with excitement. He turns back toward Skokholm, leaping out of the water, landing right where he started.

Alfred and Verlock laugh as they see Tim start to love his magic, legendary powers.

Personnel from the watchtower notice a few intruders on the island who have not properly notified the Wildlife Trust of South and West Wales.

"Stay there. Halt." Personnel start running toward their location.

Tim grabs his messenger bag as Verlock and Alfred, still in the bodies of puffins, walk off in a hurry, laughing at the personnel coming. Tim jumps back into the water, swimming toward Grassholm Island at a fast speed. It takes him nearly five minutes to reach the island, where he rises to the surface on the opposite side of where the gannets live.

Tim looks around, wondering which one of the gannets could be Ellington.

Without notice, water begins to bubble near his location, and a huge ship lifts itself out of the water. Covered in seaweed and tons of mud, the name SS Walter L M Russ runs along the side of the ship. Dirty water flows out of the ship as it glides through the air, parking itself on the island. Running over to the ship as it towers above him, Tim leaps high in the air and lands on the deck of the ship.

A huge slam comes from a metal door, which opens and closes toward the captain's quarters. Stratford walks out of the door wearing clothes from the 1940s. He appears with a mustache and slick black hair. His clothes are sparkling clean as he steps over dirt and seaweed.

"Ellington won't be able to make it, so you have come for nothing,"

Stratford taunts Tim as he rubs his hand over the edge of the ship. "I might need Amelia to make a few needed interior changes around here. What, did you think I would be somewhere near Skomer? You thought wrong, my boy. You are making me stronger than ever. I can feel the magic of the third Galon. You have one more Galon to find. The last one will be harder than you think. I am eager to see how challenged you are. Can you handle pressure, Tim?" Stratford gets very serious. He can taste the victory of his wicked plan.

Tim grins with unbelievable confidence as Stratford's eyes look almost shocked. Tim is not afraid of him. Stratford raises his arms. In the process, the SS Walter L M Russ begins to fix itself up. Stratford wants Tim to realize what he is up against by making the metal on the ship bend and scream loudly as the ship moves slowly back into the water. As its stern splashes into the water, the gannets begin shouting high-pitched noises from their narrow beaks. Bull seals off to the side of the dark brown rocks of the island begin jumping back into the water.

Something catches Tim's attention. It is a woman's voice, singing in Welsh. Looking toward the bow of the ship, the music sounds like it is coming from a vintage record player. Stratford makes his way from the side of the ship toward the bow.

Stratford uses his Meteryn spell, turning everything back to normal. The SS Walter L M Russ disappears back under the water, leaving Tim to fall into the water. Merlin HC3 helicopters hover over the coast of Grassholm. The pilots look through their cockpit window for any suspicious activity; they had received a call from a local fisherman who noticed something was going on. The only thing the RAF aerial team sees out the window is the gannets flying through the air. One of the gunners on the helicopter swirls his arm to call off the search.

Another RAF helicopter, a Griffin HAR2, turns around and follows the Merlin HC3. The sound of the helicopters drifts off, lower and lower, as they head toward the horizon.

TIM HARTWELL: Open Your Heart Trilogy (Books 1-3)

The Last Galon

Melodies from All Saints' Church begin to ring out. Tim finds himself lying on one of the benches inside. Its roof of aisles and nave are concealed by the battlemented parapets. The ceiling is paneled inside. Tim wakes up and rubs his eyes to the loud sound of the bells ringing.

Some lights shine through the stained glass inside the abbey in Basingwerk, which is located off the banks of the River Dee below the Holywell in Flintshire. The bells keep ringing with both eights as Tim looks around, noticing his messenger bag on the floor below the bench. He quickly stands and picks up his bag. The sound of the bells slows and dies down.

"The year is 1875," says Eleanor, speaking from the seventh Galon. "Quickly, find the last Galon before time moves forward once more. This is the last of the Seven Wonders of Wales. Now find it. Hurry."

Tim begins to search All Saints', looking for the last Galon. Looking up at the chandeliers hanging from the wall, he notices the last Galon dangling from one of its arms.

He looks at the Galon key, which is made of the finest rose gold. Tim walks over and stands on top of one of the benches inside the nave. Just before he touches the Galon, time and space go forward again. Outside, the weather moves rapidly, changing from night to day as the last Galon, which is the second Galon, moves and attaches itself to the necklace around Tim's neck. Eleanor tells Tim the current time is World War II, since the bells are ringing due to possible raids. She also warns Tim that if he doesn't find the stairwell of travel before the bells stop, he will be stuck in the past forever.

Taking a deep breath, he starts looking for the door to get home.

TIM HARTWELL: Open Your Heart Trilogy (Books 1-3)

Remembering his magical gifts, Tim pulls out the fourth Galon dangling on the necklace, which makes an organ play a few magical notes in the church. Tim looks up toward light dancing through the clerestory windows, giving off a reflection that points toward the chancel. Walking over, Tim stands in front of the screen, which dives the nave to the chancel. Tim, who really wants to get home, creates a door in front of him. The sounds of the organ wind down with mere seconds to spare. Tim quickly opens the door and heads in the stairwell of travel, hoping to get back home safely.

    Voices of people cheering come from afar. Tim finds himself waking up on Ludgate Hill, down the street from St. Paul's Cathedral. As he runs to check out what the commotion is about, he notices a newspaper that has brushed itself against his feet. He picks up a Telegraph dated April 29, 2011.

Tim runs down the mall, which leads to Constitution Hill, with tons of spectators looking to see the Royal Wedding.

Making his way through the crowd coming around Grosvenor Place, Tim glances up, noticing the newly married couple walking onto the balcony at Buckingham Palace. People are cheering and waving their hands in the air. Prince William, the son of Prince Charles, has married the Duchess of Cambridge, Kate Middleton. The entire crowd is happy for them. Kate's wedding dress makes her look stunning. Tim looks up, happy for them, glad to see that William has met one of the most beautiful women in the world. The newlyweds kiss on the balcony. The crowd cheers again with excitement and happiness.

A British flag sails in the air and descends upon Tim's head. A person takes the flag off Tim; Tim notices that it's wintertime in Tenby. Tim looks up to see a teenager running off with the huge Welsh flag that had been lost due to high wind.

Tim finds himself standing on North Beach; time has moved forward a few months to around Christmastime. North Beach is packed with swimmers and spectators of the 41st Tenby Boxing Day Swim. Tim runs down the beach in the freezing temperature. People are dressed up; most of them are wearing costumes or the color red.

Making his way past Goscar Rock, Tim catches time freezing once more as day turns to night. Everyone on the beach has disappeared. The only thing still present is the bomb fire near the Boxing Day Swim location. On guard, Verlock and Alfred appear in front of Tim. They shout "Silurian" and grant him the magic of the last Galon. Both of them disappear, leaving Tim alone on the beach. A loud roar comes from behind Goscar Rock.

Locked into position, Tim glances ahead to get a better look. It's Amelia. She has turned herself into a female titan, standing tall above Tenby.

"Defeat her to find the Spinning Heart," Verlock whispers. Amelia walks in her black dress of mist, covering the beach entirely. Pieces of her dress flow into the water. Amelia raises her hands and shoots out blades the size of Tim. He dodges left, then right, trying not to get hit by her sharp weapons.

Tim screams "Firewyn," which ignites his hands in blue flames. He jumps in the air, high above her head. The blue flames around his arms create a thunder strike, which blasts Amelia in the eyes.

Amelia screams; her agony makes Tim cover his ears as he lands back on the beach. She begins to speak with regret about how she has been defeated.

"How can this be? How can this boy defeat me with one strike? My love, Stratford, help me, please. His power is stronger than I have ever seen. How can this be?"

She begins to shrink, leaning against Goscar Rock. Her voice wails through the air once more as the mist from her dress begins to move back toward her. A blast from Tim's arm hits her right in the heart, making her body disappear forever, fading into the water. Tim's body disappears as well.

In a flash, he appears on Fore Street in Totnes. He looks down at a sign that commemorates Brutus of Troy, the mythological founder of London. Then someone touches his shoulder, distracting him from reaching toward the stone. A man smiles and begins to speak. He informs Tim that he is Ellington Hartwell. His facial expression is somewhat sad, knowing that they never met at Ynys Gwales (Grassholm.)

"Where have you been? I've found all of the Galons and still, I am unclear on what this Selwyn's Chancer is all about," says Tim.

Demanding more answers. Ellington informs Tim that the power of the Galons and Tim's destiny will remain unclear due to the fact that he is a boy carrying the Galons.

Ellington also informs Tim that he must touch Brutus' stone. It will lead him to a particular castle that holds a direct route to the location of the Spinning Heart.

Tim puts out his hand, grazing the Brutus Stone, then finds himself back inside his bed at home in Tenby. Mary is fixing tea in the kitchen. Tim walks in, hoping to find a few more answers.

"Mam, where is the Spinning Heart? I must know," says Tim, unaware of the consequences if Mary continues to help him.

"I cannot tell you much more,

Tim. I wish I could. Stratford might have the power to do anything to you or the world now. Selwyn's Chancer is not just a spell, it's a game that Stratford keeps to hold family descendants. Many of them died ages ago or recently. It takes the world we are from and transforms it into a world of Selwyn's Chancer." Mary taps her spoon on her teacup.

"Well, tell me, why did Cynfor tell me something different at World's End?" Tim asks.

"Whatever it told you is an illusion of the truth," says Mary. "All it wanted was to deter anyone from reaching the Spinning Heart.

"None of us knows where it is. There are others trapped in Selwyn's

Chancer. You just haven't seen them yet. Besides, some of them are not human, and believe me, your grandmother, Lilly, told me that there are more beasts that thrive there. They are more dangerous than Stratford, even though he tricked them into Selwyn's Chancer."

Mary gets up and walks over to the faucet and runs water on her dishes. Tim is starting to think his mother has done this before; he also believes she didn't stop finding all of the Galons like she said before.

Mary can sense Tim's growing emotion, so she gives her son a clue toward the Spinning Heart's location.

"Head toward Jack Sound. It

should be somewhere near there."

The twins are watching from the other room, cloaked with invisibility. Verlock and Alfred begin to worry for Mary's life, for she has broken the rules of Selwyn's Chancer.

"Her doom will come sooner or later. I am sure Stratford can feel that someone has been tampering with his rules of engagement," Alfred says with a serious tone. Both of them disappear through the walls, filled with anticipation of Stratford's next move. Tim and Mary fall asleep during another night in Tenby.

TIM HARTWELL: Open Your Heart Trilogy (Books 1-3)

Rise of Truth

The next morning, Tim wakes up on a ship on its way toward Jack Sound.

He looks at the map on the wall that shows the body of water located between Skomer and the Pembrokeshire mainland. The ship is filled with tourists; music from Katherine

Jenkins plays over the speaker system. Most of the people are looking over the edge of the ship. Kayakers are out in the rough water, testing their skills. Tim gets out of the captain's sleeping corridor with the sun shining warm above.

The breeze of salt water from St. Brides Bay fills his nose as he walks to where the rest of the tourists are located.

A man from North Wales, by the name of Michael Beck, walks over to him, talking about the scenery.

"Good morning. Are you enjoying the weather? Trying to visit as much of Wales as I can. Me and my wife are visiting every castle and island around Wales. How about that, eh?" Mr. Beck says as he waves to his wife and four kids. "I hear the inner ward is magnificent too. The Manorbier Castle—I believe it's eight kilometers west of Tenby, Pembrokeshire."

Mr. Beck, thinking out loud, drinks more of his coffee from his silver canister with a Welsh Logo on the rubber heat protector. Tim nods and smiles but doesn't speak at first. He quickly says a few words, then goes toward the bow of the ship.

He collects his thoughts, knowing he isn't the most liked kid at school. He then looks at the water below.

Mr. Beck heads back to his family as they take pictures of Skomer Island.

Throughout this journey, Tim's sense of magic has been growing at a rapid rate. He can see and hear sounds from many kilometers away, such as the water brushing against the bow of the ship. The only thing he cannot hear is Verlock and Alfred sitting behind Tim as they chatter on.

"He wasn't supposed to achieve this early," Alfred says while sitting atop the boat. Verlock plays with a magical ball made of light and picks fish from out of the water.

Tim rests his arms on the rail of the ship. "He is the only boy before him to have the chance to achieve the Galons since Ellington," says Verlock, speaking on things that Tim doesn't know about.

"Is that so?" Amelia says, approaching from the left as a young girl, the image in which Selwyn's Chancer had resurrected her. Stratford squeezes between them as the father of the girl.

"Thank you, for we have been waiting for your mouths to slip out the truth of our families' unknown history. Now, I am still trying to figure out how you little wyverns knew this. Have you been speaking with Ellington?" Stratford asks, getting a little impatient. "I will make more adjustments to Selwyn's Chancer. Remember, this is my spell, my world."

Stratford, talking with his deep

voice, becomes displeased with the progress, so Amelia shocks them repeatedly until they become silent.

Stratford continues to speak while taking the appearance of Tim's science teacher, sharing things Verlock and Alfred have never heard before.

"You have no idea that I have control of his mother," Stratford says. "As for these two little brats, if you inform Tim about my plan, I will send you both to the Death of Ages. Do not take advantage of my Selwyn's Chancer."

Amelia nods and disappears, for she has heard enough. Verlock and Alfred look scared because Stratford has turned himself into beast form.

Leaning in with his teeth

resembling those of a vampire, Stratford says, "What do you two imbeciles have to say now? I will send him to the Senedd in Caerdydd, and you two better not show up anywhere near him. Or else." Stratford makes a hand gesture, with a knife going across his neck.

Verlock and Alfred, scared out of their minds, disappear into thin air. Stratford continues to look at Tim as the ship passes Tower Point in the bay.

A huge rock formation under the ground smashes into the hull of the ship.

Tim's body is catapulted into the air, flying off the ship and splashing into the water. Stratford had proved a point to Tim without Tim knowing it. Stratford disappears as the crew and tourists start panicking. The ship sinks in the water as people scream for help. Some of the crew members get emergency life rafts and dump them into the water, then Stratford jumps into the air, turning into a darker gannet flying away through cumulonimbus clouds.

When the journey through the stairwell of travel is complete, Tim finds himself inside the lobby of the Neuadd & Oriel. He looks right and sees two guards watching sports on the television. One of their walkie-talkies goes off. The security guard turns down the volume. The lights on the enormous timber ceiling flash on and off a few times. The television fills with loud cheers; both guards turn back to watch the TV screen.

Tim runs up the stairs through the Oriel, finally reaching the public gallery. His Galons around his neck begin flashing, filling the Siamr.

His body lifts and glides over the edge of the public gallery, down into the debating chamber. Tim kneels on a circle in the middle of the chamber, wiping his hands across the artwork, which was designed by Alexander Beleschenko.

"So this is the Heart of Wales they talk about at school," he says, tossing the necklace with all of the Galons into the air above the Heart of Wales. All seven keys divide then meld into one key. The light continues to rotate three hundred and sixty degrees and heads closer to the Heart of Wales.

Tim backs up where nine chairs make half of a circle behind him. The building begins to turn into light. The magical balance of the Galon sends Tim to the top of the Slate Dias at Caernarfon Castle. The moon parks itself high in the atmosphere.

In another flash, Tim finds himself inside the castle, sitting on an Investiture Chair. The same light inside the room goes through the window toward Eagle Tower.

Jumping out the window, Tim flies high in the air into the eagle well. The light begins to race off as Tim chases the mysterious light down the steps that lead him up from under the Well Tower. Using his jumping ability, he leaps on top of the bridge where the light still hovers over the middle of the bridge.

The magical light moves from Tim to the other side. He walks inside a small area, and as he looks to the right, he notices light entering the wall. Then a stone slides out of the wall, revealing the titanium Spinning Heart, locked in the gap where the stone used to be. Tim reaches inside and pulls it out.

"The Spinning Heart, I finally have it," Tim says quietly. The magic of the Spinning Heart sends him to a secret cave in Tenby.

Tim can't see a thing; it's pitch dark. All he can hear is the sound of waves. Taking one step, he hears something crackling below his feet.

"Firewyn," Tim says, as his arm begins to glow inside of a huge rock or cave, he thinks. He crushes some skeleton bones, which seem to have been there for a long time.

Trying not to panic, Tim moves his arms to get a better glimpse of where he is located. Looking down, he notices a book covered with dust laying on the ground inside a skeleton hand. Tim picks up the Book of Hartwell and sees the House of Hartwell coat of arms beautifully embroidered on the book. Then a glare of light turns from green to white. Using a metal sword, he picks up the pendant from another skeleton and blows away the dust, trying to figure out who these people were.

The pendant has a green coat of arms with six wings connected to a circle, with a monarch-type letter "G" in the middle of a shield.

"He wasn't a Hartwell," says Tim, brushing off more of the dust. Looking back at the Book of Hartwell, he tries to pry the book open with all of his might, but the magic of the book keeps it closed. He looks again at the floor and notices that his messenger bag is on the floor as well, except the Coat of Hartwell shield is on the front of the bag.

The floor of the cave begins to give out, throwing Tim back under the night sky of the Devil's Appendix in Snowdonia. Tim hears a roar through the sky. He's heard this music before, so he runs toward the Devil's Kitchen. Stratford is flaming at the lips, wanting to retrieve the Book of Hartwell, desperately knowing he can only get it while in Selwyn's Chancer.

Stratford begins to roar loudly with eyes glaring like the moon above. The Selwyn's Chancer spell has taken away some the magic ability of the Galon, except for the Firewyn spell for eleven days in Stratford's parallel world.

Tim begins running across the

water as a doorway of light appears ahead. He dashes up the Devil's Kitchen and notices the door to the stairwell of travel is closing. Tim runs faster, looking back at Stratford, who is right on his tail, approaching much faster than the last time he was there. Tim looks forward again, only to see Amelia in front of the door.

Wasting no time, Tim continues to run, screaming "FIREWYN!" with all his might. The blue flames lash out like wings on an eagle. The flames rise and sweep Amelia all they way toward the waterfall in the Devil's Appendix. Tim jumps toward the door as the light fades, turning back into stone.

Tim collides with the rock while

Stratford's mouth dives down to kill him. A green lightning strike comes out of the sky, electrocuting Stratford and sending him back down the hill.

A girl flies out of the dark sky, right next to Tim. Her face is concealed by the hood on her cloak. Tim can see a little bit of her hair dangling below the hood.

Stratford gets up, stumbling, swinging his arms widely as he runs across the water to get Tim and the girl. The mysterious girl is wearing a male signet ring. She raises her hands toward Stratford, sending currents of electricity all the way through the water toward Stratford's location. He begins to howl, as one hundred thousand volts travel through his body. The woman then electrifies Amelia, sending her body back up into the cumulonimbus clouds. Then a large dragon comes through the clouds, swooping them both up with its feet, putting Tim and the girl on its back.

Tim gets a better lock on the girl before she pulls down her hood, blocking his vision of her face entirely. He shrugs her off for a moment, looking down as they soar above the skies.

"Where are we headed?" Tim asks.

"We are headed toward Harlech Castle in Gwynedd," she replies, as she looks the other way.

"I think I liked you much better

when you where saving my life," he adds. She tugs part of her hood over, exposing her chin. She then turns back toward the clouds quickly and says, "Good enough?" with her callous humor.

After flying through the sky for a while, the dragon begins its descent toward Harlech Castle, landing on the gatehouse. The sun is going down as the mist covers the land. The girl jumps off the neck of the dragon while Tim follows.

The dragon flies off into the sky. "Come with me," says the girl, walking into the great hall. "We don't have much time. You must see my father. Stratford's beast will be here anytime."

They both rush into the inner area, crossing the inner ward. Tim notices there are guards who look like they are from the period of the Welsh wars. As they head into the great hall, a fire is burning; a man with royal clothes is sitting in a chair, enjoying the fire. The man begins to speak, calling his daughter by the name Ceri Gwynwell.

"So that's your name," Tim says, looking over to her. Ceri walks over to a seat next to her father, who begins to explain what is going on in Selwyn's Chancer.

"My name is Henry of Gwynwell, cousin of Stratford Hartwell. But what is most important is you, young boy. Your purpose here is to understand why you were chosen to lead your family's name.

"We are a family of many, along with your family, tracing back as far as the king of kings. I sent Ceri to protect you. She will guide you, along with many others that she will introduce you to."

"How do you know so much about our history?" Tim replies.

"It's not hard to hear about the family who uses the magic power of the Galon, along with a book full of magic that writes itself. Who do you think those skeletons were at your feet?" Henry asks while tossing another log on the fire.

"That was no cave you where

in," he continues. "You were inside Goscar Rock in Tenby. My family has tried many generations to get the Book of Hartwell from there, but has failed. I have been waiting a long time for the Hartwell boy descendant who would find the secret, hidden location of the book."

Henry's guards stop him from speaking as thousands of Stratford's beasts begin coming toward their location. Henry yells to Ceri for her to head back to Snowdonia.

"Wait," says Tim. "We are going back there? He just tried to kill us."

Henry speaks quickly. "Listen, Tim. We can show you how to unlock another world inside of Selwyn's

Chancer, which lies inside Snowdon Massif. Use Ceri as your guide. Meet my younger brother, Lancer, within the mountains." Henry slides on his mask for war, calling his personal guards to protect him.

Both Ceri and Tim run back to the inner ward of the castle. Ceri whistles for her dragon, named Drava, that descends from the sky while millions of beasts approach the Harlech Castle walls.

With ease, Stratford's beasts storm into the castle. Ceri and Tim jump on Drava's neck as they fly back into the night, heading toward Snowdon Massif. Ceri looks back at the castle covered in flames. Her eyes shine with the fires coming from the castle below. She begins to cry, weeping for her father's death.

Both Tim and Ceri remain quiet. Ceri turns her head, revealing the lower half of her face under her hood. She grabs the rim of the hood and pulls it back down as they fly toward the massif.

Ceri maintains a strong attitude and keeps her composure. Tim and Ceri both want answers about how powerful Selwyn's Chancer can really be as they blend into the dark night below.

Training in Massif

The wind is blowing over one of the highest peaks in Snowdon Massif. Rain covers the sky. A large breakaway in the mountain leads to an unknown cave in the Snowdon Massif area. Drava sweeps Tim and Ceri down into the mist, deep into the peaks of the mountains. Drava's wings flap hard as Tim and Ceri land near the entrance of a hidden cave.

Ceri lifts her hand, creating an aura around them, blocking them from the rain that begins to pour. Drava kneels to let them jump off as Ceri grabs the edge of Drava's wing so she can find her footing on the rocky ground.

Tim and Ceri stand in front of the mountain with three rocks placed on the ground as a call sign. Ceri points to the rocks and puts them in a certain order from left to right.

A huge boulder in the ground begins to fade away, revealing a path into the massif. "This way!" she orders.

Drava lunges into the sky and disappears in the rain. Tim follows Ceri as they walk into the mountains with a little light coming from outside. The , which is blocking the path, appears in its place, giving complete darkness to the pathway. Tim uses his Firewyn spell to illuminate the path.

Ceri notices a faint light at the end of the pathway of darkness. The light illuminates and darkens in a particular sequence. Tim rubs his hands over the rock walls as they move forward. Ceri looks over at him for a second, then she continues to the end of the pathway inside of the mountain.

A single candle is outside a medieval door at the end of the path. The candleholder is mounted on a wooden door, with iron nails and brackets all leading into the center. There is an oval indentation inside of a ring, which resembles the same signet ring shape on Ceri's finger.

Ceri raises her hand, pressing the signet ring inside the mounting piece. Tim glances over at Ceri, wondering if the ring is Henry's or Lancer's. The door opens, leading to large thirteenth century living quarters with arched hallways to the left and right. Tim and Ceri walk into the room, looking up and noticing a circular balcony directly above them with the flag of Wales hanging over the edge. Pictures of the eldest members of the House of

Gwynwell are mounted on the walls.

Tim looks at some of the weapons designed by some of the best hands in all of Wales. There are steel axes with leather handles, green-colored arrows on wooden crossbows, and helmets made with strips of gold along the edges of the mask.

All of the armor is inscribed with the Gwynwell coat of arms.

Lancer surprises them, as his words project throughout the room.

"If you are here, then my elder brother Henry must be dead. I knew this day would come sooner or later. Ceri, nice to see you again. You were a baby the last time I laid eyes on you. We don't have much time, so you will have to learn all of our family secrets to stay alive on the other side of Selwyn's Chancer."

Lancer moves his right hand, which had been resting on the balcony's edge. His dark cloak makes a shadow of him below. Tim notices the same signet ring that is on Ceri's hand is also on Lancer's left hand.

Tim's eyes narrow as he takes a few steps back. Ceri walks down the right hallway. Tim moves his head to the right, noticing Lancer leaving a shadowy trail of his previous movements from the upper level as he stands in front of Tim. Lancer stares into Tim's eyes, pulling back the hood on his cloak. His blond hair is slicked back. His eyes are the color of ocean water.

"Quiet, now. You are here to learn, not to ask questions," says Lancer. "I will train you on how to control your magic. We have used our ways to stay alive under Selwyn's Chancer.

"Some of your elders have been keeping secrets about your power. You have done things that no Hartwell has done before. All of the Houses know that now. I am sure you have noticed everything changing around you. Even the stop motion in time. You will not be able to understand until you master using the power of Firewyn." Lancer puts on some of his gear while Ceri walks down the right hallway.

"You killed Miniver and Cynhafar,

the rulers of the House of Cynfor. Once they figure out that you found the Book of Hartwell, they will do anything to get it, since they are trapped in here as well." Lancer walks toward the left hallway, suspiciously. Verlock and Alfred appear in the opening of the hallway as Lancer grips his medieval sword, which he keeps concealed under his cloak. With relief, Lancer begins to warn them all about breaking the Selwyn's Chancer spell.

"You have no idea of the consequences of disturbing Stratford's spell."

Alfred and Verlock point their fingers toward Lancer.

"We are here to protect Tim, you

little imbeciles," says Lancer. "Should we have let Stratford kill him?"

"My father didn't die for nothing, you two," Ceri interrupts as she walks back into the main room, eating an apple. She throws Tim an apple to eat as well. Lancer, tired of speaking, grabs one of the helmets from the wall and begins stomping toward the left hallway.

He illuminates the candles on the path that leads to a burgundy door at the end of the hallway. Lancer walks right through the door without even opening it. That's one of the magical powers he possesses. Tim notices the draped olive green side wall covered with golden holders mounted in the hallway.

"Lancer painted them all with his blood, sweat, and tears," says Ceri, watching Tim as he takes a few more steps forward in the hallway. Tim notices her smiling, as her chin is exposed below her hood. She continues to smile with a brave expression.

Tim notices she is wearing a necklace with a small pendant dangling down from inside her hood. Ceri walks past Tim in the hallway and opens the door slightly as rays of light sneak inside the hallway.

She closes the door as Verlock and Alfred begin to move between Tim and the hallway, using their wyvern magic.

They grant him the use of all of his Galon keys without Ceri and Lancer knowing. Alfred raises his arm, creating a light with his fingers, and says "Silurian Galon!" Verlock then raises his arm, creating a light with his fingers, which instantly gives Tim back his magic ability from each Galon key. The three walk toward the burgundy door.

Verlock hovers toward Tim, using his magic to reveal the virtual screen made of the future. Inside, the screen illuminates as it reveals a dark castle, located at the highest point in the Snowdon Massif.

"The House of Cynfor thrives there," says Alfred. "it has a huge army of those double-headed-dragon and lion-face creatures. The word has already gotten back to Bledri and Tomes, the only sons of Miniver and Cynhafar. They are even more ruthless, being able to read the minds of anyone who fears them. Go now, let Lancer and Ceri teach you the ways of killing them. Use your magic wisely to stay alive, for behind this door is another parallel world underneath this particular world of Selwyn's Chancer. It is home to some of the darkest monsters imaginable. Some of them are very poisonous. Remember, Stratford's beast will be able to track that location as well, so you must keep your guard up at all times."

    Eleanor's voice from the seventh

Galon begins to warn them. "Go, Tim. They have found you. Enter the stairwell of travel with the House of Gwynwell now."

A large explosion comes from the entrance of Lancer's domain. Stratford's beast has tracked the location of the bearer of the Galons. Tim opens the door to light that blinds his vision. He jumps into the light, which turns night into the brightest day.

Tim opens his eyes, noticing that he is on Crib Goch, almost a thousand meters up. The clouds are low, moving across the tip of the arete. His vision catches a distant figure riding a horse along Llyn Llydaw Lake below. Alert, Tim stands ready to fight. He's caught off guard by a voice that sounds very familiar. Lancer and Ceri appear and stand right behind him. They're almost waiting for him and this mysterious figure from below.

Tim glances up toward the sky as Ceri stands behind him, wondering what he is thinking about. Lancer begins to walk down the mountain, stepping over a few rocks.

"Your training will begin when we reach Mynydd Graig Goch," says Lancer. "Brutus of Troy will teach you." Lancer gives a few orders as Tim follows behind them. Lancer can feel the moisture in the air. He takes deep breaths as they move down Crib Goch. Tim can hear nature sounds all around

Garnedd Ugain.

A white cloud moving toward them begins to cover the flanks over Llyn Llydaw below. A male figure on his horse rides along the causeway at the eastern part of the lake. Tim, along with Ceri and Lancer, continues to walk down the mountain toward the rider on the horse. Their bodies enter part of the cloud that's dissolving into a massive amount of precipitation. They gracefully disappear below.

Y Diwedd
(The End)

TIM HARTWELL: Open Your Heart Trilogy (Books 1-3)

TIM HARTWELL
and The Brutus of Troy

Volume 2

- Original Copyright Information -

Copyright © 2010 by Aeneas Middleton

ISBN-13: 978-0615600093 (1st Edition)
ISBN-10: 0615600093 (1st Edition)
ISBN-13: 978-0-615-61899-9 (2nd Edition)
ISBN-10: 0615618995 (2nd Edition)

Library of Congress Control Number: 2012902303

Book Two (Bk. 2)

Troia Nova
— City of London —
Approx. 1103 BC

N W E S

Brutus' Palace

Temple
Of Diana
(Stone Of Brutus
/London stone)

THAMES RIVER

TIM HARTWELL: Open Your Heart Trilogy (Books 1-3)

Contents

237 Mountains of Red Rock

253 War on Glyder Fawr

274 Funeral Games in Troia Nova

343 Battle on the River Thames

364 Revenge Is Bittersweet

383 Meeting with Claudius

434 Down the Host

451 The Gates of Death

Mountains of Red Rock

Cumulonimbus grey clouds begin to clear Crib Goch above. Lancer leads the pack out of the patch of mist down to Lyn Lydaw. They all notice Brutus of Troy sitting on his powerful horse. As he rides closer, they see the horse's muscular legs and beautiful dark-brown solid color coat glowing.

God's rays shine through a

patch of cumulus clouds high above them in the sky. Brutus has mid-length hair. His skin is golden from the sun, and the sun bounces off his armored chest plate. The chest plate sparkles in every direction, almost blinding Tim as Ceri pulls down her hood to block the shine reaching inside part of her hood. Brutus jumps off his horse, sticking his sword into the ground as the sword sways from left to right. Lancer nods then calls out the name of a Trojan legend.

"Brutus, Brutus of Troy. We thank you for coming at this special time of need, for we know you are headed to fulfill more of your destiny. We are anxious to see what you can teach young Mr. Hartwell, for he is the chosen one, the boy who carries the Book of Hartwell and the magical power of the Galon," Lancer says firmly.

Lancer places his hand on Brutus' shoulder, noticing that he has a cloth wrapped around his left wrist, embroidered with patterns of ancient Troy. Brutus gives his comrade a proper handshake then walks over to Ceri, placing his hand over the top of the hood on her cloak.

"I see Ceri remains unknown to the earth. I truly respect that, little one. Even though, how can you see your opponent if he is right behind you?" Brutus asks politely.

"It doesn't take much effort most of the time. All you have to do is this."

Ceri jumps into the air, pulling down Verlock and Alfred (the sneaky twin Wyvern gargoyles) who both thought they were invisible. Ceri lands back on the ground as the Wyverns' invisibility spell wears off.

"How . . . how did you know we were here?" Alfred and Verlock ask Ceri with their necks still trapped in her arm.

"I've always heard the sound of Wyvern blood flowing through their veins," Ceri says to Brutus who is astonished with her magical ability. Then he dusts off his shoulder while getting back to the urgent business at hand.

"Lancer and Ceri, we don't

have time to waste. Tim must begin his training immediately, for my time here isn't long."

The group begins to move out, leaving Verlock and Alfred behind. Three horses come toward them on the horizon, moving as fast as the wind. They ride directly up to Lancer, Ceri, and Tim and stop in front of them so they can hop on. Each horse has the Hartwell coat of arms cloth dangling from its side, which was supplied by Verlock and his twin brother Alfred.

Time passes, then the air begins to have more mist than ever as Lancer, Ceri, and Tim reach the west peak of the Nantlle Ridge inside Craig Cwm Silyn.

"Some of the most notable crags are here," says Brutus. "This location has been used over time to train the best. Even my three sons were trained here by me. My oldest, Locrinus, loved it the most." Brutus smirks as he gets off his horse, looking at the rock formations sticking out of the ground every which way. He walks over to one of the rocks, touching it with his right hand as rain begins to drizzle from all angles. Brutus' magical horse snorts near the rock slab right next to them.

"I feel it too," Brutus says as Tim looks over toward the horse moving its front legs in a weird pattern.

"Your horse was always special, Brutus," Lancer says proudly as Brutus reaches down toward the ground, looking at the dirt.

"Ceri and Lancer, head to my palace in Troia Nova," says Brutus. "After we are done here, we will meet you there for a feast, my friend Lancer. It was a please to see yo again." He adds.

Lancer and Ceri turn their horses around and ride off toward Troia Nova, leaving Brutus and Tim at the Mynydd Graig Goch for Tim's training, which can be deadly to anyone up for the challenge.

Brutus quickly snaps his fingers, which shrinks them both to the size of microscopic insects. The rocks, which now seem large, are the size of Snowdon

Mountain. The lights come from afar since Brutus and Tim are small enough to fit under a human fingernail. The tors of rock sitting on the summit tower are jagged, and the wind is much stronger than before. Brutus starts to speak as he unsheathes his sword, suspicious of what is about to come as the rain begins to pour harder from above.

"We must make it to the top of this summit. There will be a light source at the highest point, which you have to touch to end your training. You could lose your life at anytime. No time to run from the tiger beetle which are taller than the highest tree, faster than a snake's head, and they have powerful jaws. My other son, Kamber, was almost killed by one of these God-made creatures. Keep your eyes open, Tim, and let us get there at once. You have to touch the light so we can both travel through it to get back to Troia Nova."

Brutus continues to explain the nature of the training. Tim remains confident as he walks from under one of the rocks that appears to be the height of a skyscraper in modern London. Brutus grabs Tim's shirt, pulling him back as an army of tiger beetles run past their location. Tim and Brutus fly back, as both of them were almost killed. The ground rumbles as if there's an earthquake, and the beetles' legs bash down, trampling over each other with their green-shell exoskeletons. An army of tiger beetles covers the sky. Some of the light flashes in the crack of the rock; the tiger beetles move past the rock that Brutus and Tim are standing directly under.

Hundreds of ultrasonic clicks from the beetles fill the air, one after another. The beetles disappear, allowing light to come back down from the sky. Distant sounds of them moving fill the air from other locations. It is a sound that cannot be mistaken. Brutus tells Tim to run behind him as he dashes over to another mountain rock and slides through a crack between two crags. Brutus looks around, trying to stay out of the sight of the creatures that stalk the land. Even the wind can easily sweep both Brutus and Tim off their feet.

Brutus is not afraid, and Tim keeps plenty of courage around to fulfill his destiny. He can feel the rain as it pours harder, making the earth seem like it's under a waterfall. Hanging on for his life, Tim wonders what events are ahead.

"Come on!" Brutus shouts, for the magical power of the Galon has briefly taken over Tim's emotions. The Trojan commander looks to the right, for he doesn't hear any sound from the tiger beetles, which usually means they are in full attack mode under the power of Selwyn's Chancer. Brutus and Tim wait for the perfect time to move. Tim dashes toward the next rock as a huge tiger beetle jumps out of nowhere, its legs slamming on the summit behind Tim. Brutus slides underneath a rock, protecting himself from the jaws of beetle that crept behind him. Brutus looks back at Tim, wondering if he has enough courage to follow him. Brutus yells out "Firewyn," which ignites the sacred blue flame on Tim's arms.

Tim shoots huge projectiles of light and fire toward the beetle in front of him. The fire twirls around the beetle, slashing it like a knife and burning it alive at the same time. Brutus looks on with amazement, never having seen anyone so powerful, except the gods.

The 4th Galon appears around Tim's neck and sends a magical light from the sky, blinding the beetle. Tim jumps into a lake under the beetle, which, at human size, would be the size of a raindrop. Getting back together safely, Brutus and Tim continue to run toward the peak of the large rocky summit.

Out of nowhere, thousands of tiger beetles begin storming toward them. Dashing as fast as he can, Tim begins burning some of the beetles, which fall to earth and send shock waves throughout the summit. Brutus and Tim run with all their might, jumping between another gorge, which seems more like a small cave to them. The beetles are too big to enter, as thousands of them try to get inside the crack. Even with their size, the rock's density is too strong for something so titan-like.

With no possible way to escape without being chewed alive, Brutus begins to tell Tim that he must survive. The training regime has changed, for Brutus has never seen the beetles ready to murder anything in sight before.

"I'm surprised we are both alive," Tim says, and adds some humor. Brutus says nothing but whispers a few things about Lancer, informing him of the power of Stratford Hartwell and his parallel world of Selwyn's Chancer.

The beetles disperse as the darkness transforms into light. The towering beetles leave fast as the sun begins to shine through, giving warmth to their skin.

Brutus quickly yells, "It's time to run!" He dashes across the ground, heading under rock after rock and even between them. Brutus and Tim continue to move up long paths of narrow rocks to an opening where mist flows toward the center of the opening of the path. Another light-yellow light source begins to glow in a gap directly in front of them. Tim turns off his Firewyn spell, leaving the flame to fade out over his arms. He takes a deep breath and runs to the light. As he touches it, Tim magically opens a doorway. It's the Stairwell of Travel to Troia Nova. Brutus and Tim, without hesitation, jump into the light, hoping for a conclusion to this training madness. Brutus now knows the power of the Galon has changed inside Selwyn's Chancer forever.

War on Glyder Fawr

The sky is a dark pastel blue, and clouds are drifting across the earth's troposphere. Below the clouds on the ground are Lancer and Ceri, riding through Lyn Lydaw as the air remains brisk with mist moving along the ground. Lancer wraps his scarf around his nose and mouth, dusting off some of the dirt that flew on him. They begin to ride up to Glyder Fawr. Without hesitation, thousands of red flames appear in the sky, almost like comets going across the horizon, as the flaming light gets closer and closer. Ceri looks up at millions of Diablo Archwings flying between Glyder Fach and Y Garn. The secondary fleet of Diablo Arches travel by land near a river as far as Lancer and Ceri can see off the horizon.

Lightning strikes throughout the dark night. Ceri senses trouble, so she yells over to Lancer to head for the rocky outcrop directly ahead of them. The fire-lit black arrows fly closer to them from the sky. Lancer puts on his mask and quickly says to Ceri, "You can only hear the arrows within one meter.

Some of the House of Diablo Arches ride their black horses, which stomp the ground, for war has been declared on the few remaining royal descendants of the House of Gwynwell."

Ceri jumps behind one of the many spiky rocks. Lancer does the same, just in time for one of the Diablo arrows to fly past Lancer's head, scratching off some of the gold trim on his helmet.

"Most of them explode like a hand-sized atomic bomb. You're lucky," Ceri says to Lancer as she places her hand on the rock, sending a light-green electric current through the rocks around them. The current joins into one gigantic stream of electric current, leading all the way up to the dark-blue stratosphere.

The power Ceri has summoned brings a titan, amber-colored dragon wearing a V-neck collar with the House of Trydan on the front of it. The Trydan dragon is made from pure energy that thrives inside them. This royal species evolved throughout the ages of Selwyn's Chancer. Not even Stratford could believe a new species had created itself without his thoughts. Most of the dragons only fly around the Glyderau Range, for they remain travelers of the night.

In one big sweep, the Trydan dragon knocks down thousands of Diablo Arches as they scream with agony, falling off their black horses and smashing to the ground in excruciating pain.

The head marquis commander of the Diablo Arches is Lylock. His oversized shoulders bulge from the sides of his chest plate. He waves one of his hands in the air to lead the rest of the Diablo Arches behind a huge rock to survive the deadly wing of the Trydan dragon. Lylock uses his magic power to summon their Rrysen dragons, which aren't part of a house but have the same size and functionality of a Trydan dragon.

One of the major differences between the two dragons is that the Rrysen has snake-like skin instead of the large scales of a Trydan. The Rrysen dragons give birth to thousands of four-legged Rhyfel beasts with sharp exoskeleton bodies. Most of the Rhyfel beasts detach themselves from under the wings of the huge Rrysen dragons. Most of them release quickly, thirsty for the fear of innocence of their prey, and the beasts fill the sky with their high-pitched voices. The Rhyfels have the ability to rip through metal with the tight grip of their poisonous fangs.

In unison, they climb over the land, approaching from all sides and surrounding Lancer and Ceri, who are already bracing for impact. Ceri raises her hand toward the arrows being shot by the Diablo Arches and extinguishes the flame from each red arrow as it falls dormant, snapping over the rocks nearby. One of the arrows misses Lancer's head by mere centimeters as he whips back from the arrowhead that slams into the rock and falls like the others.

Baron Milwr notices something is wrong with the Rhyfels; they are even attacking some of the Diablo Arches and killing some of the black horses as their squeals reach the skies. Lylock uses his large iron axe, which has the House of Diablo Arches coat of arms on the handle, to strike some of the Rhyfels' arrows that are coming his way. Yellow blood shoots from the exoskeletons of the Rhyfel beasts.

Lylock begins freezing another Rhyfel that almost kills him as it pounces on him. Lylock smashes his fist through the head of a beast as it approaches from behind. On the other side, Ceri shoots down the Diablo Archwings from the sky as they crash onto the ground at massive speeds and explode. Other Rhyfels chomp their way through the high wind to get their prey or anything that moves toward their direction.

"We need to get out of here. Call for Drava immediately," Lancer says to Ceri. She raises her hand, shooting long waves of electricity throughout Glyder Fawr. A metallic sound pounds with energy. An earthquake shatters the ground, creating a huge crack below the Diablo Arches that are riding their black horses.

Most of them fall deep into the crack. The ground slams back together, sending thunderous vibrations across the land. Some of the Diablo Arches are crushed near the top of the crack, with arms, heads, and even horse body parts sticking out of the ground where the crack came back together.

Ceri's powers of electricity rip through most of the attackers. Lylock's son, Baron Milwr, whose voice is deadly when he speaks to anyone, begins to slowly speak to his father. Lylock wears a rare coronet with pink and canary-yellow diamonds, which are called Emosiwn Melyn. The diamonds have a special mineral that protects Lylock from being killed by his son's voice, which is a curse of Selwyn's Chancer for wars lost in the past. That's why every time Stratford comes around them, Stratford wears the same Emosiwn Melyn coronet around his long thick neck.

Baron and Lylock command all the wars of Selwyn's Chancer, since Stratford believed there was no need for them to waste his time fighting wars between trapped royal houses in Selwyn's Chancer. But this time the war backfired on them. Ceri's magical power is too strong for them when the moon is the brightest.

The last thing Lylock wants is

the House of Cynfor moving ahead of them for the number two house in all the lands. The night becomes darker in twilight. Blood travels along the land around Glyder Fawr. Lancer and Ceri wonder how they are going to escape the situation when stars begin to sparkle on the horizon toward Y Garn. Commander Lylock yells out for the rest of his Archwings to head for the shadows of the mountains in the distance. Lancer and Ceri look on as the House of Diablo Arches flees. Baron Milwr leads them as his father, Lylock, rides into the shadow, disappearing in the nick of time as the sunrise appears over the Glyderau Range. The sun's rays bounce off their skin. Ceri picks up one of the dormant arrows from the ground then pulls her hood down further to block the sun from hitting her beautiful face. Signs of victory begin to fill their hearts as they look on.

"Until another day," says Lylock, relaying his message from the clouds as their shadows disappear gracefully. Orange sunrays begin to flow over Glyder Fawr. A peregrine falcon flies above them with its shadow gliding slowly over the ground and Lancer's face.

Ceri, remaining unafraid, removes her crossbow, which was hidden inside her cloak. She looks left and notices blood dripping from Lancer's arm.

"You're hurt!" she screams. As she helps him take off his chest plate, Ceri notices a red arrow still twisting itself into Lancer's kidney. Once an arrow has penetrated his skin, the poisoned tip doesn't take full effect until an entire day has passed. After that, Lancer's body will begin to deteriorate until his flesh becomes harder than stone.

"I knew it hit me. You are lucky you didn't get hit," says Lancer as he pulls the arrow from his body and screams loudly. The tip of the arrow cuts his skin even more as it exits his wound. Lancer looks up, noticing the peregrine falcon looking at him from a rock directly across from them. The falcon starts using its beak to clean its feathers.

"Get away!" Ceri yells toward the bird. She screams out for her dragon, Drava, to swoop them up, and within a few minutes, a shadow glides above the clouds, sweeping down toward their location. Drava quickly lands, and its talons grip the dirt and rock. The peregrine falcon looks on as Ceri lifts Lancer, who is weak from the arrow wound. His face turns red as the poison moves throughout his bloodstream. Drava roars loudly as it sweeps back into the sky, carrying Ceri and Lancer to Troia Nova. Ceri looks towards the ground below, the horses they where riding are butchered by the remaining Diablo Arches before sunrise.

As dawn breaks over the horizon, Ceri begins to think about Lancer and his health. She is silent as she sits on Drava's neck, traveling above the clouds to Troia Nova. Lancer is not dead but is in a deep sleep from exhaustion and dehydration from his injury. Lancer doesn't have much time to live. Ceri pulls her hood down further in disgrace, for Lancer and her father, Henry Gwynwell, who is now dead, remind her life is short. Drava starts adjusting its large wings due to some turbulence in the beautiful sky.

Ceri looks back and notices Verlock and Alfred have magically appeared and are flying toward her. Ceri readjusts her hood and stays alert in case the twins begin to act up. Verlock and Alfred look at Lancer's bloody injury.

"We knew it would come to this," Alfred says with hesitation as Drava flies through an altocumulus lenticularis cloud formation. "We never wanted this to happen. Please understand, Ceri. You may notice Tim Hartwell should never have been allowed to find the Book of Hartwell. The power of the Galon will take its toll on his emotions sooner or later."

A few ice crystals form along the edges of their clothes due to the cirrus spissatus arrangements in the sky. Ceri, in fear of Lancer's health, taps on the neck of the dragon three times in a particular sequence of five taps, informing it to warm its body from the inside to heat its skin for them to stay warm. The skin of the dragon becomes transparent as Verlock looks down at the organs of the dragon moving inside its body. The dragon's skull looks massive and complex. Ceri looks over at the bones inside the wing structure, which has fire traveling through its veins.

"Would you look at that!" Verlock whispers loudly to Alfred.

"Pretty remarkable for her that she has the ability to warm her skin, for her mother could not," Ceri says, trying to keep herself calm. She pulls out another blanket to lay over Lancer's body.

"He doesn't have much time left," Alfred says, remaining callous, since he knows Tim Hartwell is their main concern.

"Thanks for reminding me," says Ceri. "Maybe you two should go back to where you came from. You aren't needed here anymore. We will be in Troia Nova shortly, so please leave us. I have a lot of deep thinking to do. My father is dead, my uncle is dying" Ceri adds.

"I don't want to seem rude. I just need some time alone with Lancer. Don't use your magic to get us there faster. That will do nothing but make Stratford know our location. If Lancer does pass away, he will pass without magic. He always told me to remember that, for that is the way he wants to die." Ceri looks up at the stars as day goes to night, the bright moon sliding from behind a cloud west of them. She looks back and sees a stratus cloud covering the royal blue sky.

Ceri turns around and notices Verlock and Alfred have disappeared into the night. She raises her right hand and looks at her father's signet ring. Using her left hand, she rubs the oval indentation on top of the ring and takes a deep breath. Without guidance, Ceri begins speaking to one of the stars in the sky. On this very night, a star from the Boötes constellation shines just enough to be seen with human eyes, which is thought to be a gift so people can contact someone dear to them. The message will be sent through the heavens.

"Father, oh Father. Will you look after Lancer? For I couldn't save him from death. Father, can you hear me? I hope you are right about Tim Hartwell. He must be the one to free us all from Selwyn's Chancer. I hope you can hear my words of pain and agony. I will not fail again. I promise you dearly."

Ceri notices the star becoming brighter, for it listened to her every word. Ceri taps her Drava on the neck once more to speed up, get to Troia Nova, and have a proper funeral procession for her uncle, Lancer Gwynwell. She wipes her tears of sorrow as she and Lancer fly on the dragon through the clouds.

Ceri hopes for a better day ahead. To finally have her freedom is what she wants more than ever now. Ceri, with a serious expression on her face, is determined not to let anything ever get in her way again.

Funeral Games in Troia Nova

The sound of a commotion is coming from Brutus' palace. Early morning breaks above the horizon with a beautiful light-blue tone and an orange strip of color along the land. Some of the royal guards are in front of the temple of Diana, making sure no one enters. There is a large feast inside the palace. Brutus' top men and their lovely wives and children are sitting in their proper places to enjoy an early breakfast feast for Brutus and his unexpected guest, Tim Hartwell. The weather is cool but not too windy. Brutus and Tim sit in their places at the royal end of the table. Whispers about who Brutus brought sweep through the room. Everyone begins to eat. Children play with wooden swords outside the dinner hall, mimicking the great battles of leaders from their bedtime stories of Trojan ancestors.

    Locrinus, Albanactus and Kamber arrive in the hall, taking their places next to their father, Brutus. Right away, Locrinus, the most outspoken, begins to speak to Tim about Tim's latest adventures.

"Welcome, Tim. Our father has told us much about your journey through Selwyn's Chancer. You are safe here. We have heard about your magical power. If you need anything from us, don't hesitate to ask." Locrinus makes Tim feel at home, while Kamber and Albanactus nod their heads in agreement. Tim begins to talk about a future location in the city of London.

"In my world, or what we call my present day or time, this very palace is where St. Paul's Cathedral rests. Brutus' stone, known as the London Stone, rests here and is dedicated to the arrival of Brutus on the Thames River."

Tim continues to talk about Great Britain becoming the United

Kingdom with Queen Elizabeth II as heir. Brutus glances over, noticing his sons one by one taking in Tim's words, remembering every sentence he speaks. Brutus, in light of the situation, takes over the conversation.

"Tim, those words are food to our heart, but for now, let's talk about those moments in due time. We are all eager to hear the future of these lands and about my Trojan ancestors. But first, I haven't given you a formal introduction to my sons, Locrinus, Albanactus, and Kamber." Brutus points to each one of them as they begin to eat more of the delicious food on the table.

"Each one of my sons will take over these lands, for they have made me proud as a father." Brutus does not mention the mother of his children, for he feels it's not the right time to do so.

The entertainment arrives and catches everyone off guard. Musicians play their instruments and beautiful women dance, keeping the entire dining hall amused.

"Please, Tim. Come with me to the temple of Diana. I want to show you something I believe you would love to see." Brutus begins to unfold a few things for Tim to check out. Kamber picks up his glass, raising it for Tim in honor of his presence. Everyone at the table does the same as Brutus and Tim stand, return the toast, then proceed toward the arched exit. Brutus turns around for a quick second, raising his hand for Locrinus to take command of the feast while he is out. Locrinus nods; Brutus and Tim walk out of the palace and head to the temple.

The sun's rays glide between the columns of the temple, and the sky appears with an orange tone. Brutus and Tim walk through the pillars at the front of the temple. Brutus nods to his guards at the entrance. Tim hears the sound of a large fountain. His ears perk up as the wind comes inside the temple of Diana. A pool stretches from both ends of the temple, and a statue of Diana sits at the far end of the pool. Four torches burn, and a slight smell of incense comes from all four corners of the interior of the temple of Diana.

Brutus puts his hand on Tim's shoulder, guiding him over to the statue of Diana. Tim looks at it, amazed at the craftsmanship of the marble statue. Brutus asks the temple's interior guards to step outside with the rest of the guards so he can show Tim the reason he brought him to the temple. As the guards leave, Brutus looks at the stone wall then immediately pulls down a hidden lever in the wall.

A secret passage opens behind the statue of Diana. Brutus grabs one of the torches on the inside corner of the passage and heads down a stone stairwell. Making their way down the secret passage, Tim begins to adjust his messenger bag, wiping the sweat from his hands, not knowing what to expect. Brutus and Tim walk to the end of the passage, which opens to another marble pool area with three-meter-high ceilings. Tim notices a woman sitting at the other end of the pool. With disbelief, Tim knows in his heart that it must be someone very important. Brutus points toward the woman and tells Tim to walk over to her and introduce himself. Tim takes a long deep breath and slowly walks over while speaking to this mysterious tall woman with long brunette hair.

"My name is Tim, from the House of Hartwell." The woman turns to show her true identity as a beautiful goddess

Diana.

"I know who you are, Tim. I am Diana, goddess of hunting. Welcome to my realm. I am very pleased to meet the boy all the gods are talking about. Your courage, honor, and sacrifice already mark you as a true man of respect from mighty Jupiter himself."

"How, are you here? I mean, why in the world are you in Selwyn's Chancer?" Tim looks over to Brutus who looks on as his right hand pulls his burgundy cape that's attached to his gold breast plate. Brutus adjusts the cloth around his wrist, thinks for a moment and unwraps the cloth, handing it to his new companion. Tim, with his mouth open, is shocked that such a legendary hero is giving him anything at all.

"We are here while you strive as a reflection in Selwyn's Chancer. You will only see what your destiny wants you to see. By the way, I noticed your training at Craig Cwm Silyn went well. Brutus did well, as the gods protected him like his ancestor, son of Prince Anchises and Goddess Venus, the son who traveled from Troy to the shores of Latium..."

Diana pauses for a moment as a small tear drips down her face into the water of the pool, flashing an image of Aeneas killing Turnus, then scenes of his escape from Troy. Some of the flashes show people in Latium, then King Latium crowning Aeneas the new ruler from a distant land. In a flash, the image disappears; the water goes back to normal with a halo of blue light moving through it. Diana, lost in the moment, uses her right hand to pull her hair behind her ears so it doesn't cover her face. She quickly gets back into her right frame of mind and continues to speak with a soft but strong voice that echoes throughout the room.

"You see, here you are, alive. Like Brutus, like Aeneas, your name will travel throughout the ages in your world and Selwyn's Chancer."

Tim looks toward Brutus who is looking on with eyes that believe every wise word Diana speaks. Tim starts to think about his mother, Mary, back in Tenby, wondering about the consequences she faces because she gave him the Galon. Tim quickly focuses back on Diana.

"Stratford is getting stronger the more we speak, and things will change in this parallel world. It will eventually change your reality if you don't escape Selwyn's Chancer. Brutus, show Tim the London Stone, for he must break off a portion in two equal halves. Being the son, bearer of the Book of Hartwell and the Galon, will give you the power to succeed this obstacle. If you succeed, you will find the rope of Adamanthea with two more valuable gifts. It was handed down to me from the gods to give to Brutus as an award for reaching the shores of Troia Nova. Adamanthea's rope is one of the few things ever forged by the gods with enough magical power to get you back to your home alive.

"The power of the Galon will guide you in the depths of the Death of Ages to the Stairwell of Travel to get you back home. There is only one problem ahead of you, and that is Bledri and Tomes. You killed their father, Miniver and Cynhafar. Remember?"

Diana pulls her feet from the pool, drying them with a white cloth as she looks over to Brutus and Tim with a very serious look on her face.

"Brutus will guide you to the

entrance of the Death of Ages to meet Darryn & Darron, the rulers of the House of Scorpus. They live on the reservoir of Llyn Cwellyn. Brutus knows the way to find it. Don't forget that Darron is the smartest of the two rulers. He is the one you need to speak with about drinking the gwenwyna (Welsh: gwenwyn/poison). It's made from an ancient box jellyfish. They squeeze poison extracted from the nematocysts on the jellyfish's tentacles. This poison will make you immune to the air you breathe while traveling the land in the Death of Ages.

Only the House of Cynfor, with its part dragon and part lionface creature, has the capability to survive there, unless you're a dead soul from Selwyn's Chancer. I must warn you that if the House of Cynfor even gets a smell of your existence down there, Bledri and Tomes will lock you in their dungeon forever. Your life, as we know it, will be punished by them for an eternity. There is a mid-aged barbarian who is gifted with his magical sword. Practicing wizardry has made him one of the most deadly people in all of Selwyn's Chancer. He goes by the name of Hynwyn Reese. He is the originator of the House of Scorpus, but after confrontations over power, Stratford damned him forever to the dungeons as a human being after Amelia married Stratford. Other prisoners who have been caught are good at stealing, so watch yourself down there, even around beasts from the underworld of Tartarus.

That being said, you won't be able to do it on your own. Young Ceri will be your help, Tim Hartwell."

Diana looks over to one of the fires torches burning on the wall. Tim wonders why she didn't mention Lancer. "Besides," Diana says, "I would love to send Brutus there to help you. Unfortunately, he has to fulfill his destiny along with his three sons back in his time."

"Aren't we in Selwyn's Chancer?" asks Tim. "Didn't Lancer found these lands? You know, the city of London already existed, Diana." Tim speaks with the magical power of the Galon that incites a rage within him. His emotions continue to grow with an unpredictable outcome.

"One day you will understand," Diana slowly replies as she walks back over to Tim. Brutus tosses the cloth that's around his wrist to Diana. She ties it around Tim's wrist and says, "Brutus must honor you, for this scarf you are wearing was made by Hector's wife, Andromache, long before Brutus was even born. Hector asked her to make it, for he had a dream in which he was informed by the gods that Brutus of Troy, the grandson of his third cousin, including principle lieutenant Aeneas, would also be legends themselves discovering new foreign lands. So Andromache made the cloth, giving it to Hector to hand to the gods. Brutus wore it, and now is the time for you to have it, Tim, for you will need it more than ever."

Diana nods to Brutus with the utmost honor and respect for giving away something so priceless to the Trojan bloodline, just as the sword of Troy was given to Aeneas by Prince Paris. Diana touches part of the Trojan symbol on the cloth wrapped around Tim's wrist. Brutus is quiet, knowing he loves to help others. He nods back and sticks out his chest with honor.

"Even though the end of your destiny is unclear, be safe. Remember love, honor, and to keep loyalty in your soul to heal the world," says Diana, winding down her speech. "You will leave on the sunrise of the thirteenth day. Brutus, your son, Albanactus, is riding here to the temple to let you know about your friends arriving from their long flight escaping the attack of Lylock and his treacherous son Baron Milwr."

"You mean Ceri and Lancer?" Tim blurts out with anticipation.

"Yes, now go," Diana quickly replies.

Brutus and Tim dash upstairs to the main gallery of the temple. Albanactus is already standing by the entranceway to the temple and begins to call out Brutus' name, just like Diana predicted. Brutus pulls the lever back up to the secret passage, shutting the door behind him. They rush over to the entranceway where Albanactus is standing with the guards from outside. The two interior guards are quickly ordered by Brutus to head back into the temple and keep watch. Tim looks at some of the guards from the temple as Albanactus stands there with his armor and royal cape as well. He is always ready for war.

"Father, your guests have arrived," says Albanactus. One of them is badly wounded. Procter believes he's dead."

"Thank you, my son. Let's get

over there and see exactly what's going on. Tell your brothers to meet us at the inner courtyard to the palace."

Brutus gives a few more orders to other soldiers to watch the area around Troia Nova with the rest of the ground soldiers. Albanactus has brought two extra horses for Brutus and Tim to get back to the palace. Albanactus rides back faster than lightning, with electricity coming from the horse's feet. Brutus and Tim ride along with the sun high in the sky, and a short, cool breeze blows. As they ride, Tim wonders about his mother, Mary. Her love for him, he believes, is unmatched. Tim has flashes in his head of Tenby, Pembrokeshire, during the winter as the snow falls onto the water. He remembers drinking tea and eating his favorite Welsh bacon and laver bread.

Tim understands that love, honor, and loyalty mean more to him now than being captive in the world of Selwyn's Chancer.

Everyone arrives back at Brutus' palace. They look up at Ceri's dragon standing in the middle of the inner courtyard of Brutus palace. Walking through the entrance of the inner courtyard, Tim sees Procter, the palace's doctor, using moist cloths to soak up the blood from Lancer's body. The cloths are dipped with special ingredients called ambrosia and nectar. Inner guards of the palace make their way into the courtyard. Tim runs over to Ceri, bumping a few people along the way. He notices Lancer in the arms of Ceri, who remains cold inside. Brutus' three sons run to their father, looking toward the silent courtyard. Kamber raises his eyes, staring at Ceri's dragon. Ceri remains quiet.

"Ceri, what happened? How did Lancer die?" Tim asks slowly.

Ceri stops swaying for a moment. "We were ambushed at Lyn Lydaw. Glyder Fawr, to be exact. The House of Diablo Arches was ready for us. I'm thinking Stratford knew about our plans to get more help. If Stratford wanted you both dead you would be. He is keeping you alive, Tim. He knows you are trapped in Selwyn's Chancer. Lancer sacrificed his life, like my father, for Tim to set us free." Ceri wipes some dirt from Lancer's cold face. Brutus looks on, feeling the warmth of Ceri's words as he gives orders for procedures that have taken place since the beginning of Troy.

"First, we must give him a proper burial. We will have funeral games for twelve days in honor of Lancer." Brutus points his finger at his royal servants to attend to Lancer's body and prepare the pyre with extra wood from the royal cellar. Brutus tells Locrinus to lead Ceri to her quarters so she can dress in the proper clothing.

Albanactus shows Tim to his

quarters so he can get ready, which leaves Brutus in the inner courtyard with the dragon. He looks into Drava's large bright eyes.

"Hello, my friend. Ceri's magical power must be strong for you to be tamed."

Drava takes one step away from Brutus, unafraid but not wanting to be touched by anyone except Ceri and a few others by misjudgment.

"Are you telling me Kamber can pet you and I can't?" Brutus adds some humor, "Well, the ladies have always liked Kamber." He smiles. "Now I see why." Brutus laughs for a moment as the Drava leaps high into the air, thrusting its body into the clouds and twirling three hundred and sixty degrees. "Pretty impressive," Brutus whispers to himself, walking back to the entranceway of the palace and to his king's chamber to get ready for tonight's remembrance.

Ceri and Locrinus walk down the royal hall to Ceri's guest quarters. Locrinus wishes her well before he dashes off to get ready himself. Ceri walks through her doorway, which is made from some of the best wood in the land. A golden door handle reflects her movements as she notices a long white cloak with a hood, which is another special request from Brutus. Ceri walks over to a mirror sparkling on the wall near the closet. She sits next to the cloak, breathing for a second, then hops into the hot premade bath in the marble tub. Some of Lancer's blood, which had dried on her arms, begins to swirl in the water. Ceri pulls her hair back then raises her hand, looking at Henry Gwynwell's signet ring again. Flashes of her father and Lancer's death race through her head. Ceri begins to cry, her tears dropping into the bath water. The flashes stop when a male voice across the room sounds familiar to her ears.

"Father!" Ceri screams in panic. "Father, Lancer is dead. Mark my words Father, that after tonight, you will have to watch over him." Suddenly, her father Henry begins to speak, but not as a ghost. He's something more than that.

"I will protect him, Ceri. Your words mean so much, my daughter. Tim will be able to help you in Selwyn's Chancer. Listen to him. But remember, you are now the last living House of Gwynwell descendant." Henry pauses for a moment, then picks up where he left off. "Make us proud. Stay strong and remember not to look back to old memories. Live for the now; live for yourself. Live for the House of Gwynwell."

Henry's words fade into thin air as Ceri screams, wanting her father to stay with her. Two female servants run into the room, thinking Ceri is being attacked. Ceri snaps out of her trance and quickly shouts, "Do not enter this room!" Ceri demands them to stay in the bedroom area.

The elder servant, not wasting any time, says from the bedroom, "A thousand apologies, my lady. Are you all right? We thought you were in trouble." The younger servant breathes hard from running down the royal hall.

"My lady Ceri," says the elder servant, "It's time for you to get dressed. The pyre has been constructed, and Lancer's body has been covered in the finest silk. Bundles of roses have been spread across the inner section of the courtyard. Locrinus crafted a special torch, which he calls a priceless gift from the gods."

Ceri orders the servants to turn around so they can't see her face as she walks into the bedroom, drying her hair with a towel. As Ceri changes into her white cloak, the younger servant looks into the mirror, trying to get a better look at Ceri's face. Using a bit of magic, Ceri points her index finger toward another folded robe on a seat that lifts up and covers the servants face who is trying to look at her.

"You know, it's rude to stare!" Ceri says to the young servant.

"Don't mind her, my lady. She is young and foolish and has never seen a Gwynwell descendant before."

The older servant says to the

younger, "Now apologize to Ceri for being rude."

"With my deepest apologies, my lady. I mean you no disrespect. I admire your hair, for I wish I had beautiful hair like yours," says the younger servant while rubbing her short hair with her hands.

"I accept your apology," Ceri replies, then cuts a small lock of hair from her head and adds a green ribbon around one end to keep it together. Ceri raises the hood on the white cloak, pulling it down, covering her face as she walks over to the younger servant and places the hair in her hand. The servant cries with passion, feeling honored to know Ceri Gwynwell.

Ceri and the servants walk out of the guest chamber into the royal hallway. Both sides of the hall have guards, workers, and lower-level servants standing shoulder to shoulder. Candles glow in their hands, and some members of the royal choir begin to sing the Hymns of Torment. Ceri looks right as the main hall servant hands her the unlit torch as she walks under the open archway leading into the courtyard. Hymns fill the hallway all the way to the courtyard where more melodies are released in unison. Ceri, a bit nervous, places the torch in her opposite hand and wipes the sweat from her now-empty palm. Voices of joy and sorrow fill the sky. Ceri looks toward Tim standing next to Brutus and his three sons, their wives, and the personal counsel all dressed in white linen robes. Everyone is sitting to the left of the pyre, holding the hands and arms of their loved ones.

Hymns continue to fill the air. The sky is dark blue, reflecting onto the onlookers' skin as their white robes glow slightly from the magic shine of the moon. Everyone is awaiting Ceri's arrival. Torches are lit on a stake with rectangle edges. Orange-colored fires burn at medium height so as not to overpower the shadows. Ceri's torch is still unlit as the hymns reach maximum capacity. She walks to the side of the wooden stairwell leading to the top of the pyre. Tim knows his time has come to honor the death of a new friend. He stands with his chest sticking out and walks over to Ceri to give her some encouragement with a minor hug and two kisses on each cheek.

Tim places two coins in her hand then looks up and yells "Firewyn," igniting the blue-colored flame. Tim raises his illuminated hand over the torch with a blessing of peace. The flame turns back to its normal light-orange flame. Tim nods his head for Ceri to make her way to the top of the pyre. She walks up the stairs in a way that could seem to be slow motion. Everyone looks up at her as she screams "Father!" Her voice reaches higher than the moving clouds.

Ceri glances down placing two coins over Lancer's eyes. She looks at the pale skin on his face and body. She then looks up at the stars and puts the head of the torch inside the stack of wood that surrounds Lancer's body from underneath. The fire burns high in the sky, the wood begins to crackle, and pieces of ash with flaming tips glide into the air.

Ceri looks on with her heart in the right place. This sign of peace soothes her mind, and she finally feels all right about his safe passage with Charun to the underworld. The fire reflects onto Ceri's eyes, and the fire reaches high into the sky. Everyone looks at

Ceri, standing with her legs in a wider stance. Brutus looks over to his sons, knowing he would never want to see himself burying them. He looks at some of his council, then places his hand over his heart. The entire crowd in the courtyard is silent.

Tim begins to have a weird feeling inside. He pulls his white cloak further up one of his arms and looks toward a particular star in the Boötes constellation. Everything around Tim freezes as a star brighter than the others, which is the vision for the 5th Galon, begins to whisper in his ear. Many unknown voices tell him about the beginning of magic and the original creation of human beings, along with

Selwyn's Chancer.

The coordinates over the heart of the herdsman read:

RA14h41m24.24s D37°57'25.64'

The letters, numbers and symbols illuminate the sky over the constellation in Boötes. Everyone around Tim, including Lancer's pyre, is frozen from the power of the Galon. Tim unfreezes. Everyone, including Brutus, has no clue about what just happened. Only Tim was able to see and hear the star from Boötes. Brutus' wife, Ignoge, who loves to stay out of the picture most of the time, holds her husband's hand. Her eyes shine as hymns are sung long into the night. Royal servants bring food to eat as they continue to watch the pyre burn.

Everyone's heart is open with the utmost respect for Ceri's lost ones. Her mind is curious, even about the funeral games.

Many hours later the melodies fade out along with the fire on the pyre. Throughout the night, the entire small city of Troia Nova sleeps. The pyre has gone out in the inner courtyard. A little smoke exits the bottom part of the pyre. Silence has swept throughout the palace except for the sounds of nature. Some of the royal guards are walking their shifts to make sure everything's in order around the palace.

Dawn breaks and the sun begins to lift over the horizon displaying dark-orange, medium-dark royal blue, and grey hues. Brutus wakes up early, knocking on Tim's door a few hours before the funeral games begin.

"Wake up, Tim." Brutus shows him some courtesy before he walks in to wake him up. Tim rubs his eyes and gets out of bed, throwing on some of the new clothes Brutus gave him to wear. Tim throws his messenger bag carrying the Book of Hartwell inside a locking cabinet and heads over to the door with Brutus. Walking down a few hallways and around a few corners, Tim follows Brutus as he heads left toward his royal vault inside the his palace.

As they reach the entranceway to the vault, Tim notices nine guards with enormous shields and armor guarding the door as if their lives depend on it. Brutus salutes his royal guards as they stand down. The guards walk to the opposite sides of the vault door and lift a defensive, rectangular slab of stone from metal latches on the enormous vault door. Another guard walks in front of the left side of the large door while the other moves to the right. Both of them push the door, which splits in two as they slowly open it. Brutus and Tim walk over to the entrance, and Tim notices treasure from wall to wall.

"These are some of the most special treasures I have collected inside my own world," says Brutus. "Some of them have been through many ages.

There are also treasures from Troy that Agamemnon has never seen. My grandfather was able to get them out of the city in time. You see, much of the future we already knew. Diana told me to move across the lands." Brutus smiles, taking a few treasures as they walk over to another room inside the vault with armor, weapons, luxurious cloths, glasses, and diamonds covering extended tables that are neatly stacked.

Brutus walks over to dark royal-blue drapes with the picture of Adamanthea on them. Brutus uses his right hand to pull the drapes aside to let Tim walk in. Tim immediately looks at a simple light coming from the ceiling inside this separate marble room. There is a stone circle surrounding a milestone in the middle of the room. Brutus points to one of the stones on the floor.

"This stone in your generation will be known as the London Stone, for the smaller grey-colored stone you have already touched in Totnes. I had it placed there, cracking it away from the part of the ground when I first arrived on the banks of my New Troy," Brutus says. "Diana has blessed me to get here. That is why I thank the gods every day for helping me achieve my destiny. The secrets from the gods will now be laid upon you. My grandfather's father, Anchises, bred horses, which were given to him by Laomedon from

Zeus. Not too many mortals know these stories."

Brutus unsheathes his sword, striking the milestone with all of his might. He uses his strength and power to knock a corner slab as big as a watermelon off the London Stone. Brutus points to the stone with his sword. Tim remembers what Diana said about cracking this large stone in two equal halves.

Tim, getting some inner strength, opens his heart of courage and uses the magical power of the 5th Galon. He raises his fist and smashes his hand on top of the London Stone.

"CRACK"

"The power of the Galon proves

to be very trustworthy for you, Tim," says Brutus, pleased with the outcome as Tim stands next to the cracked stone below his feet. "The gods favor you. Cherish this moment."

Brutus shows Tim something sticking out of the cracked milestone. Brutus reaches down, picking up Adamanthea's rope along with two pieces of rubble that broke away from the same stone.

"These two small pebbles will turn into those horses given to Laomedon for Anchises. They never age or die, like Adamanthea herself. These horses, made by Zeus, are designed to never tire, never thirst, and to walk through fire hotter than the sun." Brutus notices

Tim looking down, rubbing the rope grain. "When you reach the Death of Ages, plant the pebbles in the soil and watch them grow from the earth like trees in a forest." Brutus points to some of the horse paintings engraved on the walls that show a sequence of how the horses grow from the ground.

"You and Ceri will use these horses to ride the lands of the Death of Ages. Diana knows you need these things to survive, for I learned from her about the bigger challenges in life. Understanding the obstacles in life will always be the wise man's strength. Hear me speak, as the kings before me told me to trust my heart and nothing will be able to stop me from reaching my destiny. I have heard of your great power from Lancer himself. I am now a believer of your magical ability after you cracked the unbreakable milestone with ease."

Mighty Brutus hands Adamanthea's brownish-red rope to Tim, who holds it in front of him and puts the two small pebbles in his pocket.

"What exactly does this do?" asks Tim, looking at the beautiful handcrafted rope.

"Adamanthea's rope will make your body hover between the sky, sea, and Mother Earth, Mr. Hartwell. That is the only way to escape Selwyn's Chancer, guard it with your life."

Brutus hands Tim Adamanthea's

rope, which starts to illuminate like a green aurora in the sky. The handle of the rope has a ruby cap at the bottom. Tim looks more confident than ever now that he knows magic of this magnitude. Not too long ago he was just a small, unpopular kid from Tenby, Pembrokeshire.

"The power of the Galon, along with the presence of the Book of Hartwell and Adamanthea's rope," Tim whispers to himself as his heart begins to open at the possibility of saving everyone from Stratford's Selwyn's Chancer spell. Suddenly, Tim looks around and notices he is not in Troia Nova anymore.

Tim and Brutus are suspended

between the earth, sky and sea by the power of Adamanthea's rope. They look up and see space leading toward the Boötes constellation. Tim and Brutus can see the voices of many different artificial intelligence species from planets light years away. The planets begin moving in a wide circular motion. Tim notices that the Boötes constellation is shining its light in a weird offset sequence.

"Is time really on my side?" Tim asks the star as Brutus looks over at him.

"Only time will tell," the mysterious voice replies with a deep tone.

"Using Adamanthea's rope, you may enter the sublevels of Selwyn's Chancer on your planet. Some of them have forests filled with beautiful lands, which all mimic the older times of Snowdon."

The unknown voice is cut off by Amelia and Stratford, who magically appear suspended next to Brutus and Tim. Stratford has watched enough and needs to speak his mind.

Stratford is dressed in black clothes, and a silver breastplate covers his chest. He looks over at Brutus, knowing Brutus is ready for war at any moment. Stratford moves his hand over the sword that's attached to the side of his belt. The twin Wyvern gargoyles, Verlock and Alfred, appear next to them under Stratford's control. Their eyes flame red and their faces have a dark-grey tone. Alfred snaps his fingers, magically sending everyone into the Guildhall in present time. It is night and they are sitting at a large circular dinner table. Stratford has made Verlock and Alfred his personal slaves.

"Well, well, well, if it isn't the legendary Brutus of Troy," Stratford says as he eats some of the roasted pork on his plate. A few slaves, dressed in clothes from the 1800s, continue to bring exotic-looking food. "The slaves were given to me by the House of Diablo Arches. They are helpful, aren't they?" Stratford says to Amelia before turning to Tim and Brutus who are sitting across the table.

"This gathering will be short. Tim,

if you really think I'm going to let you out of Selwyn's Chancer with the Book of Hartwell, you are wrong, dear boy. You may keep the power of the Galon. Doesn't that sound like a good deal?" says Stratford, using his sneaky tactics.

"Brutus, I am amazed to see you here. Such family history to be in my world. Such an honor." Stratford smirks while Amelia puts her arm around him, giving him a quick kiss for more confidence. "You won't last forever. I am here to make sure Tim will fulfill his very own destiny."

Brutus throws a few words over to Stratford to get a rise out of him. "Nice one, Brutus. I am no longer worried about you, for your destiny, even in my world, won't permit me to change those events in time."

Stratford looks directly at Brutus, knowing the facts. He turns his head toward Tim, as his neck turns almost like that of a cobra snake.

"Tim Hartwell, aren't you supposed to be having funeral games for Ceri?" says Amelia, wanting to pick a fight. "Doesn't she need you right now? How could you leave her alone?"

Stratford looks at Amelia to let her know he will take over the conversation. "Oh, Lancer. How much I have forgotten. The only reason he is dead is because members of the House of Gwynwell put their nose in business that didn't concern them. I am not the most evil person at heart, so you will tell Ceri she will have her twelve days of funeral games for Lancer," says Stratford, somehow showing a bit of compassion for a lost one.

"Remember, Tim, I have control of Verlock and Alfred now. They will tell me everything you do from now on. Since you have collected all seven Galons, they won't be able to help you like they did before. They already told me your mother, Mary, had the 1st Galon and that she helped you along the way. I hope she knows what she got herself into, for I don't think you could possibly understand."

Amelia hears a noise coming from inside the room. Stratford orders two beasts with trousers and linen shirts to walk into the Great Hall and pass the stone walls behind him for protection.

The chandeliers refract light near their table. Stratford looks up near the red drapes, which begin to move on the balcony above them. A dragon with the head of a dragon and the head of a lion jumps over the balcony to the lower level where everyone is sitting.

"Bledri and Tomes?" Alfred whispers to his beloved twin.

"I could kill that boy right now!" Bledri says with a mean tone.

"You don't even want a piece of him, dragon boys. Tim could put you both in your father's shoes, dead,"

Amelia says, poking fun at the new rulers of the House of Cynfor. She uses her magic to slide another long table between them and everyone else.

Bledri and Tomes are wearing steel-forged metal. Leather straps hold their chest plate. Amelia uses her magic and turns them into humans with royal clothing, including blazers with the House of Cynfor coat of arms on the shoulder.

"This should be the way you look when you're invited to dinner," says Amelia, smiling at Tim to show that she and Stratford have them completely under control. Stratford raises his hand and rubs Amelia's chin, for what she does for him goes unmatched.

"Tim, you will continue to have your twelve days of funeral games," Stratford says gracefully.

Bledri is jealous because they weren't given a special time to mourn their father. Bledri pleads to Stratford to let them bring Tim to Selwyn's Chancer and kill him.

"No! You will have your time soon enough, Bledri and Tomes." Stratford claps his hands, sending Tim and Brutus back into Troia Nova's palace so he can have a private conversation with Bledri and Tomes.

Stratford scolds them for being so hardheaded. "Do you really think I am going to let them live in peace?" Stratford points in their direction with a grin on his face. "Remember, I give the orders around here. This is my world, and I will do whatever I see fit to keep order." Stratford forces his words out, trying to prove a point. Bledri, not feeling Stratford's aggression, says what's exactly on his twisted mind.

"What about your verbal agreement with the House of Diablo Arches making them the number two house in all of Selwyn's Chancer?" Slime oozes from between Blendri's teeth and out his mouth, accentuating his nasty dragon breath. Stratford ignores what Bledri says, except for his last two points.

"First off, you imbeciles, I name who is in charge. Yes, they are the number two in all of the houses, but I can say the House of Diablo Arches has completely destroyed keeping order within Selwyn's Chancer. Lylock can be foolish, but his son has the voice to kill anyone, which I need right now so you can keep the Emosiwn Melyn diamonds flowing in the Death of Ages," Stratford says, as he reasons with Bledri and Tomes on the power of rule over the *Caves of Siôr* diamond caves.

The rulers of the House of Cynfor smile but are still unhappy about the house arrangements. Stratford gives them a chance to have something a little more meaningful.

"In the meantime, I will send

Tim's mother, Mary, to your collection of prisoners in your vicious dungeon. Keep her in the large tower of your castle. I will send many legions of Rhyfels to attack Tim and Brutus' entourage during Lancer's funeral games. I will summon Baron Milwr and Lylock to fly their Rrysen dragons over their location to drop off legions of their four-legged, slimy, and disgusting eight-eyed spiders. Let's play with Tim and Brutus' entourage. I will give Tim and Brutus good reason to come down to the Death of Ages, and you will lead them into a trap so Tim is stuck there forever and ever!"

Stratford laughs out loud and continues his rant in an evil voice.

"Mary is the key to trapping Tim, Bledri. Have you forgotten that Tim easily killed your father, Miniver, and Cynhafar? He could do the same to you both. You will have your day to avenge your father's death. Bledri, you and Tomes head back down to your castle and I will inform you when you need to get your house ready for the transformation ritual.

Out of nowhere, Tomes, the other head on Bledri's dragon body, says, "Yes, my lord master."

"Oh, my. A lionface that speaks? I see your house has been keeping up with other languages, Bledri," Stratford says, knowing it is rare for the lionface to speak. "By the way, what have you done with Hynwyn Reese? Please tell me."

Bledri begins to laugh and says, "We have him working in the Caves of Siôr. We've also been using him for his sword ability in the Carantoc gladiator games. He has made us very wealthy, I might add."

"I see," says Stratford. "Do what you must. This gives me less of a headache about the overcapacity in the dungeons. You must control the killings down there. If I hear Reese has been killed due to your petty games, I will destroy you both. Do you read me loud and clear?"

Stratford demands them to answer. Bledri and Tomes both nod as

Amelia makes them disappear back to the Death of Ages.

Amelia holds her wine glass and sits next to Stratford. They both look toward the stage. The lights dim inside the Great Hall when an orchestra begins to play. Drums pound along to a catchy melody. The burgundy curtains open to nine ballet dancers, all in their positions, who move gracefully across the stage when the strings strike. Amelia looks at Stratford, kissing him. "All this for me?" Amelia asks excitedly, for she knows what he does not: a male child of Stratford's grows in her womb as she rubs her stomach.

Brutus wraps his arm around her neck, watching the white hawk of battle performance. "Is that Gavina? I hear she is the best dancer in all of Selwyn's Chancer, except for you, my love," he says. "Would you do me the honor and dance with me?" Stratford treats Amelia with a lot more respect, knowing that without her witchcraft, he would be useless ruling Selwyn's Chancer, even if he created it.

Both of them begin dancing along the burgundy carpet while the ballet dancers on the stage, unfazed, continue their act. Stratford lets go for a moment as he dances the night away with Amelia in the Guildhall.

Back in Troia Nova, Tim and Brutus find themselves in the same royal vault as if they had never left. They walk out and head for the garden area to get the funeral games organized. Brutus tells his event organizers to have archery competitions with some of the most dangerous and fastest animals in all of Selwyn's Chancer. He then informs them to add the chariot race, along with a chasing match by the last living giant titan, Magog, the son of Gogmagog who has was found hiding in Merlin's cave.

Procter begins to speak to Brutus with some humor. "Being trampled by giants always gets your heart pumping, especially Corineus' victory over Gogmagog, my king." Procter hopes he doesn't have to do that competition, for he has never been a soldier of battle. He is fine with being the royal doctor for Brutus and his family; he is not the adventurous type.

Locrinus walks in from the right, wanting to hear more about the games. "Father, will we be ready to leave soon?"

"Yes, my son. Get your arrows ready, for I am ready to watch the games. I hear Ceri is pretty good herself. Where is she, by the way?" Brutus asks his son.

"She's still in the courtyard of the pyre," Locrinus says, looking over his shoulder wondering where Ceri is as well.

"Let's round everyone up and head over to the south bank of the

Thames River. We will start there," says Brutus to everyone around him.

"We call it Battersea Park in my time," Tim says with a confident tone.

"Is that so?" Locrinus answers very curiously. "I would be pleased to hear more about the future of these lands." Locrinus is intrigued about the future in general.

"You will soon enough, my son, for those parts of the land will be yours to rule someday," says Brutus, pointing out some of his son's future.

Ceri walks out with her hood up, looking reserved but ready to start the games in honor of Lancer. Everyone begins departing for the south bank. On their way there, a royal guard rides up to his ruler and commander from Troia Nova and says, "My king, word comes from our world at home. The Ark of the Covenant was stolen by the Philistines who are en route back to the Philistine Pentapolis."

Brutus curls his lip. "I heard of the Battle of Aphek, so the story of the Ark and the words spoken by God are true." Brutus rubs his chin as he rides his horse, ending his speech as the messenger runs back into position toward the south part of Troia Nova.

Startled, Tim says, "How can you know such things while in Selwyn's Chancer?"

"Remember, Tim, I was brought here only to train you at Mynydd Graig

Goch. After the funeral games, I am going to take you to the gates of the Death of Ages to get you on your journey home. Ceri's father, Henry Gwynwell, and Lancer are the reason I was even able to be here in front of you. Well, maybe a little of Diana's help too," Brutus laughs, giving more words of encouragement to the young and gifted wizard as they make their way down the cold river Styx.

The sky is blue and rich, and God's rays cover the land. Wild horses run along the ground not too far off. Tim's intuition begins to grow stronger, for he can smell vibes of war in the air. He knew Stratford was acting suspiciously. At this moment, nothing seems to add up about Stratford not trying to steal the Book of Hartwell. Tim knows something is up. For this, he is ready.

TIM HARTWELL: Open Your Heart Trilogy (Books 1-3)

Battle on The River Thames

All of the horses break out of a forest near the river. The royal workers have set up the funeral games' archery event. The sun is bright and shining during a beautiful afternoon with birds flying in the air. Kamber, out of the corner of his eye, notices a falcon flying above them. Ceri remembers that this is the same peregrine falcon she saw when she was with Lancer back in Glyder Fawr.

"Tim, I've seen that falcon before!" Ceri yells, giving warning to her comrades. She looks over at Tim while everyone who was riding with them is at the other end of the archery range.

Albanactus, ready to show his ability, shouts at the top of his lungs, "I will murder this creature. Observe." Albanactus quickly pulls an arrow with white feathers from its carrying case on his back, shooting it faster than thunder. Tim looks on as the main crowd turns from the range. Brutus shields his eyes with his hand to get a better look at the mark above in the sky.

Ceri notices Kamber and Locrinus looking at a cumulonimbus cloud approaching not too far off from the falcon's location in the air. The arrow hits the peregrine as a river of black feathers sprays over the land as far as they can see. The sky turns from day to night in a flash. The entire camp looks on with disbelief. Locrinus and Brutus, almost speaking in unison, scream their orders to the royal soldiers. Locrinus sends a few soldiers back to the palace to send word to all of the people in Troia Nova to stand guard, for the magic of Selwyn's Chancer has made its move.

Brutus, along with his sons and royal soldiers, gets into formation for the attack. Locrinus and Albanactus unsheathe their razor sharp swords.

Kamber notices the size of a massive Trydan dragon coming out of another cumulonimbus cloud. A dark night turns into complete blackness.

"This is not good at all," Tim says. Illuminations from small explosions brighten the troposphere up to the stratosphere. The Trydan dragon flies with a different unknown energy along its tail. Small explosions go off randomly underneath the Trydan's wings. Ceri, looking up unfazed, has seen this same action before.

Millions of high-pitched screams and explosions flood the skies. The Rhyfel spiders have detached themselves and are flying down toward Tim and the rest of the group like bombs out of a jet. Rhyfel screams grow louder and louder until Brutus commands his royal archers to start shooting their fire-tipped arrows into the sky. Ceri uses her magic power to blow the arrows like bombs to brighten the lands as they explode in the sky with deep snapping tones. Some of the arrows explode packs of Rhyfel bodies; some blow half of their eyes out of their ugly eight-eyed faces.

"Die!!!" Ceri yells with a crazy, vengeful tone. She uses her magic power to shoot green electrical currents into the sky, blasting through thousands of Rhyfels. Tim is ready to end this attack and loudly screams **"FIREWYN!"**

Brutus turns to see what Tim is about to do. Kamber, being aggressive, also kills many spiders with his arrows. Tim, using the power of the 1st and 5th Galon, ignites the blue flame in his hands. A blinding light whips through the sky, freezing every Rhyfel spider in the air. The spider bodies above them are four meters high with nasty, hairy legs and glaring spider eyes. Some of their bodies are positioned in weird ways: legs up, legs down, sideways. Some are even separated from their body parts that were hit in the sky as hemolymph, or blood, begins to ooze out of some of their bodies. Tim wonders why the hemolymph is moving but their bodies aren't.

"Now that's what I call a magic trick," Kamber says, taking a deep breath.

"Their legs are really long. Do you see those things?" Albanactus adds.

Brutus orders everyone to light their torches. The sky begins to illuminate with its darker red color at the horizon. They begin to make their way back to the palace. Ceri and everyone else feels hurt that she wasn't able to honor

Lancer's death. Stratford's lies have gotten the best of her.

Brutus tells everyone to remain close as the moon sneaks from behind one of the clouds above them. A cemetery of millions of Rhyfel spiders frozen in the sky almost creates a canopy, and there are jagged shadows on the ground. Ceri looks up past the roof of dead Rhyfel bodies and notices the Trydan dragon flying back into one of the huge greyish clouds.

"Well, aren't you smart," Tim whispers to himself as Ceri begins to unfold the history of the Trydan dragons being one of the oldest royal houses in all of magical Selwyn's Chancer.

"The House of Diablo Arches

shouldn't be ignored either," says Ceri, "for only Lylock and Baron Milwr have the magic to hatch Rhyfel spiders that live in cocoons underneath the Trydan's wings. Unfortunately, Stratford's world is changing every day around us. Once you stepped one foot here, Tim, the world began to change. Even Henry noticed it. Believe me, he was always telling me about a male descendant from the House of Hartwell who would eventually free our people from the unbearable prison of Stratford's spell.

"Fear is only an illusion. Dream big, Tim. I was born to think that way, and you should think that way too. No matter what you believe, remember to fulfill your destiny."

Brutus starts to walk the moist grounds, checking his people as the air begins to get colder by the second.

With luck, the dead bodies above them gradually clear up with only a few Rhyfel spiders suspended in the air. Thirty royal guards and event organizers are making their way out of the path of the dead spiders. Somehow, millions of spider bodies made from Emosiwn Melyn diamonds suddenly appear. Their long legs cut through the people trapped beneath them. The survivors look on with horror.

CLASHHH!

The Rhyfel bodies smash the remaining royal guards and their horses to the ground, sounding like a million wine bottles dropping onto concrete. Brutus looks at some of his people dying terrible deaths filled with pain and agony. Their screams are muffled by the blood that leaves their poor souls drifting away in the night.

The Rhyfel spider bodies are sharper than glass and break into a million pieces over the lands. The spiders were designed by the House of Diablo Arches from blueprints that came from breaking down all of the secret elements that make up Emosiwn Melyn diamonds.

Tim, Brutus, Albanactus, Kamber, and Locrinus stand there, dumbstruck at the sight of death from dishonor by Stratford, who leaves his soldiers without a proper burial. Brutus raises his hand as Tim watches Albanactus throw his father a golden box with a rope dangling from its corner. Brutus places his hand over the box, and the rope lifts without the box opening. A mist of remembrance made from a nectar oil blessed by the gods begins to flow from the box, moving toward all of the bodies that were trapped underneath the Rhyfel's when they fell. Brutus puts his hands together, and everyone follows him. One of the royal soldiers with the royal family tosses a torch where the bodies lie helpless without life flowing through their veins.

Everyone steps back, looking at the fire rising high into the air as it turns yellow from an orange-red color. It reflects in their eyes as they watch their comrades burn away up in sky.

The emotions in the camp are subdued. Tim can't even utter a whisper or phrase. Brutus, sitting tall on his horse, swings one of his arms around, giving the order to ride back to the royal palace. The pack bursts into the forest from whence it came heading back to Troia Nova.

"No funeral games for Lancer?" Ceri whispers in her mind while feelings run deep in the camp members' veins. Most of them want revenge to honor their loved ones. Their hearts are not filled with hatred, however, for most of them understand that when a person dies, one must be happy no matter what because they are going to a better place. Not one soul questions the gods at Troia Nova. All that is within them is the Trojan blood that holds the agony from one of the greatest wars of all mankind, the fall of Troy.

The sun breaks over the horizon right around the time the group makes it back to Troia Nova. Every family member of the soldiers comes running out. Wives kiss their husbands as they hold their loved ones who have made it back alive.

"The Diablo Arches will be back," Ceri says. "Everyone needs to be protected from the voice that can kill with one word. His name is Baron

Milwr, the son of Lylock."

Ceri speaks to Tim as they wash their hands in one of the fully functional water fountains nearby. "Lylock knows these grounds are his grounds, for Troia Nova only thrives in Selwyn's Chancer because you are here. Even though they are great attackers, they aren't the best thinkers since they rely on instinct like the animals they are."

Tim looks toward Ceri, for he sees her emotions have completely changed; she can barely sleep through the dark nights.

After a day of horror, everyone inside the palace, except for the guards at night, try to get some sleep. Tim is still up, in front of the fire.

He's looking at Adamanthea's rope, feeling the power as light circulates throughout his room. On the other side of the palace, Brutus lies in his bed with his arms stretched out. He slowly begins to fall asleep with his sword lying next to him. In Brutus' dream, he watches the Trojan War take place to Achilles death. Images of the past pass before him. His grandfather, Aeneas, carries the Sword of Troy from the burning walls of Troy. He also has dreams of the future in which he creates one of the biggest cities in all the world.

Brutus tosses and turns all night. In an instant, Goddess Diana floats through the window as the white sheer curtains react to her beautiful presence. Diana glances down at Brutus, kissing him on his forehead. In an instant he falls asleep. Finally at rest. Brutus' mind is in tune with the universe. Diana has given him peace of mind.

On the other side of the palace, Tim sleeps. The night is windy and there are thunderstorms on the horizon. Tim dreams of his friends at Greenhill School, especially Owen, his best friend. Tim dreams about summertime in Tenby and swimming underwater like a fish to see the *SS Walter L M Russ* that he saw Stratford pull out of the water at Grassholm Island. Tim begins to miss the ordinary things in his life that he dreams about. He especially misses the person who matters most: his mother, Mary.

Out of nowhere, the 4th Galon begins to spread its colors of light around the room. The magical power of the Galon begins to effect his dreams. He is now on the south bank of the River Thames but in the twenty-first century. Directly across the river is city hall with its oval-shaped structure. Tim's mind continues to flash images of him running on Tower Bridge. The flashing images zero in on a couple walking on the bridge with 35mm cameras in their hands. Tim hears them speaking, especially the man, who is whispering to a tall woman with blond hair. The man, who is about her size, begins talking about plans to make his Selwyn's Chancer spell take over the world.

As cars pass by, the couple continues to explore more of the bridge, taking pictures as people run across, getting some exercise. Tim notices a cop walking toward him, patrolling the bridge. Tim sees the woman open her long fur coat and pull out a letter as she points toward the river with a massive diamond on her ring finger.

The man pulls out a lighter and places it on the tip of the cigarette he took from his pocket. He pats his brunette hair that is slicked back. He is a true businessman wearing oxford shoes purchased on St. James Street.

The sound of the Thames River fills Tim's ears. The vision in his dream changes to the man leaning over to the woman and saying "Firewyn" three times in a row on the Tower Bridge.

Day turns into night as fast as a Hartwell llwynog (Welsh: llwynog/fox) when Tim snaps out of his dream in a cold sweat, finding himself back in Troia Nova's palace. He is completely out of strength and silently falls back to sleep as if nothing ever happened moments ago.

Brutus wakes as dawn breaks. He sits at his desk in his personal quarters, thinking about how Ceri's funeral games didn't happen. He thinks about the magical Galon Tim carries along with the Book of Hartwell and the newly found Adamanthea rope. Brutus remains there thinking, and he feels cured in some way. He wonders why the stress in his life has been completely taken away. He stands up and looks at the sun glowing along the horizon. Brutus whispers "City of London" to himself, smiling toward the sun, thinking about his sons, Troia Nova, his grandfather Aeneas, and how discovering new land can manifest into something very magical itself.

TIM HARTWELL: Open Your Heart Trilogy (Books 1-3)

Revenge Is Bittersweet

All is quiet in the morning in Troia Nova. Men have been lost without warning. Ceri is silently asleep in her bed at the palace. Her heart is broken, shattered into a million pieces for being the last one alive from the House of

Gwynwell. Her emotions remain the same, knowing she can not change the past no matter what she does. Nothing can bring back her family, she thinks, lying in her large royal bed.

The sheer drapes over the windows glide from side to side. Black smoke creeps into Ceri's room without her knowing. As she wakes, the smoke begins to turn into a male figure. It's Stratford Hartwell, to be exact. He appears in human form, but his eyes look like those of a panther and he has razor-sharp teeth.

"I could easily end your bloodline with a snap of my finger," Stratford says to Ceri, who has her hood over her face. "Join me, Ceri!" Stratford puts out his hand with his palm facing up. His nails extend all the way down to her hood. He tries to pull it off, for he has never seen her face. Ceri slides out of bed and does a flip to the bed near the balcony. "Don't run, Ceri. Amelia is right behind you, so please, let's talk. Or if you choose not to, you will die before anyone can save you. I won't give you another choice."

Stratford retracts his long nails and sharp teeth, morphing back to normal. Ceri, who had turned to see Amelia, now looks directly at Stratford's face. His face glows like that of Achilles, and he puts Ceri in a trance with his glowing panther-like eyes.

Amelia comes behind Ceri and

bites her neck like a vampire, injecting Ceri with her blood. Once penetrated, Amelia's blood will become two separate things: a love potion and a spell for tracking her location in Selwyn's Chancer. Ceri jerks back in unbelievable pain, screaming at the top of her lungs with her voice reaching the sky. At this very moment, no one has heard her cries in all of Troia Nova, except for one person.

Back on the other side of the palace, Tim hears Ceri screaming. He throws on his clothes and runs to Ceri's room where he sees blood coming from her neck. Tim looks up and sees Stratford and Amelia standing on the balcony near Ceri. Tim screams

"Firewyn!" to ignite the magical light-blue flame. He blasts his power toward Stratford, but it instantly disappears in a Stairwell of Travel. No one in the palace knows what is going on, for Stratford used the power of Selwyn's Chancer to keep anyone in Troia Nova from knowing where he, Amelia, Tim, and Ceri are.

Tim bends down and wraps his arms around Ceri, who is on the floor. Amelia's blood mixes with Ceri's. Tim, unaware of what just happened, screams for help, but no one comes. The royal guards are standing outside, but they're unaware of what's going on inside Ceri's room.

Stratford and Amelia travel

back into Ceri's room using a Stairwell of Travel. Amelia uses her witchcraft to keep Stratford and herself invisible to Tim and Ceri.

"Let's see you try to escape Selwyn's Chancer now, my dear boy," says Stratford. "Give me the Book of Hartwell and I will end this war against you!"

Amelia steps near the door of the room without Tim or Ceri knowing. The Goddess of Diana has crossed out the power of Selwyn's Chancer for Brutus of Troy, who is holding his sword with the thought of rushing over to Ceri's voice. Brutus walks into the room and only sees Tim holding Ceri on the floor. Brutus raises his sword to see in its reflection Stratford and Amelia standing near Tim and Ceri. Brutus throws his sword, which is aimed directly at Stratford's head. The blade goes right past his ear. Stratford turns toward Brutus, who is amazed that he was hit by a mortal man. Brutus grabs a special dagger from behind him to throw as Amelia's magic once again gets them far away, back to their palace inside of their Alynn dragon.

"What the hell...?" Brutus says with disbelief, turning his head toward Tim who is holding Ceri in his arms. They are all shocked, wondering why Troia Nova wasn't protected.

Tim goes back to normal, as people are still asleep. The guards in the royal halls wake up from a trance. Tim looks at Ceri's skin as it turns back to normal after being pale. Brutus yells out for Procter to come aid Ceri. Procter rushes from his personal chambers, down the royal hallway into her room, looking over Ceri's vital signs.

"I will heal your wounds for you," Procter says, wiping the blood from her neck. He doesn't find any scars or punctures, for they have healed.

Albanactus comes into the room with his two brothers and a few extra guards to watch the door while the three brothers try to figure out the next plan of action and defensive strategies.

As night falls, the people of

Troia Nova have high stress levels, for their sacred walls have finally been breached. Tim becomes enraged, and he runs like blazes out of the room using the power of the Galon to run faster than the wind to the Temple of Diana. Tim runs behind some bushes as he stays hidden from the royal guards in front of the temple. He picks up a small stone and tosses it near the guards at the back of the temple. Both guards, without hesitation, run to see what's going on.

Tim runs fast, burning some grass in his trail as he runs inside the Temple of Diana. He walks normal speed when passing the pool and tugs on the lever that opened the secret passage below.

He walks in then immediately closes the sliding door behind him using a lever inside the passageway. Tim walks down into the passage, which opens to where he initially met Diana, only this time he doesn't see her by the pool. Diana is nowhere to be found. The torches are still burning, and the sound of pool water hits the inside of the pool walls. Tim screams out, demanding her attention.

"Diana!!!"

Tim continues to scream the same word over and over and then speaks with rage. "There's no reason to hide now, Diana. Show yourself. Aren't you a goddess of the heavens? What are you afraid of?" Tim speaks with a very nasty tone. "Why did I even listen to your words? Why did I have to go through such misery?" Tim opens his heart, wanting to hear the truth. "If Stratford wants the Book of Hartwell, I will give it to him myself." Tim goes way across the line with that particular remark with uncertainty.

"I would be very careful with the words you choose, my dear Tim Hartwell. I think we can both see that the Galon has taken over your emotions," Diana says with a firm tone. She is still invisible.

Another voice begins to speak, catching Tim off guard since he hasn't heard this voice in a while.

"Listen to Diana, Tim," Eleanor

Hartwell speaks from the 7th Galon key, which dangles from Tim's neck. The rest of the Galon is forged inside his body. Tim has now become the Galon himself. He has become the key even with anger in his heart.

A young woman's figure made from water morphs into the goddess Diana wearing a teal-colored dress. Diana only shows because she knows Tim is under the magic of the Galon. She reveals her human self, but she remains on the other side of the pool near the shadows.

"I am hurt by the words you have spoken. All men have choices to make," says Diana. "It's how you deal with those choices that make the big difference. Remember when I told you to trust your heart? I meant every word, including Mary's actions for giving you the Galon." Diana lets Tim know the situation is not going to change whether he likes it or not.

Eleanor says her peace as the voice glows from the 7th Galon. She offers another plan of attack. "Diana, I will guide Tim in the Death of Ages," she says as she gets up and turns around to face Tim from afar.

"Eleanor, your sight and guidance may not be accurate while in the Death of Ages," Diana explains. "Mary's actions in Tenby will create new rules in Stratford's world, for you see, we are not in Wales. We are in

Troia Nova." Diana puts her legs back into the pool. "Only a Gwynwell's touch on the Gates of Death will allow them to enter without paying the Tax of Soulsynwn."

Diana pulls some grapes out of the water with her magical power as a loud noise bangs near the entrance of the passage to their location. Candlelight illuminates the inside of the passage and gets brighter, showing the opening to the pool area. Brutus has come back, knowing Tim has come to see Diana. Tim turns around and notices Diana has disappeared, and Eleanor remains dormant, not saying a word. Brutus walks over to Tim and leads him back to the top of the temple.

"I will guide you to the Death of Ages, and you will have to figure out your destiny, Tim, for before all that, all I knew was a calling from the House of Gwynwell," says Brutus, telling Tim why he has come. He was also surprised that Troia Nova has come with him to Selwyn's Chancer. Brutus really knows the best thing for Tim is to face his destiny.

The next few days nothing happened. Peace somehow is restored to the grounds around Troia Nova. As a man who never runs from fear, Brutus keeps his word and orders the continuation of Lancer's funeral games. This time, he keeps them on the grounds of Troia Nova. Brutus also reminds Tim that after the games, he will take him and Ceri to see the House of Scorpus before they go to the Gates of Death.

A beautiful sun is bright in the sky, and the archery games are packed. Ceri uses a bow and arrow and splits one of the arrows down the middle, placing a bullseye in the center. Kamber makes a few bullseyes himself, for he has always enjoyed archery.

Tim sits alongside Brutus during every game. The remaining days include the chariot race, which Albanactus wins. During the javelin games, Ceri wins with her agility and stuns everyone with her performance. Instead of the giant titan race, Brutus decides to have a running match around Troia Nova. Locrinus and Kamber tie. After the eleventh day of games, Brutus hands out all the prizes in boxes that are covered with gold paper and ribbons. Each box holds a unique secret customized for each specific winner.

Brutus speaks from a podium, announcing the winners. Ceri receives first place for her boxing match and receives a box full of Lancer's clothing that has been woven into a scarf for her. Also in the box is a dress made by Diana. Since Ceri never wears dresses, it also has a hood on it. Ceri begins to laugh with everyone since she knows she never shows her face. She walks back and stands next to Brutus' sons with everyone clapping for her.

Brutus announces that Locrinus won second place overall after winning first place in the javelin games, third place in boxing, and second place in the archery games. Locrinus walks over to his father and retrieves his box of honor, which includes one of Brutus' helmets that he used in many wars. Brutus then announces that Kamber won third place overall after placing first in boxing, beating Locrinus with a tap out. Kamber received third place in the javelin games and third place in archery. Kamber walks over to his father to retrieve his gift, opening a long golden box that contains Brutus' spear and arrows. Brutus killed his first giant when he traveled to his new Troy.

At sunset on the twelfth day, Brutus knows he must get Tim out of Troia Nova and head toward the Death of Ages. With only a few more hours until the dawn of the thirteenth day, Brutus informs everyone to be on call so he can take Tim to meet someone special before they head out on their long journey ahead.

TIM HARTWELL: Open Your Heart Trilogy (Books 1-3)

Meeting with Claudius

Brutus guides Tim into a secret passageway within the walls of the royal palace. The entrance has a narrow passage with a low ceiling. The passage leads to a midsized room with maps covering the walls. Each map is organized with a specific number or letters. Brutus picks up one of the charts, which has never been opened by anyone, including himself. It was originally given to Aeneas' father, Anchises, when they escaped the burning walls of Troy in the dark-blue night.

Brutus rubs his finger over a hardened Claudius' wax seal.

"How . . . how did Anchises get a scroll from Roman history?" Tim says quickly, looking at the Julio-Claudian dynasty seal holding the chart together.

"We are all part of the royal Crystal Dynasty," Brutus replies while he breaks Claudius' seal on the chart and rolls out the scroll for Tim to check out. Tim scratches his head, for he has never heard of the Crystal Dynasty before.

Tim glances down and notices that Brutus has something he never should have known about. Tim remembers reading some of *The Aeneid* by Virgil and understands Aeneas had a shield that told the future of his people.

Brutus, along with Tim, hears a sound that seems so far away. It is the sound of a crowd screaming the name of a Roman emperor who was born into the Julio-Claudian dynasty.

"His full name is Claudius, a name of power," Brutus says as he pulls some red crystals from the drawer built into the wall. Brutus puts nine crystals inside the leather sack on his waist. He then pours a few crystals onto a table as they roll in a diamond shape on the side of the chart. The nine red crystals appear to break apart, turning into a pile of crystal dust on the table. Brutus' eyes shimmer as he reaches over, grabbing some of the crystal dust and pouring it over Claudius' name on the Julio-Claudian dynasty family tree chart.

"I want you to meet someone special to me, " Brutus says. A red-golden light begins to flash throughout the room.

Before Tim even notices what's going on, both of them are transported to the northern area of Campus Martius, directly in front of the huge tomb, the Mausoleum of Augustus. Its stone walls with square travertine shapes for extra support were originally built by Roman emperor Gaius Julius Caesar Augustus in 28 BC.

"If anyone can help you get the proper armor to stay alive in Selwyn's Chancer, he is the person to speak with," Brutus says to Tim. Tim notices they are in the future in his own time of the early 21st century.

Tim begins walking into the huge entryway leading into the vaulted corridor that leads to the burial chamber. Dust falls from the sides and the ancient walls. Some of the dust travels up Tim's nose, making him sneeze. "The massive size of the tomb looks pretty intimidating," Tim says.

Brutus turns his head, panning

the central burial chamber while awaiting the arrival of his mystery guest. Tim begins to wrap the cloth that Brutus gave him even tighter around his wrist, for he begins to ponder the words of Goddess Diana.

Brutus pulls out a few more of the red crystals he brought with him from Troia Nova. He drops the crystals on the floor. They begin to illuminate and float near the ceiling of the chamber, traveling to the corner and gathering into a small niche. The red crystals give off a high-pitched sound when Brutus and Tim walk toward the niche. The sound stops abruptly when the stone surfaces and moves behind the enclosed hatch. A raspy but clear voice speaks to Brutus.

"Who . . . who has disturbed me from my eternal resting place? Who dares to use the power of the red crystals to wake my soul once more?"

"I am looking for Tiberius Claudius Caesar Augustus Germanicus," Brutus says with hesitation. "I am Brutus of Troy. I have used the sacred red crystals you forged during rule to travel time."

"Brutus? Brutus of Troy?" Claudius is shocked to hear the voice of the descendant of Prince Aeneas.

"Yes, Claudius. I have come to you to help a boy in need. Please tell me, where exactly is the Shield of Aeneas?"

"The Shield of Aeneas, you say?"

Claudius replies. "You ask of a priceless item from both of our families' treasures. Would Venus agree to give you such power?"

The magical power of the 5th Galon makes Tim's arms ignite using his Firewyn spell without him controlling it. Tim quickly thinks about Llangollen Bridge, where he obtained such power, when yellow-orange light fills the inside of the central burial chamber. Claudius is not alive but not dead. His spirit comes alive for a short period by the power of the red crystals Brutus brought inside the Mausoleum of Augustus. Claudius can feel the power of the Galon traveling throughout the chamber. Tim turns around, hearing some movements from inside.

Moments later, another voice comes from within the Mausoleum of Augustus. It is that of Livia, third wife of Emperor Augustus and mother of Claudius. Livia's voice echoes throughout the chamber from which they stand guard.

"He who carries the red crystals must be an honorable ancestor of Prince Aeneas of Troy." Livia begins to warm up to her guest, for she knows this must be Brutus of Troy. In honor of her son, Livia convinces Claudius to receive a gift in return before giving away the Shield of Aeneas.

"Brutus, you have heard Livia. What do you have to offer me? I am

. . . I am waiting with anticipation," Claudius stutters.

"Claudius, I offer you the rope of Adamanthea," Tim says as Brutus grabs Tim's wrist, shaking his head for him not to give up something that will help him escape the Death of Ages, even though the Shield of Aeneas could be useful. Brutus changes his mind and lets go of Tim's wrist so Tim can choose his own destiny.

"Adamanthea's rope, you say? Who is the voice that speaks to me, offering such a treasure from Zeus, or should I say, Jupiter?" Claudius says without stuttering this time.

"I am Tim Hartwell, a wizard and descendant of the House of Hartwell.

I offer you the rope of Adamanthea for the Shield of Aeneas." Tim repeats what he said earlier but with a more subtle voice hoping Claudius agrees.

Out of nowhere, Verlock and Alfred arrive but remain hidden to the naked eye as they watch the conversation Tim and Brutus are having with Claudius. Alfred whispers a few words to Verlock. "Who would have known that time travel existed in the past from Trojan descendants?"

"He's completely hatstand," says Verlock. "Tim will never get out of the Death of Ages. He better hope he doesn't get caught. I wonder if Claudius will accept their proposal?" Verlock's claw rests on the side of the wall.

"Brutus, you must have trained your pupil well, for the son of Hartwell knows how to offer an emperor like myself such a priceless gift of fortune. I will accept your offer. You may obtain the Shield of Aeneas, which I have kept within these chamber walls, away from humanity. Even after the sack of Rome by the Alarics and when they spilled the ashes of my family and ravaged these vaults, they still did not find your grandfather's most precious gift of all, Brutus."

Claudius makes himself appear as a glowing image behind Tim, catching Tim off guard. Brutus smiles as he and Claudius give each other proper respect and recognition for seeing each other for the first time in ages. Claudius is wearing the proper clothing of an emperor from his reign. He grips Adamanthea's rope with his right hand, which is given to him by Tim. Claudius walks toward another niche inside the ancient burial chamber.

Brutus and Tim follow Claudius' spirit as they pass an invisible Verlock and Alfred inside the burial chamber. Claudius stops in front of the vault of his son, Britannicus. Claudius quickly presses his left hand over the front of the niche, which opens the vault chamber, only to see a vase on a mantle with the ashes of his dear son inside. Claudius looks toward the vase, picking it up for a second then setting it back down. Claudius reaches over to the back wall inside Britannicus' vault, puts his hand inside and twists his wrist left, right, and left twice in a row. The deep sound of a boulder crashing echoes inside the vaulted circular corridor. A large rectangular stone slab built into the wall has fallen onto the stone floor, making dust fly throughout the chamber. When the dust clears, Brutus and Tim watch Claudius walk to the large stone slab, his head twitching a few times, for he was born with a limp and his head snaps with his disorder, even after death.

Claudius reaches inside the stone slab, pulling out a shield slightly covered with a Roman blanket with Venus' picture on it. Claudius tosses the shield to Brutus so he can hand it to Tim. Brutus nods toward Claudius as he moves slowly back to his resting place inside the central burial chamber. Claudius speaks before his guests from the future and past take off.

"Remember, young boy, that the shield has many magical powers. The future was written on the Shield of Aeneas way before you were born, way back in the time of Brutus' grandfather coming to the shores of Latium. Augustus was very pleased to have Virgil read him *The Aeneid*.

"Brutus, will you promise to come again and tell me more about the streets of Troy? You will be rewarded for your travel if you do."

"I will. The Crystal Dynasty will forge again, Claudius," Brutus replies as he and Tim make their way toward the exit. Tim unravels the blanket from around the Shield of Aeneas before they leave. Tim notices there are four elements that make up the shield. He rubs his fingers along the shield body, touching the engravings of the future of Rome and the creation of the universe on the face of the legendary shield.

"This shield will protect you from the fires of the Death of Ages, even though you traded Adamanthea's rope," says Brutus, who's seeing the shield for the first time. "Both of them have similarities, one of them being the earth, sky, and sea. Vulcan forged the shield for Venus by her request so she could give it to Aeneas. You will be protected against any power trying to stop you, for not even the strongest magic can penetrate my grandfather's shield. Keep in your mind honor and loyalty, and amazing things will happen for you in the future."

Brutus has flashes in his head of his grandfather fighting the Greeks as they attack Troy, as well as flashes of Aeneas fighting Achilles before almost being killed by him. Tim and Brutus walk out to the gate, which blocks anyone from entering the Mausoleum of Augustus. Brutus pulls out another red crystal from his pouch as they walk closer to the front gates. Brutus tosses the crystals into the air, and they explode like fireworks in the dark night sky. Magical dust falls from the air above onto their bodies, sending them both back to the secret vault room in Troia Nova with the charts and maps.

Before they leave, Brutus picks up one of the maps tucked underneath a few scrolls. He walks back out of the secret room into the royal hallway and behind the large lion statue. Kamber notices them coming out and walks over to them. Respecting their privacy, he doesn't ask about their whereabouts. Brutus tells his son to get his brothers and a few soldiers and meet back in the dining hall for a feast. They will go over the plans of travel to the House of Scorpus near the gates of the Death of Ages.

About half an hour passes, and everyone has eaten well. Brutus picks up his cup and makes a toast before they head off for travel. "Hear me now. Hear my words, my sons, my royal family. I will keep my promise to Diana and Lancer by guiding Tim and Ceri to the Death of Ages. Let's wish them both a safe passage through the depths of Selwyn's Chancer."

Brutus walks beside the long table, surrounded by his comrades. "I have traveled along the oceans. I envisioned a land in my dreams at the very foot of Goddess Diana at her abandoned temple when we arrived."

Everyone begins to smile, since they all love King Brutus and what he stands for. Locrinus gives his final farewell to Tim and Ceri as well.

"It was indeed a pleasure to meet you. I will pray to the gods you will return safely to your home, Tim." Kamber and Albanactus nod their heads in respect.

Everyone at the table stands as Brutus, Tim, and Ceri gather their things to head out. Albanactus glances toward the Shield of Aeneas as Tim picks it up, still inside the cloth. Albanactus' eyes are struck with sight of the shield. Procter rubs his chin, looking at the shield too. Locrinus quickly shouts, "We believe in you."

Albanactus speaks to Tim; Ceri looks at everyone smiling and waving as they head out of the royal palace. Tim, Ceri, and Brutus jump onto their horses to make the long trip toward Snowdonia in Gwynedd.

Brutus tells them to pack everything tightly on their horses, for they never know if they might meet some unexpected guests along the way.

Days turn into dark nights as they travel faster than an arrow shot by Apollo toward North Wales. Along the way, Tim uses his Firewyn spell to ignite one of his hands to light one of the torches he brought to illuminate the land during night travel. Tim ignites another torch, handing it to Brutus and then lights one for Ceri.

"So, where are the gates in the Death of Ages?" Tim asks.

Brutus looks up at the sky as he turns toward Tim and Ceri to explain. "The House of Scorpus thrives near the Snowdon Massif, near the lake of Llyn Cwellyn toward the east. The castle only appears near the Llyn Cwellyn and Mynydd Mawr at twilight. The Gates of Death are underneath the castle. The only thing in our way is the water that allows you to travel there. At twilight, the ferryman, Charun, will take us to the castle of the House of Scorpus.

We must hurry toward the reservoir to make it in time. Let's get there to reach Charun before the end of twilight over Llyn Cwellyn."

They continue to rise along the grounds of Llyn Dinas, passing Llyn Gwynant. Toward the left, they notice Crib Goch, the same arête they walked down the first time they met one another. Ceri begins to ponder why Lancer never mentioned the secret location of the House of Scorpus would be near we he thought the House of Cynfor would be located. But apparently, the leaders of Cynfor has taken their castle down into the Death of Ages.

As twilight approaches, they

hear the sounds of large beasts coming toward Llyn Cwellyn from the direction of the Glyderau Range. Brutus, Tim, and Ceri jump off their horses and they quickly gather their weapons. Ceri watches Brutus pull out a beautiful wooden dial with triangle-shaped carvings on the top. The sounds of beasts begin to get louder. Brutus, Tim, and Ceri know they do not have much time to get on the ferry with Charun before the armies from the House of Diablo Arches on their black horses reach their location.

Brutus kneels down and spins the wooden dial on the water, which hovers over the water at Llyn Cwellyn. An ancient horn on Charun's ferry blasts sonic waves that reach as high as the skies. Tim looks behind them and notices thousands of beasts approaching, guided by the House of Diablo Arches, with revenge on their minds. A ferry arrives through the mist toward the end of the reservoir. Brutus tosses three golden coins toward Charun, who grabs them with his half-decayed hands, putting them inside the pocket of his black shredded robe.

Charun moves his hand in a gesture to let them know they have paid their price and may enter the ferry that he only uses on the Llyn Cwellyn. They jump onto the ferry with some of the bones that make up his ferry begin cracking but standing strong.

Charun, using his oar, moves them at a decent pace toward the other end of the reservoir. Brutus howls to scare off the horses so the animals won't be murdered by the beasts that approach the Llyn Cwellyn.

The ferry glides halfway across the reservoir as the beasts make their way to the water. Baron Milwr and Lylock look on with disgust, for they missed their chance once again. Tim looks toward Lylock, whose eyes are glaring in the night, along with the eyes of his son, Baron Milwr. Ceri notices Lylock is wearing a Emosiwn Melyn diamond coronet, which illuminates the ground they are standing on, even under the dark night. Ceri reaches in her pouch and gives Brutus and Tim two Emosiwn diamonds to put next to their ears so they can be protected. They all cover their eyes when Baron Milwr screams out a killing note that shatters the ears of some of the House of Scorpus. The beasts standing next to them without their diamonds fall to the ground, dead. With luck, the House of Scorpus' castle appears near the base of Mynydd Mawr where it meets the Llyn Cwellyn. The howling of Baron Milwr begins to fade away when twilight, at its peak, opens a hidden pocket within Selwyn's Chancer between the Mynydd Mawr and Llyn Cwellyn.

    The mist begins to clear as they notice the same mountain hidden in a layer of the parallel world of Selwyn's Chancer. They see a massive stone castle with a wooden gate that goes down into the water. The gate begins to lift when Scorpus' guards notice Charun holding up his left hand with a pendant dangling from a silver necklace. Tim looks on both sides of the ferry, which has bones from some of the House of Diablo Arches who misbehaved. Those stubborn devils. They never learn.

With his mind, Charun moves the six oars inside the ferry. The only treasures he keeps inside are the spirits that bribe him to cross any of the rivers in Selwyn's Chancer, including the Gaia that humans and the river Styx in the underworld.

Large crackling sounds fill the air as Brutus notices guards with human-looking bodies and large scorpion tails waiting for them at the other end of the rigid tunnel leading into the royal Scorpus inner ward.

Guards from the battlements above appear with arrows pointing toward them. There is a west and east tower with fire torches burning high into the night sky.

The eleven-foot Scorpus guards **(eleven feet = 3.3528 meters)** have eight legs. Their claws fit between their elbows and wrists, but they have human hands. Their tails with their stingers spread out along the inner ward stretching twenty-eight feet

(twenty-eight feet = 8.5344 meters). Their stingers are deadly. A spirit with direct knowledge of Selwyn's Chancer cannot deny that.

"Scorpus exoskeleton bodies always make a crackling sound, always move in perfect unison," Brutus whispers to Tim. Ceri holds onto Tim's hand when a larger defensive guard from the east tower begins to blow an alphorn, sending a T. Rex roaring sound across the sky. The guard blows on a weird-looking conical bore instrument that they push their wind through. Only Scorpus blood can dilute the poisonous reeds on the instrument that make such a distinct prehistoric sound.

Charun parks the ferry near the

docking station. Ceri turns her hooded head toward one of the guards, which makes the Scorpus guard a bit nervous. He growls at Ceri.

"Ceri don't look into his eyes. He will kill you, even if I know his rulers," Brutus says as she grips Tim's hand a little tighter. Tim notices Ceri has changed since the death of her loved ones.

Ceri looks toward the castle, which has long banners draped with the House of Scorpus coat of arms on them. All of the guards have the Scorpus coat of arms on their body armor and weaponry, which shine like their exoskeleton bodies.

Eight Scorpus guards have helmets over their eyes. Their long spears have millions of small stinger needles covering the spear, except for the leather handle that was added as a grip. Four of the Scorpus guards escort them into the castle while the other four break away in formation. Tim looks down at two of the guards' hands. One hand looks human, and the other has a large scorpion claw that can snap any object in two.

    The Scorpus guards enter the castle and head into Stywyn Hall and then into the Hall of Judgement where the rulers Darryn & Darron await their guests. Tim begins to ponder the location of the Death of Ages. "It must be around here somewhere," Tim whispers to himself. He looks at the silver railings and massive Emosiwn Melyn diamond chandeliers above them in the middle of the Hall of Judgement.

A lead defensive Scorpus guard greets them in the *Hall of Judgement* and, being a bit nosey, looks at the shield Tim is carrying. Tim switches the shield to his other arm while the guard makes a chomping sound, since he wasn't able to get a better look at what type of shield Tim was carrying.

Darryn & Darron are sitting in two oversized chairs that allow their tails to go through so they can sit in human form. Their twenty-eight councilmen watch from both sides as Tim, Brutus, and Ceri walk down the carpet to the other end of the hall. Darryn, the most outspoken, taps his scepter to the ground like a judge in a courtroom.

"Oh, my brother, do you see what we have here? A hero from Troy and a hero to London. Do I also see a boy Hartwell descendant? What mother has broken the rules in Selwyn's Chancer?" Darryn can't believe Brutus of Troy and the carrier of the magical Galon is right before their eyes. "We can truly believe our eyes, brother, for we must believe our eyes." Darryn has a slight mental problem, which makes him unable to remember who people are. But he never forgets someone who screws him over.

While tensions begin to rise for a second, Darron, the smartest of the two, welcomes his guests properly, for he knows them well, he thinks.

"Brutus of Troy, welcome. Please excuse my brother for his minor sense of humor and memory loss." Darron makes his guests laugh a little while Darryn's head swings back and forth. Darryn's ego makes him arrogant, and he wears a massive Emosiwn Melyn diamond on his hand that once belonged to their original ruler, Hynwyn Reese. Darryn trapped Reese in the Death of Ages when Reese took control of how many spirits he would let through. Darryn's payment was huge amounts of Emosiwn Melyn diamonds from the rich lost souls who weren't granted access to entrance of the

Gates of Death.

"Guards, you may stand down, for these are our guests," Darron says, looking over to his defensive general. Darron waves his hand for them to walk out of the Hall of Judgement, except for his personal royal Scorpus councilmen. "You must have traveled a long way here, even though we know you wouldn't be here if someone weren't trying to get into the Death of Ages." Darron looks toward Ceri and Tim, trying to recognize them.

Darryn notices the Coat of Hartwell on Tim's messenger bag and immediately rubs his jagged hands with much excitement. "Anyone who can make Stratford's words of rage travel across the lands of Selwyn's Chancer may speak to me anytime he wants."

Darron laughs, for he doesn't like Stratford too much himself. "Speak, my boy. Let me hear the voice of the boy who killed the ruler of the House of Cynfor.

"My name is Tim Hartwell, son of Mary, member of the House of Hartwell. This is my friend, Ceri, from the House of Gwynwell." Tim is not afraid of their ridged bodies as they look at young Ceri with her hood up.

"This might call for a celebration. A Hartwell, a Gwynwell and a Trojan. I must be dreaming," Darryn says, adding more humor. Brutus remains unfazed as Tim begins to speak again.

"Darron & Darryn, your excellencies, we are here for the drink of the gwenwyna."

"Gwenwyna you ask for, dear boy? We apologize, for we only have a fraction left. It won't be enough for you three, only two of you," Darryn lies while keeping a disappointed look on his face.

"I will not be heading with them, you see," says Brutus. "I am here to do a favor for an old friend who has passed."

"Death of a friend, you say?" Darron says with some concern. "I will grant you two glasses of gwenwyna, even though I know my councilmen won't agree with anyone undead traveling there, for only the dead of Selwyn's Chancer live there. But . . ." Darron stands up, along with his brother. "It will take approximately six hours for their bodies to heal from the effect of gwenwyna. While their bodies rest, I will show you how to get back to Troia Nova without being seen from the House of Diablo Arches."

"No need, but thank you, for the goddess Diana will lead me home," Brutus says as Darron's face looks weird with his eyes bugging out a bit.

"No apology needed, for if Goddess Diana is around, we know you will be safe," Darron replies. "After they drink the gwenwyna, I will show them the hoist in the *West Tower*. It leads to the Death of Ages. Follow us to the *Chamber of Gwenwyna*. We will have to strap their bodies onto the beds to keep them from killing themselves. Unbearable pain is a side effect for humans who drink gwenwyna because the poison runs through their veins. But they will survive."

Darryn waves for their councilmen to ready the Chamber of Gwenwyna at once.

The Scorpus rulers, along with Brutus, Ceri, and Tim, head toward the Great Hall that leads to the opposite end of the Chamber of Gwenwyna. Darron begins to speak about a few things none of them might of heard about the Death of Ages.

"I hope you are fast on your feet. Members of the House of Cynfor are growing to the size of titans down there, and only their lungs can breathe the air," he says looking at Tim.

"Stratford will know you are there once Tim steps on his most precious land. The House of Cynfor won't expect to meet such a powerful wizard as yourself, I might add. We have heard about your victory in defeating the powerful Miniver and Cynhafar."

They pass many rooms with different symbols covering each door. Darryn & Darron notice that Tim is carrying a shield, but they don't recognize it as the Shield of Aeneas. They continue down the Great Hall, which leads to arched metal doors with a large metal locking system. The Coat of Scorpus is forged onto the top of the door. Darron unlocks the door with a special sequence of metal buttons. Darryn looks toward Ceri, still trying to figure out what her face looks like beneath her hood.

"She must be one of the ugliest girls in all of Selwyn's Chancer," Darryn says.

"Excuse my brother. He must watch his tongue," Darron says.

"I didn't know scorpions have tongues," Ceri says, giving some humor back.

"Feisty little one, I see, Brutus. She must be the daughter of Henry

Gwynwell to speak the way she does," says Darron.

"You knew my father?" Ceri asks.

"We didn't know your father, but we know where his spirit is located," says Darron. "Henry is locked in the dungeon of Bledri and Tomes, we have heard from some of the bribers coming our way. You would be surprised what you can learn from someone who hasn't been given approval to enter the Gates of Death."

"We must find my father at once!" Ceri demands as she looks toward Tim. "That means Lancer must be there as well," she adds as she loses it for a moment, thinking she can see her beloved again.

"Yes, but you cannot save them now, for they are already locked in a horrid place," says Darron. "The only person who can free them is Stratford. Just don't make a deal with anyone in the Death of Ages. Stratford knows everything." Darron stops talking as he leads them into the Chamber of Gwenwyna.

The Scorpus councilmen appear wearing navy-blue robes with yellow trim and the Coat of Scorpus on their chest, which they wear proudly. Each councilmen is holding a candle as he faces two stone slabs, which look like beds. Darron points toward the slabs, which are for Ceri and Tim to lie upon for the gwenwyna process.

Dawn breaks as the sun's rays sneak from behind the walls to shine through the stained glass depicting the fallen kings through the ages of the House of Scorpus. Tim and Ceri walk near the beds and lay their things on the rock slabs.

"Stay strong, you two." Brutus gives words of encouragement as Tim and Ceri lie down, looking at the ceiling of the chamber. Two Scorpus councilmen lay yellow linen over Tim and Ceri, which has Scorpus symbols of witchcraft and wizardry. Darryn & Darron take their royal seats, pointing toward Brutus to join them to watch the ritual of the Gwenwyna.

All twenty-eight councilmen walk

into the chamber. Two of them hold a metal platter with two ridged glasses with oval bottoms. The councilmen break out of formation in unison and walk down both red carpets leading to Ceri and Tim. The other twenty-six councilmen begin repeating their words over and over.

"Gwenwyna, gwenwyna"

The Scorpus councilmen yell the name of their poison faster and faster as the cups get nearer and nearer to Tim and Ceri. The councilmen raise the metal platter high in the air, then bring it down in front of them. In mere seconds, the councilmen stop singing, which makes Tim and Ceri a bit nervous. Tim and Ceri grip the stone slabs as the

Scorpus councilmen lift the yellow linen sheets over both their heads in unison, then pour the gwenwyna poison directly into their mouths through an opening in the sheet. Four guards walk over to Tim and Ceri; two hold down their arms and legs so they can't get away.

Within a few minutes, Tim and Ceri begin screaming with dreadful pain as the gwenwyna travels throughout their bodies. Their voices echo throughout the chamber. Both Ceri and Tim's eyes begin turning light orange as the gwenwyna poison circulates evenly throughout their system. Ceri screams again, and her voice shatters the crystal cups the guards carried the poison in.

Brutus, along with Darron & Darryn, is amazed that her vocal octaves can reach that high. Tim begins screaming along with Ceri, tossing and turning as they try to free their bodies from agony. Tim and Ceri feel like their bodies are being burned alive. Everyone looks on as the gwenwyna poison continues to take effect.

Some unexpected Wyvern guests appear high in the rafters and look down at the entire group in the chamber. It's Verlock and Alfred, the protectors of the Galon and the Book of Hartwell. Both of them remain invisible to the crowd below and keep an eye on them. Otherwise, Stratford will kill them.

"They must be completely hatstand!" Verlock whispers, seeing the pain Tim and Ceri are withstanding could kill any normal human being.

"If Brutus wasn't around, I am sure, Verlock, they both would have been stuck in Selwyn's Chancer forever," Alfred replies as his claw grasps one of the rafters and he jumps to another to get a better look. "Why didn't Stratford destroy the House of Scorpus when he had the chance ages ago? They must have made a deal with him to survive over the ages. If Tim gets inside the gates of the Death of Ages, we will have to protect them, no matter what Stratford thinks."

"Yes, my brother, but Stratford will

lock us in Bledri and Tomes' dungeon if we do. I am willing to die for Tim. We cannot be afraid of Stratford or Amelia any longer," says Verlock.

"I am tired of being slaves to them," says Alfred. "We need to be free."

Alfred and his twin jump onto another rafter, then fade into thin air. Just before they disappear, Verlock whispers, "Tim has acquired the Shield of Aeneas. Who would have known it was still inside the Mausoleum of Augustus?"

"Yes, I know," Alfred says, waiting for the right time to come back again. The twin Wyverns are content with each other. Their eyes sparkle as they disappear into another part of the world in Selwyn's Chancer.

TIM HARTWELL: Open Your Heart Trilogy (Books 1-3)

Down The Hoist

Brutus, along with the rulers of the House of Scorpus, remains very quiet inside the Chamber of Gwenwyna.

Four councilmen who are holding down the arms of Tim and Ceri begin to slowly let go of them in unison. The remaining Scorpus councilmen who are singing begin to slow down, along with the councilmen who are letting go of Tim and Ceri. All of their voices lower while everyone looks at Tim and Ceri lying down. Darryn & Darron are especially curious to see who awakens first.

Brutus' eyes are slim as he looks toward Tim, who is beginning to move around, groaning from the pain he withstood. Tim leans up from beneath the sheets, using his right hand to pull them off. His eyes turn from light orange back to their normal brown color. Tim swings his legs around the edge of the stone slab and rubs his hand over his head, trying to get his senses back to normal again.

Ceri starts moving around beneath her sheet. Her hood almost slips, revealing her face, but with a quick reaction, she pulls it back down to keep her identity a secret. Brutus steps forward to make sure they are all right. Darron warns Brutus to wait until the effects of the poison completely wear off Ceri. Brutus takes one step to the side when Ceri gets off the stone slab, looking at Tim beginning to collect his things that are still next to the base of the stone slab.

"*Wait!*"

Darron's voice projects throughout the entire chamber. He orders his guards to stop Ceri, for all Scorpus councilmen must see her eyes to make sure the gwenwyna worked correctly.

"The girl must take off her hood and reveal her eyes. Show us your eyes, young girl. We demand that you show your eyes immediately," Darron says with a stern voice but meaning no harm to their guests.

Ceri turns and faces the direction of Darryn & Darron. "I will show my face to no one. Not you, not anyone, except for the House of Gwynwell. Since you know I am the last one, neither of you will see," Ceri says with a lot of emotion.

Darryn claps his hands together

in a particular sequence, which alarms more of the army that storms into the Chamber of Gwenwyna. Brutus unsheathes his sword, putting his blade to Darron's neck, for he believes the royal rulers of the House of Scorpus are up to something.

"Why must the girl reveal her face? Why is it so important for her to reveal herself to you both?" Brutus yelling out.

The Scorpus guards jump fast into position, holding their sharp scepters toward Ceri. Darryn, fearing for his brother's life, explains the reason for the special request.

"If her eyes remain light orange, she will be forced to be the watcher of the Last Fairy Maze Forest in the Death of Ages. She will turn into a fairy who cannot see. Only by movement will she be able to hear. She will trap herself in a forest that never ends, with roads that lead nowhere except right back to the back entrance of the castle."

Ceri's tone changes, for she just might have to reveal her identity after all. Brutus retracts his blade from Darron's neck and sheathes his sword. The Scorpus general defensive and the rest of the guards lower their defenses.

"Ceri, please do as they say. I know how much your identity means to you, but I guess you don't have a choice," Tim says as he calls off his Firewyn spell and the flame extinguishes. Ceri walks between the rock slabs, looking up toward the rulers. Tim walks over to Brutus as they look on, for they have never seen her face. Ceri pulls down her hood, going as slow as possible, for the pressure to show her face is overwhelming for her. As the hood slides back, her beautiful brunette hair is exposed. The entire chamber whispers. The councilmen are shocked to see her eyes with the light-orange color. The councilmen inside the chamber begin to whisper louder when Tim notices something about Ceri that no one else in the chamber sees, except for him.

"Zoe? How can this be?" Tim notices that Ceri is also Zoe Beckham from his Greenhill school.

"Yes, it's me, for I am Zoe Beckham in your world, but my real name is Ceri Gwynwell in Selwyn's Chancer."

Tim almost falls down in shock, knowing that the girl he had a crush on at Greenhill has been helping him on his journey the entire time.

"I have been watching you, Tim," says Ceri. "My family has known about you ever since your birth. I am sorry if you are disappointed in me for not telling you the truth all along."

"You have more problems now than an identity crisis," Darron says. "There is only one person who can stop the transformation of you becoming the sole watcher of the Last Fairy Maze Forest in the Death of Ages."

Darryn, with a serious tone, says, "No one will be able to free her from the maze."

Darron pauses for a moment to order all of his councilmen and guards out of the chamber at once. They walk out, whispering to themselves, for they know something is up. The guards close the high chamber doors behind them to give their new guests some privacy.

"You both are now physically capable of breathing the air in the Death of Ages. But, we are breaking a bond with Stratford to let you go free, young girl. Only for Brutus have we decided to lead you to the hoist in the

West Tower, which will take you down into the earth under Mynydd Mawr to the Death of Ages. Gather your things and come with us immediately," Darron says as his scorpion tail sways back and forth.

Darryn & Darron walk over to the Great Hall, which leads to the West Tower. The walls are covered with battle achievements and skeleton heads as trophies. In the West Tower, there is a wooden door that Darron opens to reveal the hoist attached to a long chain that is connected to the peak of the West Tower. Darron sways his hand toward the hoist for Tim and Ceri to get into.

Brutus looks at both of them

inside the hoist and says his farewell, for he knows this might be the last time he ever sees them alive. "Be safe, you two. It was an honor for me to help you along your journey. I will always remember the stories you told me about the lands that I discovered growing into something magical. I will continue to pray for your safety. Remember, Tim, you use the shield well. Trust your heart. Always remember that. Ceri, protect Tim the best you can, for he will find a way to heal you from being the watcher of the maze." Brutus puts his right hand over his heart.

Darron reaches inside his long robe and pulls out a medium-sized canister that contains liquid. "Young girl, this will help slow down the process of your fairy transformation," he says as Ceri grabs the canister and pulls her hood back up, getting ready for what they might face in the depths of Selwyn's Chancer.

"Thank you for caring, even though I know you don't have to," Ceri says as Tim glances over to her with a different look, since he now knows she is Zoe Beckham from Greenhill.

Darron shuts the metal gate to the hoist, pulling a metal switch that makes it descend into the mountain of Mynydd Mawr. Brutus looks down and salutes them.

The metal hoist clanks as it descends into the ground. Tim screams out

"FIREWYN"

This ignites his arms with a light-blue flame so they can see inside the hoist going down the shaft. The air becomes thin as they ride further and further into the earth, both not knowing what to expect next. All of a sudden, a strong gust swoops through the shaft, blowing the edges of their clothes. Tim and Ceri stand guard, for they don't have the slightest clue what to expect during their journey, besides the evil castle of the House of Cynfor.

Ceri pulls off her hood and quickly gives Tim a kiss on the cheek, which catches him off guard.

"What was that for?" Tim says.

"I've never kissed a boy in my life, so if I'm going to die, I might as well kiss someone while I'm still alive," Ceri says, pulling her hood back up.

After a few minutes, the hoist drops faster into the shaft, going thousands of meters inside the earth's crust. Tim and Ceri crouch down, bracing for impact as the hoist continues to descend. They close their eyes, for dust begins to fill the shaft from the speed of the descent. The temperature inside the shaft gets hotter and hotter the further they descend down into the earth.

Without notice, the old hoist begins to slow down, and a red-toned light illuminates beneath it. The air almost smells like nectar and ambrosia, which are the same substances the gods use to wash and cleanse the sinful flesh of humans before they are reborn. The smell gets stronger and stronger the more they descend. Tim and Ceri look at each other as they begin to hear the sound of a river.

"Is that the sound of water?" Tim says as they stand up.

"I believe so," Ceri says as she ponders how water could be in the depths of Selwyn's Chancer.

The light becomes brighter beneath the shaft. The hoist screeches a bit while it transitions to a stop.

"We must be getting closer to the end of the shaft!" Tim says loudly as the hoist clanks against the rocky walls of the narrow, dusty shaft.

BOOM!

The hoist slams loudly on the bottom. Tim and Ceri open their eyes as the dust clears, noticing a reddish world in front of them that almost looks like Mars. The powerful River Styx is down a medium-sized hill ahead of them.

"The Death of Ages?" Tim says as they step onto the red sand ground. As they look back, they notice a huge train behind them, and the hoist they rode down on is inside one of the train's cars. Tim and Ceri look up to a dark, blue-toned sky, wondering where the shaft or mountains are. The sky turns from blue to dark orange many times during a day's cycle in the Death of Ages. Tim and Ceri look at the sky, wondering exactly what they've gotten themselves into.

The Gates of Death

The door of the hoist that was behind Tim and Ceri slams shut as the rugged train begins to move again. Tim looks right and notices two beastly figures called Vonixra. One stands more than six meters high. Tim looks up at one of the mysterious characters who wears a long black trench coat that goes all the way down to his large feet. The other Vonixra beast is about three meters tall. They speak to each other in their strong native language.

Vonixras are immortal, and their sole purpose is to control the traffic of dead spirits traveling to the Death of Ages. Both of the beasts are laughing about something, for they haven't even noticed Tim and Ceri looking at them. The taller beast begins to speak in his Vonixrian language.

"Ana Carantoc gugin fulira."
(The Carantoc gladiator games will be fun to watch later.)

Another train made from old rugged steel moves into place. More dead spirits walk out of the train as its horn blasts into the air. The Vonixras begin pushing the spirits toward the long line of dead spirits gathered along the River Styx down the hill below.

Tim and Ceri wonder why they haven't been noticed. They begin to walk in the opposite direction of the train. Tim uses the power of the 4th Galon to tap into his vision and look down the hill past hundreds of different beasts gathered at the wooden station of Charun on the river Styx. Tim looks across the river to large gates, which are connected to high-level battlements that travel as far as the eye can see in either direction over the horizon.

"We need to find a way to the other side," Tim says as they continue in the opposite direction of the train.

Ceri notices the air has gotten thicker. "This truly is the River Styx," she says, looking toward the water. "The Styx is wrapped around the earth nine times." She stops speaking as they notice a large black ship crossing the river approaching the Port of Charun. Tim's hearing has improved, and he can now hear the train that dropped them off stopping not too far from their location.

Ceri wonders why they aren't going with the rest of the souls onto the ship, which is docking in the port, for they will never be able to cross the River Styx without the help of Charun.

"I have another idea," says Tim. "Do you see these small pebbles? These will help us get across the dreadful river."

"Well, how and the hell are we going to do that?" Ceri replies as Tim pulls her arm so they can run down the hill and be closer to the river. As they run, Tim notices a section of the River Styx that's smaller than the rest.

"This is the perfect spot," Tim says as he holds the two pebbles in his hand that Brutus had given him. Ceri looks on, wondering what in the world Tim is going to do. Tim plants the pebbles in the sand just like Brutus told him to. In a matter of seconds, the pebbles begin to grow as the sand spreads out into two large oval shapes. In a flash, the shapes drop back into the desert without anything happening.

"I guess they were broken," Tim says lightheartedly. Suddenly, two large horses leap out of the desert with their two front legs high in the air. The horses have saddles on their backs and metal helmets over their heads for protection. The helmets have ancient symbols on them, which were engraved by Jupiter. Their eyes flame with light, and their muscular legs grind into the sand. The horses are trained to immediately obey the individual who planted them. Jupiter's horses stand in front of Tim and Ceri, awaiting their orders.

Down on the other side of the River Styx, some of the dead spirits begin boarding Charun's ferry. Tim uses his vision to once more zero in on Charun with his rugged body and the same torn, sheer robe, except this time, Charun is using the main oar to steer the ship. Charun notices that some of the dead spirits have not been buried properly and are trying to sneak onto the ferry along with the approved spirits. Some of the disrespectful spirits bombard the ferry since they want to wander the sands of the outer regions of the Death of Ages.

One of the outer regions is called Emosiwn, which is where the high-pressure and high-temperature Caves of Siôr are located. They are also the same deep caves where the precious Emosiwn Melyn diamonds are mined.

"In a secret vault, Stratford keeps the largest pink and yellow diamonds from the caves," says Eleanor, speaking from the 7th Galon that appears around Tim's neck. "He deports spirits from the dungeon of Bledri and Tomes to mine at the *Caves of Siôr* for an eternity."

Down near the river, one particular spirit from the House of Diablo Arches, who died in war, is causing a disruption on Charun's ferry as the spirits fight to board the ship. The lost spirit rips apart some of the other spirits on the ferry with his huge arms and oversized muscles. Charun, having enough of their child's play, begins to throw spirits into the River Styx. The spirits scream for their lives, for they will drown in the river and stay there for an eternity. Their cries reach the skies as they scream for mercy as they are tossed one after another into the river Styx.

Charun begins to laugh as the lost souls drown, for they are completely helpless. Charun grips a scepter that was next to him and screams into the sky as thick black smoke comes out of his mouth. The smoke pours high into the sky then turns into liquid acid as it descends onto all the lost souls who should be crossing on the ferry. The acid eats their spirit bodies until nothing is left, except for their skeleton bodies, which are made of light. All of the approved spirits in the ferry are left unharmed by the acid, which stops descending from the darker blue-orange sky as dusk approaches.

Charun grips his scepter and starts smashing the skeletons, sweeping them into the river as they clank off his ferry and dissolve into the River Styx. Charun, for some reason, starts saving the spirits who were supposed to get a lift and pulls them back into the boat.

"I guess he has a heart after all," Tim says as they continue to watch from afar.

Tim begins to get restless and jumps onto his horse, then tells Ceri to follow his lead by doing the same. Down below, Charun has gotten all the spirits together and is making his way across the river near the Gates of

Death, which have long iron beams going up and down. A huge Trydan skull is positioned on the front of the gate for intimidation. That particular Trydan was killed by Bledri and Tomes' lionfaced father, Cynhafar, even though the dragon-headed Miniver always took the credit.

Large, dark, iron and steel ride makes up the top of the gate. Tim notices a moat with slime oozing from the bailey. He and Ceri hear men and women screaming on the other side of the battlements. They look at each other as they wait for the right moment to cross the heavy-flowing River Styx. Moments later, Charun parks his ferry on the other side of the river, pulling an oval handle connected to a rope attached to an ancient bell mounted on the top of the long sacred ferry.

When Charun pulls the handle down harder, two large Cynfor dragons appear on the top of the barbicans, which connect the sides of the Gates of Death. The Cynfor dragons with their two heads look down to make sure everything is safe below so they can open the gates. One of the dragons blows a large horn that produces a loud sound and steam. Tim and Ceri cover their ears as the horn's power makes the water overflow the banks near the Gates of Death. Both of the Cynfor dragons, who are gatekeepers, growl as they open the locking system from the other side of the Gates of Death.

Four Cynfor dragons push open the gates as the dinosaur skull slides up, allowing the gates to open like suicide doors.

Two Cynfor dragons, who are third in line to the throne, walk out to meet their new batch of fresh spirits that are entering in one line through the Gates of Death. One of the Cynfor's names is Derilyn, and it has a dragon head; the lionface head is named Geulia. The other Cynfor dragon's name is Fyanicrum, and his lionface head is called Jupira. The Cynfor's approach the ship carrying their humongous swords in their hands.

The swords are so big they could cut down even the largest dragon in one swipe. Derilyn uses his tail and sticks the large blade into the ground, trying to intimidate the dead spirits of Selwyn's Chancer, for most of them are afraid of any Cynfor.

Some of the spirits used to work for Stratford and Amelia and failed in their duty or were killed in wars orchestrated by the House of Diablo.

Tim looks as Ceri moves her hood back so half of her lower face shows and her eyes can be seen. Tim notices Ceri's eyes are still a light orange color. He wonders whether he will be able to cure her from becoming the watcher of the Last Fairy Maze Forest. Ceri keeps

Tim patient while they sit on Jupiter's horses. Tim looks down at the Shield of Aeneas sparkling on the side of his horse. He reaches inside his messenger bag and pulls out the Book of Hartwell. Ceri looks at him, shocked to see such magical power in her presence.

"So, that is the Book of Hartwell. Why haven't you used any of its magical power?" Ceri asks as she continues to watch spirits enter the Gates of Death to the castle of Bledri and Tomes.

"I can't open it," Tim says to Ceri. "I thought once I found all seven Galons I would be able to see what my family has hidden throughout the ages. Even the spells have been written by the book itself, for it has become alive somehow." Tim tucks the book back into his messenger bag, and a place flashes in his mind.

"The Peninsula of Roseland," Tim says to himself, for he knows where he must go to open the Book of Hartwell so he can find a way home. First, he must rescue Ceri from her doom. Second, he must find Hynwyn Reese. And third, they must escape the Death of Ages.

Tim along with Ceri wait for the Cynfor dragons to leave before they go back through the entrance. Fyanicrum screams as the gates shut completely, and no one can hear his screams on the inside. Tim and Ceri continue and ride their horses to the front of the gates of Death. Ceri touches the dinosaur's skull on the gate. Her father's signet ring slowly illuminates on her right hand. The power of her Gwynwell bloodline magically opens the Gates of Death to the House of Cynfor where Bledri and Tomes are secretly awaiting their arrival.

TIM HARTWELL: Open Your Heart Trilogy (Books 1-3)

TIM HARTWELL
and The Death of Ages

Volume 3

- Original Copyright Information -

Copyright © 2010 by Aeneas Middleton

ISBN-13: 978-0615612485
ISBN-10: 0615612482

Library of Congress Control Number: 2012904215

Book Three (Bk. 3)

Goddess Venus

Love

MOTHER TO AENEAS OF TROY

Contents

- 491   When Twins Are Born
- 505   Emosiwn Melyn Diamonds
- 518   When a Fairy Is Born
- 538   Find Hynwyn Reese
- 596   Love From Venus
- 603   Mary's Escape
- 618   Jealousy From Across
- 649   When A Kingdom Falls
- 715   The Bluebells Forest

TIM HARTWELL: Open Your Heart Trilogy (Books 1-3)

When Twins Are Born

Bledri and Tomes, the rulers of the House of Cynfor are standing in front of hundreds of Cynfor dragon gatekeeper soldiers. The new rulers of the House of Cynfor are sitting on their royal thrones inside chamber *Cynforanyth Senate Hall*, which is perpendicular to the Gates of Death. The sound of old metal ships having it's parts ripped away for demolition catches Tomes attention as gust of winds fly through the Senate Hall where titan-sized Cynfor dragons are patiently waiting with their Cynfor coat of arms on their armor, and helmets sparkling in slight darkness of the Cynforanyth Senate Hall. Fyanicrum and his lionface Jupira are sitting in their royal seats next to Derilyn and his lionface Geulia.

"Here me, here me!" Bledri says. Pounding his scepter which has a *Emosiwn Melyn* diamond the size of a grapefruit on top with the Coat of Cynfor engraved midway through the handle. Bledri looks over towards Tomes direction, eager to inform his men on the news that has come from Stratford. "We are now in-control of the biggest mines in all of Death of Ages!" Bledri shouts out as the low-level Cynfor Gatekeeper dragons stand guard around the chamber, tapping their swords on the ground making fire sparks. The Gatekeepers continue to tap their large human size blades on the stone floor as Bledri continues.

"The power of the *Caves of Siôr* are under our control effective this very day, therefore we will punish any spirit in the Death of Ages that believes they can smuggle our precious Emosiwn

Melyn diamonds to their outer regions. As you know the House of Diablo Arches have been controlling the Caves of Siôr from the beginning of Selwyn's Chancer." Bledri expresses the anguish their race has been going through over the money, power, and control generated from the Emosiwn Melyn diamonds. For they will keep every single slave as currency given to the House of Cynfor from other houses to make a profit in the gladiator games.

"We have new fighters and slaves in the chamber I see." Bledri pointing over to many of the fighters who are below them looking up. "Most of you have abandoned your race, even ashamed your house names. But not here. You will fight in the games and you will mine our diamonds for an eternity. Nothing more, nothing less." Bledri continuing as Tomes, the lionface head nudges Bledri about a few things he hasn't pointed out. Bledri shakes his head left to right, and continues to speak on what Tomes is referring too.

"As of today, we are expecting two guests to be arriving very soon. First, a boy wizard descendant of the House of Hartwell, second a young girl, the last descendant of the House of Gwynwell," Bledri says. When a neck of another dragon comes from behind the royal drapes that reach high above the Cynforanyth Senate Hall ceiling behind them. The Cynfor

Gatekeeper whispers in Bledri's ear, then he whispers in Tomes ear. Jupira looks on very suspiciously on what is being said but can not make out the Gatekeepers words.

Bledri slams his scepter on the floor once more, ending the introduction to the Death of Ages meeting. In a instant, Bledri and Tomes follow the Gatekeeper behind the curtains while the remaining low-level Cynfor soldiers start pushing the new spirit slaves towards the freezing cold dungeons.

Derilyn and Fyanicrum shout out to the top of their lungs towards their low-level command to get ready, ordering all of them to head towards

TIM HARTWELL: Open Your Heart Trilogy (Books 1-3)

the Caves of Siôr. Everyone leaves out the Senate hall when the Wyvern twin-gargoyles Alfred and Verlock decloak from invisibility rubbing their hands together with excitement. The Wyvern twins quickly disappear back into thin air whispering to each other. "Their completely hatstand," Verlock says. Before they jet out towards the stone battlements of the legendary House of Cynfor castle.

On the opposite side of Selwyn's Chancer, Stratford whispers; "Tim Hartwell" to himself as Lylock walks into the library of Amelia's Chamber which is inside of Amelia's fortress located inside the belly of her titaness Alynn dragon.

The personal guards who walked Lylock inside the chamber closes the large doors behind him. The father and ruler of the House of Diablo Arches, Lylock is wearing his infamous pink and yellow Emosiwn Melyn diamond coronet which is sparkling through the room along with the epic chandelier above them. The fortress rumbles for a second, for the Alynn dragon is getting tired in flight as it descends out from a patch of Cumulonimbus clouds to rest near a hidden section of Foel-goch, a massive mountain in Snowdonia, Wales.

Stratford is sitting down in human form thanks to Amelia's magic. Lylock looks around the ancient library with many books that go back as far as early human and dragon civilization. Stratford continues to look down towards his chess pieces playing with a few of them with his fingers. He has gotten word that Amelia is going to birth his first child, and he is overly excited about the magical powers his child might have when conceived. Stratford has been overly stressed given the short amount of time waiting in the library. He personally invited Lylock to play a few rounds of chess with him while he waits for Amelia to go into labor.

    Both of them remain quiet as they begin setting up their chess pieces one by one. Each chess piece is made from Emosiwn Melyn diamonds, except for the Queens. Which Stratford keep as precious red rubies that remind him of Amelia's, favorite stone on mother Earth. Lylock glances at one of the paintings with a disturbing look, since he isn't used to seeing Stratford in human form very much. "Are you comfortable with my appearance Lylock, you seem a bit edgy," Stratford says. "Humans are ugly creatures, I must say. Their bodies are so fragile, you know our race looks upon that as a weakness." Lylock thinking about how complex human anatomy is at the same time. "Well if you where human maybe you wouldn't like your beast appearance either." Stratford snapping his fingers turning Lylock into a handsome mid-age man, which startles Lylock making him jump out of his seat looking at his hands, Stratford snaps his fingers once more making two beautiful blond and brunette archangels appear next to him.

They begin to rub Llyock's shoulders and caress his auburn human hair. Lylock for a moment is pleased with all of his new company, but hating his appearance with a passion. Stratford snaps his fingers making the women disappear turning Lylock back into his Diablo Arch beast form. "That's more like it!" Lylock says rubbing his jagged hair on his head. Looking at himself in a mirror to the left of him. "Okay, since your the guest, make your first move," Stratford says. Lylock stares down at his chess pieces moving his pawn in a conservative manner to A3. Stratford puts his hand on his chin to think for a moment, he adjust his thoughts and moves his pawn to B5.

After an hour of playing, the fireplace begins to dim leaving only a few pieces left on the chessboard with Lylock surprisingly in the lead. "It looks like you might walk out of here with a sure win," Stratford says firmly. He suddenly thinks about his unborn child as he chooses his next move wisely. Lylock in his best interest, abruptly brings up some disturbing news that has been going around the House of Diablo Arches. "Lord Stratford, I wonder, why have you not killed the son of Hartwell? The boy you call Tim Hartwell," Lylock says. Stratford looks up at him wondering why he would him a question his authority especially in at this time.

"Be patient, my friend. For even the House of Cynfor wants Tim dead after killing Miniver and Cynhafar at World's End, Bledri and Tomes wonder why I am keeping your vicious House alive at all in Selwyn's Chancer. Thanks to me, I understand that wars in the Death of Ages have gotten out of control. Why do you think I made your House second of them all even though you failed again miserably at Llyn Cwellyn," Stratford says to Lylock about their rational decision making.

He always felt the House of Diablo Arches needed to be more organized during war. "If it wasn't for Brutus of Troy, we would of captured that little brat." Lylock trying to explain his failures.

"I don't want to hear that, I know you guys can handle the business. But your house failures have now forced me to honor the royal House of Cynfor in full control of your Caves of Siôr.

"You have done what!!!"

Lylock screaming to the top of his lungs. "Sit down or would you rather me reverse my decision of your house being number two," Stratford says with a callous tone. "I had to give them something down there, besides, your house has been controlling the trades of Emosiwn Melyn diamond for ages. If you can do me a small favor, I will return the favor a million times fold." Stratford trying to give Lylock an even better proposition.

"How would you like to be the rulers of the Death of Ages in Selwyn's Chancer forever?" Stratford giving a piece of his final plan to his best friend King Lylock. "I need for you to gather your house and start a war for me, a war beyond anything you have ever done for me, my dearest Lylock," Stratford says with much ambition and revenge.

"Tell me Lord Stratford, for I am eager to know what I must do to control such power." Lylock expressing a deep passion to fulfil his duty of finally controlling a god-like power inside Selwyn's Chancer. Stratford looks directly into the eyes of Lylock, reaching over to Lylock's chess pieces on the board. "I want you to kill a King, two heads to be exact," Stratford says as he slides out of his seat looking over to his enormous book collection. He looks up towards the second level walkway with a spiral staircase going up to a secret room that no one except Stratford, and his wife Amelia has been into. A secret room that Stratford keep a spell over for it can never be opened by anyone except him and his beloved mate Amelia.

King Lylock stands up quickly

to his feet, almost not knowing what to say, he doesn't know exactly what Stratford is talking about. "I want you to kill every descendant of House of Cynfor, you will control the depths of Selwyn's Chancer if you succeed. Can you do that for me Son?" Stratford says with a sparkle in his eyes. "Lord Stratford, I have been waiting many ages for those words to come from your mouth, you have chosen wisely to believe in the House of Diablo Arches my master." Lylock roars loudly with joy as he walks around the room to where Stratford is standing.

"When I call for you, you need to act quickly, and the Death of Ages will be yours, just remember that." Stratford replies as one of Stratford's personal guards interrupts him about Amelia going into labor. Before Lylock walks out, Stratford calls for him once more to say a few more words. Stratford notices Baron Milwr peaking inside of the doorway, Baron quickly stairs at the pink and yellow Emosiwn Melyn diamond coronet around Stratford's neck for protection against his voice. Stratford looking back at him with a larger Emosiwn Melyn diamond on his hand to show off a bit. He d moves his head when Lylock notices the Coat of Hartwell tattooed under Stratford's human wrist. Stratford morphs back into his beast form keeping a human torso, arms, and legs.

"Make sure when you attack the House of Cynfor, you better return Mother Mary to me alive. The wizards mother;

Do you hear me?"

Stratford screams out loudly, still thinking about his unborn child on the way. He re-adjusts and speaks to Lylock who truly is his best friend in a more respectable manor. "Mary must remain alive when you attack the castle to the House of Cynfor. Don't fail me now Lylock, for your future kingdom will be set with you and Baron Milwr, and of course all of the House of Diablo Arches," Stratford says quickly." He looks directly into Lylock's eyes for some reason he doesn't mind his House failures at this moment. The power of Tim Hartwell has opened up more realms inside of Selwyn's Chancer, he can feel it. Stratford gives a few more orders while in the presence of Lylock, but Baron can only think about the Emosiwn Melyn Diamonds as precious fruit to his mind. Stratford waves them off, getting back the task at hand, running to see Amelia while Baron and Lylock quickly fly like a rocket jet out the stomach, thru an opening of the throat escaping the fire and phlegm inside the mouth of Amelia's Alynn Dragon. They both bank towards the upper region of the Cumulous grey clouds above Pembrokeshire Coast National Park. The enormous Alynn dragon wings soars high above huge Cumulus Nimbus clouds towards St. Guards fading into the sky pass St. Brides Bay.

    Back inside the Alynn Dragon, Stratford flies down the royal arched hallways where large drapes on every edge with the Coat of Hartwell embroidered on them. The for wings and the key hole centered between them. The red drapes flows throughout the master royal bedroom chamber where Amelia is located. Stratford transforms himself into his human appearance, his eyes are glowing slightly as he rushes to hold Amelia hand.

"My love is that you?" Amelia whispers towards Stratford, his medium sized ears can hear every word crystal clear.

Amelia takes full control of Stratford's mind without him even knowing while he holds her hand whispering, "I Love You." She makes her self fall silently asleep, while her body is fully awake and functional.

A white flash magically turns into a magical spirit which begins to speak to Stratford, as it appears to be an Obstetrician the way she is dressed. "She is due any minute now". The woman explains she is Amelia's spirit Megan Lynelle, a resurrected spirit from her **Alynn-tusk spell** which allows her to split her spirits in two. Amelia was always untrustworthy of anyone to touch her unborn baby with their hands, especially someone who would try to assassinate her first born. Amelia's mind silently as her body continues to push the baby out of her womb, Stratford look on for he knows this has been her dream for as long as he can remember.

    Stratford stands there almost unfazed by Amelia's second spirit, he holds Amelia's warm hands while he stands by her side gripping her hand for support with his conscious still under control giving Amelia insurance of safety while Amelia body pushes with agony. Eight hours pass and Amelia still hasn't given birth, stress levels are skyrocket high in Amelia's birthing chamber. Stratford is sweating heavily on the side of his face, for he is awaiting patiently the arrival of his heir to the throne. Fifteen minutes pass by while Lynelle raises her right hand signaling in the air that a baby's leg is coming from out of Amelia's womb.

"It's a boy!"

Stratford yells out loudly while Lynelle holding a cloth in one hand, pulls the baby from the legs first completely out. "He was born feet first," Megan Lynelle says. Stratford smiles from ear to ear amazed at the very sight of his son who has brunette hair, but with a golden lock right behind his right ear. Lynelle wipes the boys blood from it's skin as she points towards the body of the baby using magical sterilized scissors to cut the umbilical chord.

TIM HARTWELL: Open Your Heart Trilogy (Books 1-3)

Lynelle holds the baby directly in front of Amelia's sweaty face for her to see her son, then she hands the boy infant to Stratford to hold when Megan raises her hand once more. Lynelle does the same sequence with her right hand noticing the top of another baby's head that is beginning to poke out of Amelia's womb from her body.

"There is another!" Lynelle shouts loudly, Stratford holding his newborn son in his hands as Megan Lynelle speaks to Amelia's body waking her human spirit back up. Stratford under Amelia's spell begins to lift, he looks towards her for a quick moment thinking about why Amelia didn't bring out Megan while Tim was in the castle previously, he thinks maybe Lynelle knows something he doesn't know, but dismisses those thoughts snapping back into the moment holding his newborn son while Amelia cries for she has never seen something so angel-like in a dark world they thrive in every day, especially being secluded inside of her enormous, but precious Alynn Dragon.

At the same time, Lynelle begins to pull the second baby out and notices that it's not a boy. "It's a girl?, They are fraternal twins?" Lynelle speaking frantically as she looks at the baby girl infant with tropical blue ocean colored eyes, and blond hair. Megan begins to tend to the baby, doing all of the necessary things for the second baby to be stable and healthy, for a new heir prince and princess have been born.

A few hours pass, Stratford inside of the birthing chamber with Amelia as she sleeps totally exhausted. Amelia's second spirit Lynelle tends to the babies while giving the son to Stratford and the girl to Amelia, Lynelle's spirit disappears which means Amelia's spirit is whole again. Amelia looks so proud to have a daughter as well.

"Twins? What shall we name them my love?" Amelia's silent words move through the chamber, Stratford looks down at his son while looking over to his daughter exchanging them between each other. He begins to think real hard for a boy name that sounds strong to reign his empire through the ages. The large castle sways a bit inside of the belly of the Alynn dragon, as the dragon begins waking up back near the mountains high above the clouds of Snowdonia, in north-west Wales. "We shall call our beloved new prince, **Cayne (Welsh: Spear).** He will be my new heir, we will also make a statue of them both at the next Carantoc Gladiator Arena in the Death of Ages, I will then, make sure everyone knows he will rule at the right age," Stratford says with upmost confidence for he knows his son will have his very own magical powers that will reveal themselves soon enough. Amelia looks at Stratford to continue for he knows his daughter must have a name just a honorable, so he names the Princess of Selwyn's Chancer after his dear love Amelia.

"She will be called **Amelia II**. She will be an equal ruler besides Cayne until he comes of age to rule the royal throne of Selwyn's Chancer. Our little princess will control all dragons and ice when Cayne becomes King. She will have some control, it could be decent for the both of them in the long run. They both will be a forced to be reckoned with." Stratford can feel the endless knowledge of the parallel world within Selwyn's Chancer looking at them. Stratford glances at Amelia's beautiful eyes, love has sprouted from their hearts, Stratford always knew he needed the presence of knowledge, and the only way to be a true King, is having a true Queen.

"Open Your Heart, Trust your Heart"

Stratford whispers to himself, reciting one of many House of Hartwell old family quotes.

Stratford grabs both children to let Amelia sleep, her twin spirit Lynelle illuminates one more to take care of the twin babies. Stratford with a clear mind with peace traveling through his heart, for his new children and beautiful Queen. He walks back out of the bedroom chamber, all the way outside to the gates of Amelia's Chamber to the castle.

Stratford walks towards the

heart of Amelia's Alynn dragon, which is beneath a glass floor below his feet where the dragons heart is thumping loudly. He just stands there with his pink and yellow canarie Emosiwn Melyn diamond coronet around his neck, his enormous ring shining in peace. At this moment, Stratford is thirsty for all of the hidden power in the parallel world of Selwyn's Chancer that has created itself, thanks to Tim's mother giving him the 1st Galon key, he thinks to himself about the magical possibilities that will occur. Stratford looks down at the Alynn's dragon heart smothered in Lava beating like a wild drum, some of the lava splashes against the other side of the glass below his feet. Stratford smiles knowing that he has ceased the moment of future power, like he did before trapping the House of Cynfor in the Death of Ages forever. Stratford drinks some wine in a oval glass as he continues to stare at the beauty of the dragon heart, beating with its heart beating with a deep tone, he imagines if his children will have twin-telepathy while he looks up at the Diablo Arches on top of the castle with their flat heads, bodies of black edged bodies standing on top, guarding the purple toned crystal castle.

    The huge panther Sylkin, catches Stratford's eye and tries to make an impression for a quick snack. Sylkin jumps up with excitement forgetting the large chain connected to its collar around his neck that brings his panther-like body slamming back down to the rocky ground. Stratford points on the side of Sylkin magically creating a Tyrannosaurus Rex appear right in front of Sylkin. In a flash, Sylkin goes in for the kill at lighting speed leaping towards the Tyrannosaurus that roars back not afraid. With a quick attack, Sylkin teeth sink into the neck of the Tyrannosaurus using his razor sharp teeth to take hold and snaps the neck of the T-Rex, pulling half of the neck with the head completely off. Stratford begins to think about a genius idea of using Sylkin to help along with the House of Diablo Arches when they invade House of

Cynfor as twilight passes the sky outside North Wales.

TIM HARTWELL: Open Your Heart Trilogy (Books 1-3)

Emosiwn Melyn Diamonds

Deep inside the raging world of the Death of Ages lies the Caves of Siôr, resting below another patch of clouds drifting across the Earth's troposphere. Below the clouds are large waterfalls in the middle of the desert outer skirts. At this very moment, the House of Cynfor for the first time in The Death of Ages have control of the precious diamonds that shine like no other diamonds in the universe. Each diamond keeping the House of Cynfor very happy about the control of such the Caves of Siôr.

Bledri and Tomes egos are through the roof as they arrive outside the Caves of Siôr with dragon Fyanicrum, his lion-face head Jupira, including their partners are third to the throne with another Cynfor dragon named Derilyn and his lion-faced head Guelia. Standing behind them all are their royal personal guards including a few Gatekeepers from the Gates of Death. All of them are draped in armor with capes dangling from their backs, which has the royal House of Cynfor coat of arms on all of their armor, weaponry and apparel. Tomes has gotten excited somehow from his born-drunken slumber. One of the main reasons why their father wanted to make Derilyn and Geulia second in line but for politics over the senate, Miniver and Cynhafar where named third in line to the throne.

Tomes at this very moment feels the triumphs of power, he magically straightens up his neck looking through the 5th level window to see a mountainous cave interior that stretches a path into darkness. Tomes lion-face head seems more intelligent at this very moment.

"How could this be?" Bledri whispers to himself watching his brother Tomes look around sniffing the air for any scent of a trap by the Diablo Arches, he knows a few of them can never be trusted for their strong ties with Stratford. Bledri and Tomes both understand that Lylock and Baron Milwr and their House of Diablo Arches have been in control of the Caves prior to their arrival in Selwyn's Chancer. As everyone continues to look around the 5th level chamber, Fyanicrum and Jupira notice a letter nailed to a wooden stake in the ground towards the lower exitway chamber. The letter has a candle wax seal as the letter sways side to side from the gust of wind they creeps its way up from the lower chambers.

"This seal is from Nessa and Elle Milwr, the daughters of Lylock and sister to brother Baron Milwr," Fyanicrum says. "Nessa was almost killed by the voice of her own brother Baron Milwr as her Emosiwn Melyn necklace had fallen off a cliff where they were arguing one night for I have heard." Bledri replying to Fyanicrum.

"If it wasn't for Lylock, Nessa would be dead, I was shocked to hear Lylock had enough time to wrap a spare coronet of Emosiwn Melyn diamonds around her neck to save her, for her eardrums are still severely damaged." Tomes speaks unexpectedly for none of the other Cynfor lionface heads can speak.

"So that is why their father Lylock has given Nessa and Elle the power of being speakers of the house and over business throughout the Caves of Siôr for Lylock and Baron don't know how to write words after all," Fyanicrum says with laughter. "But they can still read!" Bledri says with a firm voice as he waves his arm for Fyanicrum and Jupira to snap back into formation to read the letter out loud to their rulers Fyanicrum and Jupira who pull the letter from off the wooded stake, as they walk into formation reading the letter out loud.

"The House of Cynfor for this day forth will inherit leadership of the Caves of Siôr. All of the slaves or beasts who mine in the Caves of Siôr are locked up in their cells occupying 2nd and 3rd low-level chambers. All monitoring, logs, security-line sequencing are left inside of the master guarding chamber on 4th level chamber ,which controls most of the complex. Watch your back for the prisoners have become restless as you transform more of them into the cells. We are sure your house will due fine in this manner. Sincerely, The House of Diablo Arches." Fyanicrum reads when another patch of Gatekeepers sent from the Castle to Bledri and Tomes to restore order in the Caves of Siôr to their liking. In some way Bledri and Tomes are still wondering why Stratford would freely give away anything, especially control of the pinnacle of wealth in Selwyn's Chancer. Both Bledri and Tomes shrug off the idea as Stratford predicted their instinct race would to perfection. Genius.

The House of Cynfor make all of the necessary **Trancynformation** inside of the Caves of Siôr including schedules for feeding all the spirit slaves, while Bledri and Tomes walk through the 2nd and 3rd level chambers looking at some of the slaves in their cells for they haven't been given access inside the Gates of Death. Most of them were caught by the House of Diablo Arches while others made deals with the House of Scorpus. Only to find themselves in the Death of Ages to get caught by the Vonixra beasts, later sold to the House of Diablo Arches for Emosiwn Melyn diamonds.

Bledri and Tomes start mapping out the remaining cave interior which is the size of the *Ogof Ffynnon Ddu* caves in South Wales. They head back up to the 4th level chamber walking out onto the balcony which oversees the 2nd and 3rd level chambers that have over three-hundred cells. Bledri grips the safety pipe along the balcony and begins to address all of the slaves about their new Twenty-three hour work schedules, giving them one-hour for leisure time so they can still fight each other in the annual *Carantoc Gladiator Games* which are coming up tomorrow early afternoon.

A few hours past as a small Cynfor runner who looks like a lizard with branded Cynfor Coat of Arms on their backs. The runner informs their rulers of possible intruders within their castle grounds. "I told you we should of stay back at the castle and come here tomorrow, but no... You had to see this place today, I knew I should of listened to my first intuition." Bledri blaming Tomes for them leaving so soon without capturing Tim's Mother Mary before the arrival Tim Hartwell and Ceri Gwynwell.

Bledri orders Fyanicrum and

Guelia to stay guard at the Caves of Siôr and to keep them informed on the progress of mining through the caves, for they have some very important business to take care of including the treatment for the Carantoc Gladiator games. Bledri and Tomes wrap things up and head back to their castle to capture their intruders for they know who are, except for the rest of the royal House of Cynfor House.

"Bledri and Tomes have already broken a few rules by not including the Senate hall on situations involving the house," Verlock says to his brother Alfred the Wyvern gargoyles who are spying on them for Stratford, for they magically appear with their eyes illuminating, but remain completely invisible hiding inside of the chamber.

As Bledri and Tomes head back to Cynfor castle, Fyanicrum and Jupira walk back up to the 5th level looking at all of the Emosiwn Melyn diamonds in the cave once more, Derilyn and Guelia pull the levers for all of the slaves to get working and start mining more diamonds for them.

    At this very moment, tension between slaves and the House of Cynfor has risen for the slaves really understand even more now, this has to be the worst thing for them to happen in ages, even under the leadership of the House of Diablo Arches. Fyanicrum looks on as the royal Cynfor dragon personal guards stand guard in their places. The slaves holding torches, form lines leading down into the pits of the caves. The light from their torches begin to illuminate further down the cave from the royal observation side-chamber. "The fire of their torches are burning fiercely," Fyanicrum says to Jupira. "I hope their inner-fire can last forever, for now the House of Cynfor will grip the power for our beloved Bledri and Tomes forever in the Death of Ages, for we will put our lives on the line for such a treasure, agreed Jupira." Fyanicrum continues speaking as his lionface head Jupira nods and continues to look down at history in the making

When A Fairy Is Born

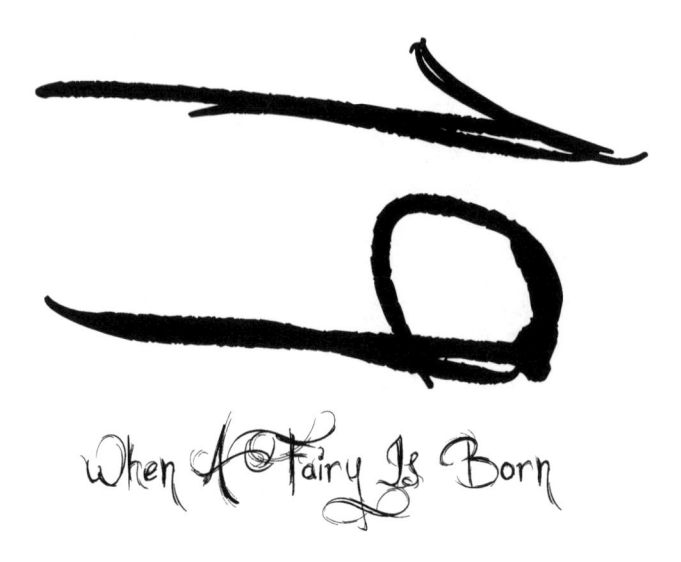

On the other side of the castle to the House of Cynfor, Tim is watching the Gates of Death open up slowly as the T-Rex dinosaur skull slides up while the Gates begin to open as light begins to blind them. In a quick flash, both of them open their eyes to see no one there, except a long path directly in front of them, with trees stretching as far as they can see from left to right. Tim and Ceri both look further down the path ahead of them noticing a castle far off in the distance. Tim, becomes very suspicious for he doesn't see any of the Gatekeepers or Cynfor dragons anywhere in near sight.

"How could they disappear so quickly?" Ceri says. "They must be using some type of magic to transport themselves to different parts of the Death of Ages. The Gates of Death slowly shuts themselves with a loud bang as they shut completely. Out of nowhere, Ceri grabs her chest and begins to feel the transformation of her becoming the watcher of the Last Fairy Maze Forest. With hesitation, Ceri quickly pulls out the canister that Darron. One of the rulers from the

House of Scorpus had given her to slow the process down. Ceri quickly pulls out the cork and drinks some of the liquid, Ceri begins coughing hard for the taste of the liquid abstract made from poisonous leaves grow outside the castle of the hidden House of Scorpus in North Wales.

"This is some of the unpleasant stuff I ever drunk in my life," Ceri says. She tucks the canister back in her cloak, both of them are still sitting on Jupiter's magical horses waiting for their next command. "Good thing they gave it to you, for if it wasn't for Brutus of Troy, we would both be trapped in the upper region world of Selwyn's Chancer in Snowdon. In a flash, Ceri begins screaming to the top of her lungs for the liquid that Darron had given her isn't working correctly, it has speed up the process of her fairy watcher transformation.

"How, how could they do this to me? They have betrayed us!" Ceri says. Screaming as her body slowly begins illuminating. She begins to fade away as her body falls of the horse onto the ground. Tim quickly jumps off his horse to help her, but notices that her body has faded away into the ground. He looks up at Jupiter's horse Ceri was sitting on noticing that both of the horses have merged into one horse, for the power of Jupiter must know exactly what is going on. Tim screams in the air with revenger as he looks at the ground picking up her cloak, but her signet ring is hovering slightly in the air above the ground with her necklace that has a charm with the Coat of Gwynwell engraved on it. Black crows begin to fly from the tree tops to other parts of the forest. Tim, not sure what to do screams out to the top of his lungs;

"CERI!!!"

Tim breathing erratically, feeling the betrayal once more, he should of known the House of Scorpus were not to be trusted. Tim in his mind, builds rage in his heart to meet the rulers of the House of Scorpus, Darron and Darryn and pay them back for what they have done. Tim looking up noticing the sky changing from orange to blue, the wind begins to pick up, the young wizard jumps back onto his horse not sure where to go next. Without warning Tim hears a voice laughing, echoing to the top of the skies. The voice is very familiar, it's the voice of Ceri but sounding sinister, for she has become the watcher of the Last Fairy Maze Forest after all. The voice begins to speak from inside of the forest directly ahead. Tim puts all of Ceri's belonging into a sack on the side of the horse, then immediately dashes down the path.

Tim rides Jupiter's horse down the path where the path splits with a huge tree in the middle of the path. There is a wooden Wales Coat of Arms nailed to the tree, with a young girls face poking through the center of a key hole of the shield. Only the nose and mouth are exposed. Tim walks his horse over to the tree jumping off his horse, he picks up the Shield of Aeneas of he side of the horse for protection and walks over to this mysterious female coat of arm object. "What are you?" Tim says as he rubs his left hand on the side of the shield, out of now where the girls face begins to speak;

"STAND BACK"

The girls voice shattered through the air, with a smooth but ruff tone. "Ceri is that you?" Tim asks the fairy watcher who doesn't have eyes. "Ceri is no more, she is gone forever, you will never escape my forest young wizard. You will be trapped here for the rest of you miserable life." The voice of Ceri as the fairy watcher replies with a rude tone, her spirit is controlled by the magical poison from the *Gwenwyna*. "Ceri, it's me Tim, don't you recognize my voice?" He says. With a respectable tone hoping she will understand. "Why are you asking question to answers you already know. Choose your destiny, left or right dear boy." Ceri giving Tim his options of travel through the forest. "Which way can I find Hynwyn Reese, for I know he can help you?" Tim says.

"Hahahaha, the mighty barbarian, he should he fighting in the Carantoc Gladiator Games very soon, he can't help you now." She replies then going dormant not saying another word. Tim's eyes looks more determined than ever. He looks left, then looks right, noticing both paths seem too similar, he is not sure which way to go. Before he chooses, Tim hears two voices he knows very well, they appear behind him, the twin Wyvern gargoyles Alfred and Verlock.

"Look what she has gotten herself into now, for she was the last bloodline to the House of Gwynwell," Alfred says. Tim out of rage picks Alfred up and slams his back up against a tree demanding answers. "I told you he was completely hatstand," Verlock says as the power of the magical Galon begins to make him more enraged. "We, we can't help you save her, only Hynwyn Reese knows how to transform her back. We can tell you which way to go, but that will be all for now, Stratford for sure has his eyes on us all at this very moment. Don't you know Amelia has given birth to a girl and boy fraternal twins, they will have some of the power of the Galon themselves, for now you know you Mother Mary should of never given you the Galon back in Tenby. Tim holding Verlock by the neck, let him go has he slides him down to the ground. Tim lets the Shield of Aeneas slide off his right arm onto the ground next to him. Jupiter's horse snorts on the ground as soon as he does, knowing he is loosing some of his confidence and needs to shape back up.

"Don't give up now, young wizard for you have much journey ahead of you, especially since you gave away Adamanthea's rope, you should of never traded it with Emperor Claudius," Alfred says. "Don't order me around!" Tim screams back at them, some of the birds chirp in the background distracting them for a second. "Verlock and Alfred look at each other, remembering to keep their promise to help Tim no matter what, even if it gets them killed. In their heart they are tired of being slaves to Stratford Hartwell.

Okay, fine you must go left, this way will lead you to the Castle, but you must remember there will be a storm ahead, but you will survive trust me. Going right will have you lost forever even though it leads to the Gates of Horn, but not the right way, if you can understand. "Alfred twisting his words up a bit. The fairy voice begins to speak for she won't except anyone tampering with her knowledge of the forest, in a mere seconds, tree vines fly towards Verlock and Alfred grabbing them both pulling them deep into the forest as they scream for their life, but for their sake are able to disappear in thin air before the vines crush their bodies like toothpicks.

"Holy Tenby," Tim says. Noticing the forest is very well indeed alive.

"Listen to them if you must, but you will never escape my realm," Ceri says. Trying to discourage Tim to go down the right path. Tim trusting his twin-wyverns, gathers his things, jumps back on top of Jupiter's horse, and rides down the left path as fast as he can. Electricity sparks on the ground as the horses ride faster and faster down the path to the back entrance to the castle of the House of Cynfor. Tim continues to ride down the path when he notices more and more wooden coat of arms repeating themselves with Ceri's face appearing on one tree after another, for she is blind but can hear every movement of the horse riding through the forest. Tim not giving in, continues to ride faster and faster, the sky turns from blue to orange once more with Noctilucent and Cirrus spissatus undulatus clouds starting to appear above him far ahead.

"This must be the storm Verlock and Alfred was talking about, the voice of Ceri as the fairy begins to laugh louder and louder until he approaches part of the forest path that has mist blocking his sight as he rides closer. Tim pulls on the reigns on his horse to halt to a stop with dark mist directly in front of him, almost as if the clouds where lowered to the ground on purpose. Tim not sure what will be waiting for him down this misty path, hears another voice, that he for sure would never forget.

"You must continue to believe Tim, for fear is only an illusion," Goddess Diana says. She appears on the side of him as a mere glow for day become night in seconds. The forest is completely dark which is going to make it harder for him to travel within the Last Fairy Maze Forest," Diana says as another female made of light appears next to Goddess Diana and begins to speak. Hello Tim, I am Goddess Venus, mother of Aeneas from Troy, I am here to give you a bit of knowledge thanks to Diana informing me of the situation you have been forced into," Venus says. Her and Diana are as tall as some of the trees. Their glance down at Tim with their bodies illuminating the ground area around him.

"Use the Shield of Aeneas to guide you through the storm, it will help you in many ways as it did Aeneas when he needed it most in Latium," Venus says. Tim not really sure what to say, utters a few words out to see exactly what he must do next. "Tell me what I have to do Venus, and thank you Diana, I never expected to see you again," Tim says. When a Galon key appears around his neck dangling from his neck, it's the 7th Galon the guiding voice of Eleanor Hartwell who begins to speak. "Tim you have the power of the Galon use it well, listen to them both for they can help you, besides I am not sure what fate Ceri will have, you might not be able to save her, but you must escape the Death of Ages with the Book of Hartwell, that is the upmost importance right now." Eleanor speaking from the power of the 7th Galon once more, Venus looks towards Diana and both of them agree with Eleanor. Venus begins to speak informing Tim about the magic the Shield of Aeneas has to offer him as he continues his journey to fulfill his magical destiny.

"First young wizard, I would like to inform you if and when you escape from the Death of Ages, you will have to return the Shield of Aeneas back to it's proper owner. For Claudius has concealed the shield for generations without our knowledge. It must be taken away to a safe place for it must never be in the hands of evil in Tartarus or Selwyn's Chancer. Do you understand me young wizard?" Venus asking with a serious tone on her voice, Tim replies with a simple nod and bows to the goddess of love and beauty.

"Hold the Shield of Aeneas in front of you, look at it natural beautiful golden color, feel the engravings over it, note the triple triumph of Augustus below its center. Nothing can penetrate the shield for it has been forged by Vulcan under my consent for my son

Aeneas. Now you will hold this power in your hands and remember the truth from it. That is the only way for the true magical ability to shine along with the power of your magical Galon ability." Venus unfolding more of the truth about the shield. Tim eager to ask more questions cuts her off not intentionally, as he glances over to Diana with her arms crossed wondering what exactly he will say next from his lips.

"Oh dear Venus, please tell me why did Virgil have Aeneas go through the Gates of Ivory instead of the Gates of Horn, for that has been a mystery since the days Virgil." Tim asks politely for he hopes he isn't being rude for wanting to know one of the biggest mysterious in mankind history. Venus curls her lip, surprised to hear such wise questions coming from a young boy from the House of Hartwell. "I will answer this one question, and that is all for you must be on your way," Venus says quickly.

"Virgil was correct indeed, Aeneas' spirit was one of the very few to do so, it was based only at the time Aeneas traveled through the Ivory Gate. Aeneas happened to be born on a leap year, which allowed him to be able to travel through the Gates of Ivory for the dreams he would see would be his future, not lies. Don't forget Aeneas was alive when he traveled through the underworld. For this was the reason he could have images that would rise in his dreams to remember for when he was reborn, for all souls are cleansed of their sins and memory. Aeneas would be reborn and his dreams would be the map that will guide him to Latium and his destiny. This will be all I reveal for now" Venus smiling at Diana.

"Now back to the Shield of Aeneas, if you look at it now, you will see it has a map of the Death of Ages on it, look... Don't you see?" Venus pointing towards the shield engravings magically turned into a map of all of the Death of Ages. "Look now young wizard for we must go now, you must travel your life as you see fit. Arma Virumque Cano," Venus says in Latin to Tim. "You are the chosen one my dear boy, you will turn Tenby into one of the greatest cities in the future, as Aeneas did for Rome. Oh and by the way, we see Jupiter's horses has helped you out tremendously," Venus says. Before Goddess Diana makes wind appear around them in the shape of a medium sized tornado making them vanish swiftly into thin air. Tim look both ways left and right towards the trees. He notices Ceri's face on a near by tree behind him, watching his every moves in the Last Fairy Maze Forest. Parts of Ceri's face are made with small leaves from the forest while her lips smile towards him, as if she knows something he doesn't.

Tim unafraid, looks down at the Shield of Aeneas before he slaps the reins on the side of the body of Jupiter's horse riding off into the mist path towards the castle of the House of Cynfor. "Oh Ceri for I will save you, I will find Hynwyn Reese to bring you back by my side, I must save you," Tim says to himself. Wondering if he can really save Ceri at all. Tim also ponders why Venus didn't mention the Book of Hartwell, but shrugs off the notion feeling the signs racing through the clouds of mist praying that he will get to the castle in time. For the dark night is approaching the Death of Ages, the forest is filled with all types of mythical beasts, poisonous creatures, lost spirits that are dangerously awaiting to find any new prey inside of the vass lands throughout the Last Fairy Maze Forest.

TIM HARTWELL: Open Your Heart Trilogy (Books 1-3)

Find Hynwyn Reese

Night flows from a long daylight of blue and orange hues, the earth is quiet, the air seems a bit more thin the closer Tim gets to the castle of

Bledri and Tomes. He notices the cloud of mist opening up ahead of him with altocumulus lenticularis cloud formations above him even with dawn breaking from the dark knight horizon. Thanks to the 5th Galon, the *Firewyn spell* illuminates light-blue colored flame around his arms, lighting up the land around him. Tim continues riding Jupiter's horse down the Last Fairy Maze Forest path, finally reaching the back of the castle of the House of Cynfor. He notices the fairy watcher's coat of arms on the last tree facing his direction. Tim looks at the height of the battlements , and length which stretches as far as the horizon like the previous Gates of Death when he first arrived with Ceri into the legendary Death of Ages.

Tim more determined than ever, looks left, then right noticing he is located at the west Gates of Death which doesn't have a large Trydan skull mounted on the front of the titan size wooden suicide gate doors which are directly in front of him. There is a large steel Cynfor coat of arms hammered onto the gates. White smoke is drifting from underneath the gates door that catches Tim attention, there are a few skeleton body parts buried on both sides of the western Gates of Death. Each skeleton has one of their arms chained to the wall of the battlements as if they where placed there to be killed by the Cynforian dragons.

Large roars with earthquake thumps on the ground from an unidentified dragon is coming from behind Tim from the misty path. Ceri's Fairy Watcher voice comes from the right side of him.

"Are you prepared to die? It's coming for you, there is no escaping the Last Fairy Maze Forest for I am the watcher, you will die where you stand young wizard." Ceri's voice sounding scratchy for the magic which has transformed her, she has complete control of the mysterious forest. More howls continue to get louder coming from behind him, he looks back not seeing a thing through the thick mist down the path when two unexpected guests, appear perched on the top of the Gates of Death looking down at Tim from high above.

"Use the power that Brutus of Troy has taught you Tim, for these doors can only be open by a House of Cynfor or by a House of Gwynwell blood descendant. Once you are small enough, you should be able to walk underneath the west Gates of Death," Alfred and Verlock, the twin-wyvern's shout down at him. A quick snap of Tim's fingers makes him and Jupiter's horse along with his belongings shrink to larger than microscopic size right next to the west Gates of Death. The leaves and dirt from the ground seem larger than life. Pieces of dirt are the size of his apartment building back in Tenby, Pembrokeshire.

Tim's ears pick up the howling but this time sounding like a titan, almost hurting his eardrums from the huge power from of the unknown dragon stomping towards his direction. The Fairy Watcher screams out for she does not know where Tim has gone to, wondering how could he disappear so quickly without her knowledge of hearing.

"Where are you? Where have you gone in my realm," The fairy watcher says. "Tim on Jupiter's horse rides faster than lighting underneath the Gates of Death, but at his microscopic size it takes him a few minutes to completely underneath the gate doors. A few microscopic Cynforian bugs that where living underneath the gates notice Tim traveling to the other side. Looking like the perfect meal, they get into attack position from the bottom of the Gates which seem as high as the St. Paul's Cathedral in City of London.

Tim with quick reaction shoots out his light-blue flame from his *Firewyn spell* towards six bugs that are pouncing down towards his location. The fire-flame scorches the Cynforian bugs one by one, burning them as they fall down as hot as a burning volcano shooting out rock from it erupting. Their bug legs pop off, their bodies explode like popcorn into a million burnt pieces of exoskeleton shards, Jupiter's horse eyes turn into an electrical current and shoots out lightning electrocuting more bugs on the side of them trying to sneak attack. Tim looks down at the horses eyes surprised that Jupiter has given them some of his own magical god-like power.

As they safety ride underneath the west Gates of Death to the other side, Tim snaps his fingers turning him and his horse back to normal size when a loud sound shocks them both.

BANG!

"What was that?" Tim screams out as he grabs holds of the reins for the mysterious dragon beast had slammed it's body against the opposite side of the Gates of Death but without them seeing. When Tim turns around he notices that he standing between the battlements and the lower bailey to the dungeon of Bledri and Tomes.

"Holy Tenby," Tim says to himself using the words of his best friend Owen from his Greenhill School back in Tenby. As the beast smacks the gates from the other side once more, Tim turns around once more looking up at the back end of the castle where the entrance of the dungeon leads down into the dungeon cells of the castle. "This must be where all of the spirits are locked up, Hynwyn Reese must be here, I have to save Ceri," Tim says to himself noticing there aren't any Gatekeepers guarding the western Gates of Death. He looks up noticing different Cynfor mid-level Dragons patrolling the top of the castle, but unaware Tim has infiltrated the grounds into the lower bailey as they look further over hearing the sound of the Gates being smashed onto by the mysterious dragon on the other side.

Tim quick to think, races towards the walls outside of the castle to hide from the sight of the Cynfor dragons above him before they notice his intrusion. Tim sitting on top of Jupiter's horse remains still on the side of the castle with his face towards the stone entrance to the dungeon on his left-hand side leading down into the main entrance way where more Cynfor Gatekeepers are guarding inside. The House of Cynfor haven't had an intruder on their grounds since the legendary war between the House of Scorpus, before Darron and Darryn gave up Hynwyn Reese to the House of Cynfor as an offering of peace between the two different Houses to remain in peace with each other for the time being. Both houses agreeing not to commit any type of viral act of war or high-treason against the House of Cynfor.

The twin-wyvern gargoyles, Alfred and Verlock appear on top of the battlements, with their legs draping over towards the lower bailey looking down at Tim, who is breaking inside of the dungeon that houses all of the dead spirits known in Selwyn's Chancer and some from Tartarus. The dungeon by myth is impossible to escape by any spirit locked up. Some of the slaves have worked their twenty-three hours of the day and Tim just happen to be going in when they have one hour of leisure time from working at the Caves of Siôr. The vicious prisoners inside are slaves who compete at the Carantoc Gladiator games where a raffle is drawn, a certain amount of gladiators are picked to fight against each other until the death.

"He's completely hatstand for going in there alone, is he really going to try and save Hynwyn Reese, I wonder what the House of Scorpus will have to say about that," Verlock says to his twin-brother Alfred speculating. I can tell you this my brother, if he escapes, that will open up pandora's box, many of the spirits there will believe they can escape as well. I wish him luck for it is pretty brave of him for trying to save Ceri, for she is the last bloodline to the House of Gwynwell. Do you think he an do it escaping the Death of Ages?" Alfred asking Verlock as the continue to look down at Tim who is gathers his things off Jupiter's horse and walks down the steps to the humongous entrance to the deadly dungeon.

Alfred's eyes cue in on Tim

holding the Shield of Aeneas as he uses his power of the 4th Galon to walk trough the locked wooden door which has metal brackets that are unbreakable. Only the strength of Cynfor Dragon Gatekeepers with their oversized shoulders can open the locking system to bring in or let out slaves for the gladiator games or mining Emosiwn Melyn Diamonds. Verlock looks up in the air and notices the titan Cynfor dragons patrolling on top of the large **Cynforian Keep Station** with their tree-size bow and arrows which can kill any titan with one pull of the giant-size arrows as thick as tree trunks found in Snowdonia National Park.

"Look at the size of those things!"

Verlock relaying back to Alfred before they disappear into the night, Jupiter's horse shrinks to a microscopic size on it's on to avoid being captured awaiting for Tim's return from the dungeon. Before the wyverns completely disappear. "Let's pray for them," Alfred says a few more words of curiosity.

"Only if he didn't trade Adamanthea's rope he would of escaped the Death of Ages by morning. Oh well, it looks like his journey will he harder than we planned," Alfred says. "Planned? Hogwash!" Verlock whispers. "There should of never been a boy descendant to carry the Galon, what if didn't.." Verlock cuts himself short, as they notice there are some visitors entering the lower bailey from the main bailey. The top Cynforian members of the Cynfor Senate Hall, Ceiro-Eira the dragon head, and Valmai his lion-face head arrive to check up on the living conditions of the prisoners, just incase they need to be disciplined for killing other prisoners during the leisure time during their lunch break in the lower bailey. Ceiro and Valmai's main objective for this very day is to maintain the prisoners endurance and health, keeping their muscles toned for mining or fighting in the gladiator games.

How much pounds do you think our House will make our majesties when the games begin," Ceiro says. With his red spiky mohawk leading all the way down to the end of their tail. Valmai nods his head for being a lion-face he hasn't learned how to speak only a few words which he never can pronounce anyway, so he nods up and down for Ceiro, giving a gesture that he agrees with his dragon head party of their rugged looking body.

"The entire House of Cynfor has complete control of the Caves of Siôr, I am so excited for the Senate Hall, I can see fortunes in the near future. It has been long overdue that the House of Diablo Arches have been controlling the precious Emosiwn Melyn Diamonds," Ceiro-Eira says. While they continue to walk towards the entrance of the dungeon slowly.

Ceiro-Eira barks a distinct sound, which alarms the Cynfor dragons at the *Cynforian Keep Station* to open up the doors for them to enter. Bledri and Tomes changed moved the lock switch to open the dungeon doors into the Cynforian Keep Station for more protection when they became rulers of the House of Cynfor.

Somewhere in the lower levels of the dungeon, Tim Hartwell is searching the long underground levels of the dungeon for Hynwyn Reese unaware they he could be caught at any moment and locked in the dungeon of Bledri and Tomes for an eternity.

Tim walks down a narrow

underground path which leaves to second lower-level of the dungeon, there is only one way down to the third-level which is marked on the Shield of Aeneas, the engravings on the shield have completely change d due to the power of the Galon. Tim looks down at the shield which has map of the entire dungeon. There is a path that connects the main chamber all the way back to the lower gates to transfer more prisoners underground instead of above ground. Tim hears some voices coming his way, he dashes over to a shadow hidden pocket, as he watches Ceiro-Eira walk directly pass him into the **Snowyn Chamber** that keeps ice which melts and creates a cool ventilation area thought out the castle including drinking water system. Ceiro-Eira points towards the ice while Valmai points over to a large map on the ceiling showing the locations of the Snowyn mountains not too far from their location, the only place in the Death of Ages that naturally makes ice for the entire House of Cynfor.

"The ice needs to be restocked immediately," Ceiro-Eira says to some of the low-level Cynfor dungeon guards. The guards move in formation to head out to the entrance way of the dungeon with a long and wide carriage that carries the large slabs of ice back to the castle.

"Halt!!!"

Ceiro-Eira says. Looking towards his lion-face head Valmai. "Do you smell that?" Ceiro-Eira opening his nostrils wide. "I think, I think, I smell living human tissue," Ceiro-Eira replying back to Valmai when Fyanicrum and Jupira, third in-line to throne arrive to see Ceiro-Eira.

"You smell what?" Fyanicrum says loudly towards them suspiciously. "It's nothing your majesty," Ceiro-Eira says. Keeping a tight lip for the last thing they want is for Fyanicrum and Geulia to think they aren't doing their job by watching every meter of the dungeon. Fyanicrum barks towards the rest of the Cynfor dragons to disperse out of the *Snowyn Chamber*, and head towards the main building which is attached to the ***Carantoc Gladiator Colosseum***.

"You will be able to finish your work later, it's time to watch the games" Fyanicrum reassuring Ceiro-Eira and Valmai there is nothing to worry about. The entire group leaves out of the Snowyn Chamber into another hall that leads to another entrance of the dungeon. Tim Hartwell unnoticed, is almost frozen to death from the cold temperatures. Tim yells out **"FIREWYN"** to warm his arms up with his light-blue flame. The young wizard walks down some of the cold isles to see if anyone of the prisoners is Hynwyn Reese since Tim has never seen a picture of the magical barbarian and original ruler of the House of Scorpus.

"Hynwyn Reese, Hynwyn Reese" Tim Hartwell whispers out, using his left arm to illuminate the light-blue flame from the *Firewyn spell* of the 5th Galon to brighten the isle hallways. "Shh, keep it down will you little twerp, your going to get us all killed" A raspy voice coming from one of the dark cells, most of the other prisoners are laying silent in their cells staying obedient.

Tim walks slowly over to the dark cell trying to get a better look at who has the courage to speak. "Keep it quiet" The voice speaks once more when Tim looks into the left-hand corner of the cell to see a shadowy figure with long arms and short legs named Caledfryn, he is an old hard-nosed Cynfor dragon with only one head, for his lion-face head Dazeryn was chopped off for high-treason, stealing a large amounts of Emosiwn Melyn Diamonds selling them back to the House of Scorpus while keeping all of the profit for himself.

Caledfryn still has the large thick scar on the side of his neck where the neck of Dazeryn lion-face head used to be. Caledfryn eyes have remained bloodshot ever since he was punished. The old Cynfor dragon looks down at Tim outside of his cell with one claws holding onto the frozen prison bars. "What is a living soul doing in the dungeon of Bledri and Tomes, how are you even breathing down here?" Caledfryn asks, but before Tim can answer, he asks another serious question for he notices the House of Hartwell coat of arms on Tim's shirt.

"You are the boy descendant of the Galon, you are the one, what the heck are you doing here? What the heck are you doing here?" Caledfryn repeating loudly, while Tim raises him hand in the gesture for him to keep it down before alarms on of the Gatekeeper guards.

"I am looking for Hynwyn Reese, tell me where he is in this dreadful place. "Tim asks holding the Shield of Aeneas with ease for the weight is as light as a feather for him to carry long distances. "Hynwyn? You say? He isn't here dear boy, he should be preparing for the Carantoc Gladiator Games near the main building his number was picked, but you won't get anywhere near there. Besides, I would watch your back, I am sure someone knows you are snooping around here, didn't you see Ceiro-Eira and Valmai almost sniffed you out?" Caledfryn says, acting worried for reasons of being punished badly again.

"Head up the spiral staircase, there should be another hallway where they keep the gladiators waiting. There is a dormer window you can crawl into and sneak into the colosseum from the roof. Make sure you do not fall off into the moat, there are demons that lurk near there. Their favorite dish, eating Diablo Archers who are thrown down off the castle as a simple game of fun and trickery. So if they had a taste of your human flesh, I am sure they would go crazy, so watch out," Caledfryn says. While backing away back into the dim shadow behind him to lay down following dungeon rules. Caledfryn bodies disappears in the shadow completely, for he doesn't want to escape, he knows that not having a lion-face head, he will never be excepted in any populated region of the Death of Ages.

"Go now boy save us all from this hell, it's about time for us to have some action around here, I am sure

I will hear the stories of your great victories throughout the ages, we have already heard your victory killing Miniver and Cynhafar, you know that sent shockwaves throughout the House of Cynfor, for we never knew the day would come when a boy descendant from the House of Hartwell would lead the people in Selwyn's Chancer to freedom." Caledfryn says his last words before remaining completely quiet in the shadows. Tim not sure what to say, puts his fist over his chest showing respect, then rushes out towards the spiral staircase which will lead in the direction of Hynwyn Reese, Tim is hoping he can meet him before he has to fight.

Tim walks through a few doors using the power of the Galon, and freezes a few Cynfor guards on the way who where sitting at a room-sized table playing cards drinking a special liquor called Cya. Tim continues to run through the halls trying not to be noticed. At the same time, his mind keeps thinking about his Mother Mary, and Ceri being the watcher of the Last Fairy Maze Forest. He even thinks about his legendary trainer Brutus of Troy racing through his mind while he makes it through the another spiral staircase inside of the circular turret. A path with two hallways splits towards the second level of the main building where there are two Cynfor Gatekeeper guards watching an arched door. Tim can hear chants coming from outside which must be filling up with guests from all over the outer regions of the Death of Ages and above.

Tim looks at one guard who has a large iron skeleton key on the side of his metal locking belt attached to the lower part of his iron chest plate with the Cynfor coat of arm engraved on the chestplate. Both guards are carrying razor sharp weapons, so Tim decides not make a huge scene and freezes time, with the magical power of the 1st Galon. He walks over to the Gatekeeper with the iron skeleton keys, and lifts it off his belt while they are frozen in time. Without wasting a second, the young wizard opens up the huge arch door and walk right into the large holding room that has orange light glaring inside of the room, which quickly turns to blue as the day cycle changers once more. Tim notices a gap through the edge of the colosseum in clear view through the window. Tim looks up towards a large muscular scorpion male figure standing near a large window with one hand human and the other a scorpion shaped claw. Tim knowing his time is limited, so he begins to speak with urgency knowing Carantoc Gladiator games will begin at any moment.

"Hynwyn Reese, my name is Tim from the House of Hartwell, son of Mary.

I have come a long way traveling with Brutus of Troy and speaking with Goddess Diana, even meeting the House of Scorpus who kind of help us to get here," Tim says.

"Us you say? Where is the other?" Hynwyn says with a deep voice replying back. "Brutus of Troy is the only reason I even knew the Death of Ages even existed, but getting back to the point, my friend Ceri, the last bloodline of the House of Gwynwell has swallowed the Gwenwyna poison with me to get down here, but she is now the watcher of the Last Fairy Maze Forest. I need you help, I need to save her now," Tim demanding Hynwyn for some answers.

"If what you say is true, then

there is nothing that can save your friend. If Brutus helped you get here, there is only one thing I can tell you, leave this place immediately. If you are the boy descendant of the Galon, the best thing for you is to escape. For I am surprised you where able to get into the castle so easily, I guess this proves you are who you say you are..." Hynwyn taking a few moments running his human hand over a long razor sharp blade he uses to fight in the games, which has kept him alive this long, even though he wishes he lost sometimes.

"Okay, since you are the true bearer of the Galon, there is one way for you to save your friend, but it might take your destiny in the act.

You are too important, my advice save your own life. I always knew the House of Gwynwell would help out if the prophecy was true. There is only one person can save you, and that is Goddess Venus, for she carries the answer that can break the spell of the watcher of the Last Fairy Watcher.

"Venus? I just saw her before I came into this castle. Are you telling me she didn't tell me how to help her then?" Tim scratching his head not sure why Venus wouldn't help him. "No, no, no," Hynwyn says. Almost whispering his words. "She wanted you to find the only female of the House of Cynfor, the only princess to be exact. Her name is Nia, she was born human, but with the blood of the Cynfor dragon in her veins. You must find a way to get her to fall in love with you, for only her heart in true love, can lift the spell over the power that hold the watcher to the Fairy Maze Forest. It was a curse given to her from her father that your murdered, Miniver and Cynhafar dreaded anyone to make her fall in love with their human daughter a long time ago. Princess Nia is the only one from the House of Cynfor that can free your friend. After the games, you will have to summon Venus to give you the **"Love of Venus."** Princess Nia's curse forbids her to fall in love, only that power from Venus can make her do so," Hynwyn says. He starts wrapping up his speech turning around to get a better look at the boy who can change it all. Hynwyn notices that Tim is carrying the Shield of Aeneas, and for this very moment he smiles because he is astonished such a magical symbol of power and truth really actually exist.

"It looks like you have been very busy I see, you have recovered the shield that can even change human history as you know it, but you must leave immediately, it's almost time for me to head out to kill another beasts with my sword. Jump out dormer window and find your way to see Princess Nia, Venus will show up sooner or later I am sure of that," Hynwyn says. Grabbing a huge axe with his scorpion claw, he picks up his helmet that has the House of Scorpus coat of arms on it which he still wears proudly.

Noises start to come towards the door, Gatekeepers guards outside notices that the previous guards are still frozen. Tim quickly snaps his fingers to unfreeze them which sends them toppling over each other outside of the room. Tim nods towards Hynwyn Reese for his help, for he didn't expect the meeting with him would lead to the answers he was looking for.

Tim mounts the Shield of Aeneas on his back and leaps out the dormer window with all of his might doing a front flip to a back flip which leads him standing on top of the main building looking over the at colosseum, he wonders where Princess Nia's private balcony could be. At this very moment, he is tired of it all. Tim misses his Mother Mary more than ever, he knows her doom will come sooner or later, for somehow he believes she is will captive in the hands of the House of Cynfor any moment now.

TIM HARTWELL: Open Your Heart Trilogy (Books 1-3)

Love from Venus

Large white and light-greyish Cumulus mediocris and stratocumulus castellanus cumulogenitus clouds are hovering above Tim from the sky above. Dawn is beginning to break across the horizon when Tim looks up and notices;

RA14h41m24.24s D37°57'25.64'

The exact same star coordinates illuminating high in the blue sky from the same constellation in Boötes once more, Tim remembers the last time he saw these coordinates was when he was at the funeral pyre for Lancer's Death in Troia Nova.

"Oh God hear me now, I am here to fulfill my destiny, I trust my heart and spirit more than ever. I trust Mother Mary to lead me into a world of the unknown. Now I fear my friend and mother may be lost forever. If you grant me the power of courage to stay afloat in times of conflict, I will do nothing but return the favor to my family and my country of Wales," Tim says rushing over to a cement block which is mounted on top of the roof. He hides from the view of the Cynfor dragons in the Keep Station looking over to his location, but also distracted as they hear the cheers and trumpets blaring from the colosseum. The orchestra brass sounds are filling the skies while the first part of the *Carantoc Gladiator games* are about to begin. Tim not waiting for another chance to be noticed anymore, unexpectedly looks at a small puddle of water resting on the roof, he looks down at the water and notices that his reflection is not there. The magical power of the Shield of Aeneas has given him the power of invisibility. Tim looks up at the skies for he notices the star from the Boötes constellation is blinking at him, granting him another god-like power.

With his new power, Tim begins his way down the side of the roof to the main building which leads to an overpass into the colosseum. Tim stands guard as he watches all of the elite House of Cynfor, followed by the Senate Hall members making their way into their private royal booths. After they all head in, Tim climbs down the side of the overpass holding onto the edge, swinging his legs into the walkway for him to land safely on the stone floor. Tim leaps out of the way for one of the huge Gatekeeper guards almost steps on him with their enormous feet. Tim kneeling down, notices another split hall which leads to the outer ring of the colosseum where only the elite are only allowed to privately pass through.

Trusting his heart, Tim heads left around where no one can bump into him, long drapes are covered inside of the hall with the House of Cynfor coat of arm embroidered on them. Loud cheers fill the arena while trumpets continue to blare out their distinctive sounds.

A large amount of Cynfor dragons are making their round through the pass and are completely covering the hall, Tim looking very alert with his instincts, he better get out of their way before he is crushed to death. He quickly turns around looking for the closest archway for him to run into. Tim notices there are Bluebell flowers inside of a Emosiwn Melyn crystal flower vase mounted just outside one of the arched doorways. Tim runs towards that particular entrance way, where a silk curtain is hanging in front of. Tim dashes to the side, where he barely escapes from being trampled to death, jumping back into the curtain not knowing that he happens to be in a royal observation room where Princess Nia watches the games. Luckily for him, no one has not entered yet, there is a long bench that overlooks the center of the colosseum. Tim looking towards the crowd, notices Bledri and Tomes observation booth directly across from Princess Nia's area.

Tim looks down at the battle area when he notices Hynwyn Reese being walked out for the first death match followed by two Gatekeeper dragon guards who shut a metal fence behind him. The Carantoc announcer *Grunoktyn, the dragon head* and his lion-face head *Bevan* who is holding a royal scepter with fire coming from the top, walks out to the center of the grounds where Hynwyn is watching him from the opposite side with his axe and sword in either hand.

"Welcome to this years games, Sponsored by our royal highnesses

Bledri and Tomes. We bring you the *Carantoc Gladiator games*. First, may we introduce the extraordinary longtime, undefeated champion Hynwyn Reese in the right corner," Grunoktyn says. The crowd goes crazy for they know Hynwyn is by far the mightiest soldier to be captured in the dungeon. "In the left corner we bring you *Juvelian*, an outcast of the Diablo Arches who will fight to the death on this very day," Grunoktyn says. Juvelian stands there with his rugged body and tarnished armor with a half scratched away House of Diablo Arches coat of arms on his chestplate.

Juvelian's weapon of choice is none other than a large spiky chain, that has a metal triangular handle that he can swing around with ease, connected to the end of a chain which a large angled blade on the end of it. Juvelian muscular back has spikes coming out the back, which were surgically implanted by the House of Cynfor just for the games. Grunoktyn continues to speak with his arms stretched out pointing towards both opponents.

Tim continues to watch for he is eager to see what everyone has been talking about, for Hynwyn uses magic as well when he fights, he is a true warrior of battle. Grunoktyn returns back up to the royal box where he sits next to the Fyanicrum and Guelia, along with

Derilyn and Geulia.

Before the fight begins, Bledri and Tomes stand up to make a special announcement for they have a special guest that will be sitting next to them to watch the games.

"To all of the House of Cynfor and other special invited guests. We have the mother of the last boy descendant of the House of Hartwell in our very presence, Bring her out now!" Bledri orders his personal guards to bring out Tim's Mother Mary.

Tim on the other side puts his hands on the edge of the balcony, wanting to scream to the top of his lungs with agony that his very mother is finally paying the price for what she has done. He know can see that she should never given him the first Galon Key, now paying the price. Tim's emotions are building up with rage as he ignites the *Firewyn spell* on both of his arms to try and kill the rulers of Cynfor while still invisible. Just before Tim has the perfect aim without his mother being caught in the way as she is being brought out, chained to the wall to watch the games on Bledri and Tomes balcony. A voice speaks to Tim with female arms gripping his wrist stopping him from attacking.

"This is not the right time to save your mother" The voice of Goddess Venus standing right next to him invisible to everyone as well, except for Tim. He is a tad confused wondering why he can't avenge his Mother Mary.

"They are too powerful together my dear boy, you mother is under the spell of Selwyn's Chancer now," Venus says as she takes out a small diamond shaped box from her sheer dress. Venus whispers a few words inside of the box, making it illuminate around the edges with a pink light. Venus places the diamond box in Tim's hand instructing on exactly what he need to do at this moment.

"Follow the words of Hynwyn Reese, for he already told you the route you need to take at this very moment," Venus says looking up at her with his eyes shedding a few tears for his Mother Mary. This is the **"Love of Venus,"** give this to Princess Nia, once you do, she will fall in love with you. This is the only way to save her, for Ceri will be crucial in escaping the Death of Ages, but it will take longer than you think to achieve this goal. Trust me as you did Diana, Henry and Lancer Gwynwell, especially your trainer Brutus of Troy.

Goddess of Diana has already informed me that your emotions are starting to take over. Don't make the same mistake of moving before you are supposed too. Many heros have died in the path by doing do, including Julius Ceaser. Take his life as an example, if Ceaser never assassinated, Rome wouldn't of had it's first emperor

Augustus. Every happens the way it supposed to, life has it's challenges and even the smallest steps in the wrong direction can change everything," Venus says with her last words before she disappears. Movement behind the drapes pushes them forward. Tim moves to the side noticing Princess Nia walking into her observation balcony, her beautiful blond hair, with blue eyes that resemble a tropical sea amazes Tim with her every movement. Princess Nia sits down, right next to him without her knowing. She waves for her guards to leave and stand guard outside in the hallway.

On the opposite side of her location, Bledri notices she has entered so he throws a white cloth down into the arena to start the match, he never starts until she is in attendance.

Juvelian dashes fast towards Hynwyn Reese, Tim looks down at the action which seems like they are moving in slow motion getting closer and closer. Juvelian swings his spiked chained towards Hynwyn who does a backward flip while the tip of Juvelian's blade barely missing Hynwyn's back while he lands a few feet back. The blade swinging through the air gets stuck into a large stone, used for defensive purposes during the games.

Hynwyn taking notice of the moment, leaps high into the air and throws his axe towards Juvelian, the axe has a magical seeking ability that will find it's opponent no matter where they stand. The sharp axe slices through Juvelian tight leaving his body slumped over in agonizing pain. The crowd screams with cheers for Hynwyn has wounded his opponent with ease while the trumpets blare out with each step Hynwyn makes towards Juvelian's body. He looks down at Juvelian who is huffing and puffing, while he screams out for mercy with his bloody hand in the air. Hynwyn faces Bledri and Tomes awaiting for their approval for a quick kill. Bledri points his hand downwards, Hynwyn takes his sword thrusting it into the body of Juvelian leaving his body lifeless.

The crowd goes crazy once more, cheering on the champion that never looses. Bledri whispers something in Tomes ear about Stratford on their way into the colosseum without their prior notification. Bledri waves towards the crowd for the next match to start, the Cynfor guards raise the metal gate to escort Hynwyn back into the dungeon. Bledri and Tomes don't want Hynwyn around when Stratford shows up. At the same time, two other guards grab the body of Juvelian dragging him back through the metal gate before it completely shuts.

Back inside of Princess Nia's observation balcony, Tim places the **"Love of Venus"** diamond box on the bend where Princess Nia is sitting as she watches the eight on eight battle. Princess Nia turns back over and notices the diamond box sitting on the bench, she quickly turns around to see who placed it there but see no one in sight. She picks up the diamond box and looking at it's shape from eye level.

Princess Nia slides open the top of the box but it only opens halfway, she lightly shakes the box near her ear when a whisper sounds into her ear. In a flash, an invisible pink light from all of the spectators covers the entire royal box without anyone in the colosseum knowing. A body double has been placed in her spot, when her and Tim magically appear in a oasis in the desert of the Death of Ages. Princess Nia awakens a few minutes later not sure what exactly happened, she look towards Tim standing right in front of her.

Princess Nia rubs her eyes which sparkle, for the **"Love of Venus"** has made her instantly fall in love with Tim as soon as she lays eyes on him. She runs over to him, wrapping her arms around Tim who is wearing royal clothing from the early 1900's.

"Oh my love, for I have found you so, tell me you love me so I can assure my heart to sing back to you," Princess Nia says with her real emotion taken completely over her mind and heart by hearing the whispers of Venus' voice coming from the diamond box. She is wearing a white linen dress holding Tim as tight as she can, with her arms wrapped around him. Tim unsure how to react, utters the words she must hear from his mouth.

"You have found me, I am yours, my love," Tim replies, as they walk over to the pond sitting down to speak more. Food appears next to them, when a white unicorn appears walking into the oasis, somehow it has managed to travel down into the Death of Ages. The unicorn gallops over to the pond for a drink of water when Princess Nia begins to speak.

"Oh look my love, a beautiful horse from the gods, what a true sign of passion coming towards our presence," she says. While Tim thinking about his mother, and Ceri in the back of his mind, feeling quite awkward about this entire situation, but staying true to his word and believe Goddess Venus he gives in to love Princess Nia.

Without them knowing, the twin-wyvern gargoyles, Alfred and Verlock appear on the opposite side of the pond behind a tree looking at the new romance unfold before their very eyes.

"Goddess Venus has become involved now, how can this be? I wonder what Stratford will think about the gods interfering with his parallel world and devious plans," Verlock says to this brother. "It looks like the gods favor the young wizard after all, but we will see," Alfred says watching the unicorn drink more of the pond water from the oasis. The wyverns both look toward Princess Nia and Tim speaking to each on the other side of the pond wondering what her fathers Bledri and Tomes will think about their new love affair. "We better get out of here, Stratford will get the best of us if we don't report back to him soon," Alfred says. Snapping his fingers twice making him along with his twin brother disappear in thin air.

Back at the Carantoc colosseum, Stratford makes his way into the main royal box where Bledri and Tomes are sitting, Stratford dressed in full royal portrait clothing, resembling something King George VI would wear during his time of reign.

"I see you have captured Mother Mary," Stratford says. Walking over to her, but not feeling the way they have her chained up like an animal. "You imbeciles, is this how you treat her?" Stratford for some reason acting with compassion, possibly because he is not worried, since he is a new father with children that could inherit the same power Tim Hartwell has achieved through Selwyn's Chancer. With a wave of his hand, Stratford magically turns the stone bench Mother Mary is sitting on into a plush couch, also turning Mary's clothes from 21st century into a 13th century red plush luxurious long dress. Bledri and Tomes are looking wondering why Stratford is being so generous to Mother Mary, who is supposed to be captive by their liking.

"My lord, we have done as you asked, but for some reason we have not found Tim Hartwell anywhere within the Death of Ages," Bledri says to Stratford trying to explain some of their failure of the day. "That boy is around here somewhere, you must find him immediately! I don't care what it takes," Stratford says as Mary looks at him still not saying a word. "You should of never given Tim the 1st magical Galon Mary. You will have to pay sooner or later, but not now, I want you to see him die right in front of you." Stratford speaking impatiently.

Cheers from the crowd as another beast has been killed on battle area continues on. Stratford is wearing his large pink and yellow Emosiwn Melyn coronet around his neck. Bledri looking at Stratford with his eyes glaring while Tomes speaks a few words before Stratford leaves.

"Master, why not have Tim fight against Hynwyn Reese when we capture him, it would be the ultimate battle in your honor," Tomes says wit his slurred voice. Stratford amazed, whips his neck around to speak "Now that is one of the best ideas I have heard in a long time, you better watch yourself Bledri, Tomes may be smarter than you think," Stratford says loosening up adding some humor before heads back to the Alynn Dragon in the upper levels of Selwyn's Chancer back to Wales, where Amelia is taking care of their new twins. Just before Stratford leaves out, he turns around and reminds the rulers of the House of Cynfor to not put Amelia in the dungeon, he informs them to put her in the secret watch tower.

Bledri and Tomes nod their heads as Stratford disappears in thin air, Mary looks on with disgust for she can't wait to find a way to escape the castle herself. While Bledri and Tomes are distracted, Mary picks up a metal nail that Stratford left her on purpose for some reason, she thinks another plan is going to be in happening very soon. She quickly slips the iron nail under the sleeve of her dress without anyone noticing. Bledri waves his arms in a motion for the Gatekeeper guards take her away to the secret watch tower of the castle.

TIM HARTWELL: Open Your Heart Trilogy (Books 1-3)

Mary's Escape

Patches of Cumulus mediocris and stratocumulus castellanus

603

cumulogenitus clouds are gliding above Princess Nia and Tim, who are still sitting next to the pond as the white unicorn finishes drinking the water from the pond. Goddess Venus resting on a cloud high above, looking down at their very move making sure Tim Hartwell is doing what he needs to do to fulfill his destiny, which is leaving the Death of Ages in one piece. Venus is happy with her results, she moves her right hand in a waving pattern which sends the duo back into the *Carantoc Gladiator Games* without anyone back at the colosseum noticing. Mother Mary has already been taken back to the secret watch tower, the interior of the room is filled with silk and velvet under lock in key where she is planning for her escape.

At the colosseum Princess Nia stands up with Tim being visible, both of them visible to the crowds, except no one has noticed yet. She grabs hold of Tim's hand while she screams to the top of her lungs for her father's attention.

"Father!!!!!"

She calls out, the entire crowd including the fighters on the battle ground stop moving as if something had gone wrong. Bledri & Tomes look towards their daughters booth, noticing the person they have been looking all along is holding hands with their very own Princess. Bledri face appears furious. He goes into survival instinct roaring loudly for all of his guards to run over towards his daughters balcony thinking she is about to be harmed in some way.

In a matter of seconds, every Gatekeeper available make their way towards Princess Nia' private booth area, Fyanicrum and Jupira are one of the first ones there holding large swords directly towards the intruder. Derilyn and Geulia have been waiting a lifetime to marry Princess Nia even though she is human girl, even though she has been promised to Fyanicrum and Jupira before Miniver and Cynhafar died.

"What is this, grab hold of the carrier of the Galon now!" Fyanicrum says displeased of what he sees,

Princess Nia holding Tim's hand as if they where a matched pair.

"What is this madness? Are you siding with a Hartwell now?" Fyanicrum ordering Princess Nia for answers while he points his fingers towards her out of rage and madness. Everyone in the entire colosseum looks on shocked at how Fyanicrum is totally out of line. Bledri and Tomes finally make their way through the crowd, everyone in the colosseum including the gladiators still alive on the battle ground are looking over at Princess Nia's balcony. Bledri has heard enough of Fyanicrum speaking reckless towards their daughter. Bledri and Tomes grab Fyanicrum and Jupira by the neck and toss them over the edge of the balcony making them smash onto the battle ground of the colosseum. Due to their size, they are only left with scratches and bruises stumbling back to their feet.

"Everyone leave the colosseum immediately, the Carantoc games are over. Fyanicrum, you and Jupira will head towards the *Snowyn* mountains for more ice. Derilyn and Geulia, you will depart for the *Emosiwn* mountains, and make sure those prisoners mine double of the minerals, or else!" Bledri and Tomes stomping their foot down on the concrete floor. The entire crowd leaves out the Carantoc Gladiator Colosseum as fast as they wind, no one wants to disappoint their rulers, even if their lives depended on it. Bledri looks over his shoulder for Ceiro and Valmai, ordering them to fetch Hynwyn Reese and bring him back down to the colosseum. Bledri looks at Tim with the Shield of Aeneas on his back, but not knowing that it's the same shield from Aeneas of Troy.

Tomes, with his deep voice orders a few Gatekeepers to bring some Cya to drink at the royal box. Bledri and Tomes are eager to speak with Tim instead of killing him right away, only they truly fear what is about to come next. As everyone makes their way back to the royal box, Tim begins to ask a few questions before the royal Cynfor leaders can.

"Where is my mother?" Tim asks a few times while Bledri and Tomes remain silent looking at Princess Nia holding Tim's hand not letting it go. Their minds are racing, wondering why she is so extremely affectionate towards the young wizard.

"We are bound to keep Mary at our castle there is nothing you can do to help her now. Why do you ask these questions? You should know the answer to your riddles dear boy." Bledri answering with a calm voice. Princess Nia's emotion have fallen deeply in love with Tim, even though their young age, Nia has chosen a mate for marriage all thought would never happen.

"Father, I have chosen Tim

Hartwell to be my husband, for I will love him with all of my heart, and bare his children at the right age in Cynfornia. He will be my King, for when you and Tomes pass. I will lead our kingdom to the far edges of the Death of Ages" She says. "Arrrgh!" Bledri says as his tail whips down a bench behind him. They know they have no other choice for it has been written in stone in the **Royal Cynforian Chapel** by their father Miniver and Cynhafar. Once Princess Nia she chooses a mate, their is no reversing it. Bledri and Tomes have to accept their daughter's wishes provided to her since birth. "My precious daughter, how can you do this to us? Stratford runs Selwyn's Chancer, he will declare war upon us if we allow such blasphemy." Bledri pleading with her while he cracks his knuckles in anguish.

"You have heard my words loud and clear. You will marry us at once and send us to the *Bluebells Forest* in Cynfornia. If you decline, I will release the *Soulsynwn dragon* and the vines from the Last Fairy Maze Forest to destroy this castle..." Princess Nia making threats towards he father for the **"Love of Venus"** has her heart and mind locked on her decision. Bledri and Tomes nervous, sweating from her heads. Picks up a large cup filled with Cya juice to make them ease their fears from the wrath of Stratford. They both know the Last Fairy Watcher and the Soulsynwn dragon power together can be even worst to them.

Bledri and Tomes looks over at Tim not saying a word as just yet, but knowing they have to agree with her terms. The Senate Hall will surely convince them otherwise if they do not. The love for his daughter he must agree with her terms they ponder. The Gatekeepers have finally brought Hynwyn Reese out to the center of the battle ground. He looks around wondering why the entire colosseum is completely empty. Bledri makes a few decision to ease his anger.

"Guards send Hynwyn Reese to the Last Fairy Maze Forest, make him suffer for the pain I must adore by accepting my daughters proposal. Someone must be punished and I choose him," Bledri says. Tim looks down at Hynwyn in the center of the colosseum sad that he can do nothing to save him. The Gatekeepers shove Hynwyn in the middle of his back as hard as can. Pushing him towards the back of the castle which leads to the Last Fairy Maze Forest. Bledri smiling while Hynwyn is being pushed along turns his neck around looking at Tomes. They both look down at their daughter and Tim Hartwell and continue to speak.

"I accept your proposal on the premised of Tim fighting with us against Stratford and the House of Diablo

Arches. When the time comes, we hope he knows war will come sooner or later," Bledri says. Drinking more of the Cynforian Cya juice with it's blue color that is extracted from the Bluebells that have been brought over from an unknown region to any house in the Death of Ages, except for them. The Bluebells forest resembles Dockey Wood, Ashridge in England.

"I will fight with you," Tim says. The Galon beginning to take over his emotions a little more each day. They all toast to the new fiancé of their princess. Then, one of the gatekeepers comes running back with his arm bleeding badly. Bledri and Tomes stands up wondering exactly what happened.

"Explain yourselves you fools," Bledri says. "Your Highness, Mother Mary has escaped from the tower, she has killed some of the Gatekeepers who where transporting Hynwyn to the forest. Some horses grew from the ground splitting in two. Mother Mary and Hynwyn rode off into the Last Fairy Maze Forest, for we tried to close the Gates of Death in time, but they both escaped," the Gatekeeper explaining.

"You must be joking, how did his happen? How did she escape?" Tomes says. "Let them be, we have bigger issues at hand," Bledri says. Tim is smiling, happy that his mother escaped at least with someone that can protect her while in Last Fairy Maze forest. "Order the ceremony at once!" Bledri says. Still enraged that Tim has killed their father Miniver and Cynhafar but what can they do now, but except the changes of events at hand.

The only thing Tim isn't aware of is the blood of Amelia bite still runs through Ceri's veins, once she gets the wind of his marriage to Princess Nia, Ceri will be furious. Even though Princess Nia controls the land she has been cursed to live in forever. Mother Mary and Hynwyn Reese who are already lost inside of the Last Fairy Maze Forest, began looking for a way out. Luckily Hynwyn knows of a secret path back into the castle if they can find it.

TIM HARTWELL: Open Your Heart Trilogy (Books 1-3)

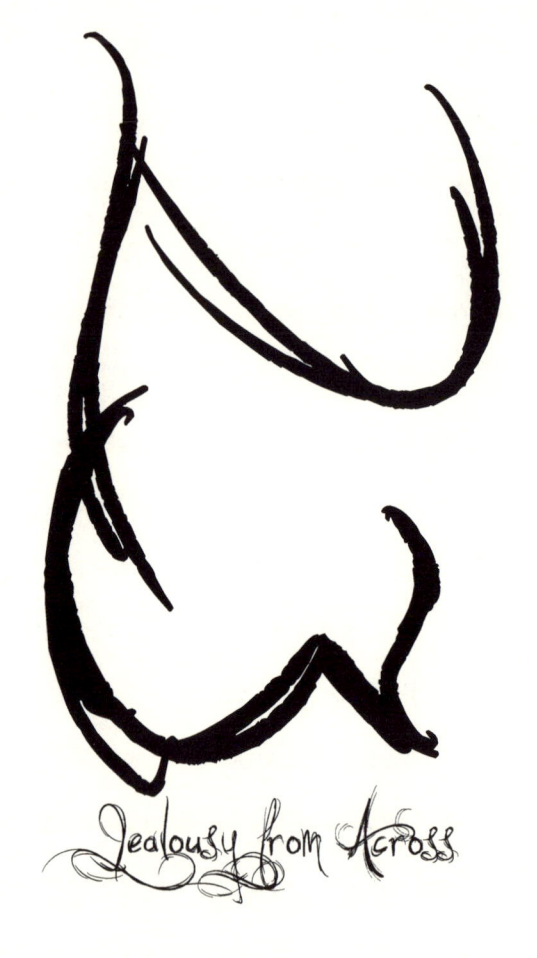

Jealousy from Across

Night has fallen across Snowdon, in North Wales, the Alynn dragon which holds the Amelia fortress inside of the belly of the dragon is flying high above cumulonimbus clouds. Where lightning strikes beating the sky. Rain pours on the shoulders of Stratford who is watching the rain drop into the Llyn Cwellyn reservoir in front of him. The rain is cold as it bounces off his Emosiwn Melyn coronet around his neck. Lylock and his son Baron Milwr are standing next to Stratford. Amelia remains away resting in her chambers inside of the Alynn dragon which is making circular pattern above more cumulonimbus clouds that approach their location. The entire House of Diablo Arches standing behind all three of them dressed in full battle armor with the House of Diablo Arches coat of arms on each of their chest plates, helmets, and weaponry.

"It's time Lylock are you ready to take charge and bring me the heads of Bledri and Tomes. You and your arms will storm the walls of the House of Cynfor. Leave nothing but dust for you to rebuild your realm, you will regain control of the Caves of Siôr diamond trade," Stratford says. Standing in human form, but with his head in beast form.

"I am ready my lord. We will crush them with all of our might. We will not fail you, I have been waiting again to retake our place in the Death of Ages controlling the dungeon of dead spirits once more. Baron Milwr speaks to his soldiers, who are wearing Emosiwn Melyn diamonds to protect themselves from his deadly voice.

"My soldiers, we are ready to attack. We will enter the east Gates of Death that leads into the colosseum. They will never expect us," Baron says. Unaware the House of Cynfor are ready for war. Stratford among the crowds near Llyn Cwellyn has already foreseen victory. In his mind, he thinks about helping Mary escape. He doesn't want her killed just yet. Not until the Book of Hartwell has been opened. Stratford aware of Mary's escape with Hynwyn Reese. He is very disappointed in Alfred and Verlock, for not giving him all of the information about Goddess Venus interfering with his plans. Those bloody Wyverns," he says looking at the rain hit the water below his feet.

At twilight, Stratford uses his power to send the House of Diablo Arches through a portal which will lead them directly into the Death of Ages instead of traveling through the House of Scorpus hoist. Lylock and Baron Milwr swing their arms for their army to move out. Some of the Diablo Arches riding their Diablo black horses into the light of the portal. Stratford whistles for the Alynn dragon to swoop back down from the sky as the army moves through the magic portal. The Alynn dragon lands back on the ground opening his enormous mouth. The dragon's bottom jaw lays flat on the ground. Stratford walks into the mouth of the dragon heading back into the cumulonimbus clouds above disappearing in the mist of the dark night.

Darron and Darryn who are eating in the *Hall of Judgement,* hear word from their Scorpus soldiers that war has been declared on the House of Cynfor. Darron along with Darryn, laugh as hard as can be when they hear the news. As long as it's not them, they don't care less. They have always been nonchalant and callous towards other house affairs.

Back down in the Death of Ages, inside of the Cynforian chapel. The senate are sitting behind *Preacher Ifor* and his lionface *Vaughn*, who is waiting at the mantle for the ceremony of marriage to begin. Cynforian balled music is flowing through the chapel. A long isle with luxurious carpet and drapers flowing through the chapel. Everyone with importance to the royal House of Cynfor are watching the ceremony. Waiting for Princess Nia to walk down the Isle. The Cynforian marriage bell-clock rings loudly inside of the chapel. Since the beginning of Selwyn's Chancer, Preacher Ifor holds the bridal scroll with both hands as the bell-clock winds down. The bells leave a middle-pitch ringing sound, serving as a marker for the bride to walk into the chapel. Everyone inside the chapel turns around are looking back towards

Princess Nia, who is wearing a beautiful wedding gown that is designed from a high-end taffeta organza. The appliques on her bloom down the hem have been stitched with perfection.

The bridal music ringing dies down as Princess Nia walks down the royal aisle. At a steady pace, with young captured fairies from the Maze Forest holding the hem. Tim in a formal suit from the 13th century. Glances back at Princess Nia, she is more beautiful than he could of ever imagined. He's very nervous for he knows Ceri was showing her love for him. Now, he almost hates that he was not able to comfort her after she saves his live. Now she is cursed, he thinks to himself. To be the watcher of the Last Fairy Maze Forest. Bledri and Tomes meet their daughter, holding her hand proudly down the royal aisle.

Princess Nia finally makes her way down to Tim. Reaching her out for Tim to hold. The young wizard holds her hand , while the both face Preacher Ifor and Vaughn for them to begin the vows. Two unexpected guess appear on the side of the chapel but completely invisible to the crowd.

"He must be completely Hatstand, Tim must be out of his mind. I guess the Goddess Venus knows what she is doing. Allowing something like this to happen. Who would of known, the Princess of Cynfor's engagement would bring an alliance with the House of Hartwell. I don't know what Stratford will do," Alfred says. "I guess he is not worried," Verlock replies. He look toward Alfred who happens to be eating some of the sugar bread displayed on the side of the chapel. Alfred usually is the focused one, loves Cynforian sugar bread cookies more than anything in Selwyn's Chancer.

"How can you find the time to eat? The House of Diablo arches are on their way toward the castle from the outer regions. They already taken full control of the Caves of Siôr," Verlock says. Smacking the rest of the food out of Alfred's mouth, trying to get him to pay attention at the matter at hand.

"I don't know what to say this time. Matter of fact, we should head to the forest and see what Mother Mary and Hynwyn Reese are up to. Hopefully they aren't dead by now," Alfred says. He snaps his fingers magically sending them into the Last Fairy Maze Forest to see if they are still alive. Princess Nia and Tim are holding hands as Preacher Ifor finishes up his speech before Tim repeats the royal vows.

"I promise to love you, no matter sickness until death do us part. I do," Tim says. Preacher Ifor looks towards Nia to finish up her vows. "And do you Nia, promise to love Tim, no matter of sickness until death do you part," Ifor says. Looking towards Princess Nia who has a tear coming from her eye with complete happiness. "I promise to love you, no matter sickness until death do us part. I do," She says. Preacher Ifor lets Tim know he may put the 20 carat Emosiwn Melyn diamond wedding ring. Tim slides the ring on her finger, given her a formal kiss on the mouth. Preacher Ifor continues his last few words. "You may now kiss the princess bride," He says. All of the Cynforian spectators scream with joy. They know the prophecy of her marriage will save their people from Selwyn's Chancer. Bledri and Tomes, along with the rest of the Senate Hall members, continue clap their hands with excitement. Except for Fyanicrum, Jupira, Derilyn, and Geulia who are sick to their stomachs, about the very notion of Tim becoming second in-line to the throne of the House of Cynfor. Everyone continues clapping while the newly married couple heads for the arched exitway. The royal bell-clock rings only a few times which marks the ending of the wedding.

A white beautiful carriage that has yellow and pink canarie yellow Emosiwn Melyn diamonds encrusted all over the carriage pulls up to the front of the royal chapel. Princess Nia and her new husband step into the carriage. Tim looks inside noticing the Shield of Aeneas and the rest of his belonging are inside. Princess Nia has magic of her own, including the power to be able to life or move heavy objects with her thoughts. Including control of all things in the Last Fairy Maze forest, except the mind of the Fairy Watcher, for that is controlled by Ceri doomed curse.

Everyone waves off the newly married couple to the Bluebells forest in Cynfornia, located in the far end of the Death of Ages. The air is completely different there. Not other house for the House of Diablo Arches breath the air there and stay alive. Only the House of Cynfor princess and the husband through marriage are allowed to breath the potent air. More poisonous all of the air in the Death of Ages. This was a fail safe to protect the future of the Cynfor throne, where a new kingdom will be born.

The royal white carriage makes it way pass the northern Gates of Death. Entering the unknown region to the Bluebells Forest. Princess Nia and Tim will live there for the five years, but are forbidden to have any sexual contact until their sixteenth birthday. By ritual, Tim must bare Princess Nia an heir to the throne of the new kingdom Cynfornia.

Night falls turning into a very dark blue sky with cirrus and cirrostratus in the Death of Ages. Bledri and Tomes are sitting on their thrones planning a strategic defensive plan for the arrival of the House of Diablo Arches. They are sitting on a round table which allows all of the Senate Hall including the royal heirs to speak together. Bledri and Tomes orders metal spikes to be placed all around the castle. Including a layer of oil which they will ignite once the intruders are outside of the walls.

An hour passes by when the war horn in the Keep Station alerts. Noticing the intruders are visible from a distance. The frontline Diablo Archers have lit torches coming from their scepters marching towards the castle of Cynfor from a distance. One of the mid-level Gatekeepers who escaped the attack on the *Caves of Siôr* has made his way into the main building with a few others. Breathing hard for they where almost killed in the worst possible way.

"Your highness, the House of Diablo Arches have taken over the caves, we have failed you my lords," the Gatekeepers explains. "Others managed to escape, are heading towards the *Snowyn* mountains for refuge," the gatekeeper continues. Fyanicrum receives a scroll from his lieutenant from the Keep Station, stating the House of Diablo Arches are approximately eight-hundred meters away from their exact from the castle ***(miles: 0.5 , meters: 804.672.)***

"Destiny has made our daughter Princess Nia save our race. I fear not Stratford anymore. He has planned for our removal from the Death of Ages some time ago, we have heard. My brothers, we will fight until the end. We will fight until there are no more, we will win in our hearts no matter what. Do not fear the power of Stratford's Selwyn's Chancer world. We will live on, we will prevail!" Bledri says. Everyone stands up from their seats, heading for the curtain walls where all of their weapons are mounted. Tons of Cynforian guards load their bow and arrows, the size of trees that can take down any large amount of enemies at once.

    Bledri and Tomes order their entire army to stand guard, waiting for death to approach their castle. Their mission, to protect their throne from complete annihilation. Tomes looks out into the night. The moon has parked itself high above Altocumulus lenticularis clouds forming in the distance of the shadows above them.

Legions of Diablo black horses are pounding against the rugged ground towards the river Styx. The frontline of Diablo Arches begin their way down to the river.

Lylock and Baron Milwr stand on top of the small hill with their own royal guards. Some of them are holding staffs that carry the flag with the House of Diablo Arches coat of arms glaring in the night, lighting up the skies around them.

"Attack!" Lylock screaming out. They watch the front lines get closer to the River Styx. Bledri and Tomes, knowing they are completely safe while inside of the castle, watch the Diablo Arches mount their camp around the eastern side of the castle.

Bledri orders Derilyn to fetch him the scroll of Charun, allowing them to be able to control the movements and magic of Charun. A special power granted them three wishes from the *psychopompoi* of the underworld.

Derilyn fetches the scroll from the sacred locker in the Keep Station, rushing back over to their ruler for the next plan of attack.

The frontline of the Diablo Arches have all parked themselves on the border of the River Styx. Bledri spreads open the scroll, reading the first wish he has been granted from Charun. The scroll was a gift from him for giving so many souls that have paid him well during the ages.

Tomes looks at the scroll along with Bledri and they read the first wish out loud which is composed in Welsh dactylic hexameter;

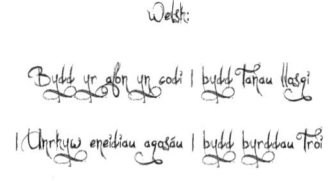

Welsh:

Bydd yr afon yn codi | bydd Tanau llosgi
I Unrhyw eneidiau agasáu | bydd byrddau troi

English:

The river will rise | fires will burn

I any approaching souls | Tables will Turn

Bledri reads the words slowly and very carefully. Any mispronounced words will make the wish void. With every word spoken properly, Charun appears from out of the dark night on the Styx. Arriving towards the *Port of Charun*, slamming fast into his dock station. The frontline of the Diablo Arches stand there unafraid, but with no clue of the aftermath that is awaiting them.

Charun places his oar down and raises his scepter in the air with his right skeleton arm. His left hand rests on the oval handle connected to a rope with the same ancient bell, he uses to inform the House of Cynfor to open the Gates of Death. This time, Charun grants Bledri and Tomes first wish. He stands on his small black ship wearing his torn sheer black robe, that drapes over his body. Charun screams in the air raising his scepter in a swift upwards motion towards the sky. The ancient bells ring three times making the water levels of the River Styx raise high into the air forming the shape of a large hand. Bledri throws a torch, igniting the hand with fire from the oil he had his Gatekeepers put there from earlier.

    Lylock and Baron Milwr look in fear for the first time in ages, they have never seen magic coming from the river Styx so dreadful. The titan black hand made fire and essence of the river Styx. Pounces on top of the entire frontline of the House of Diablo Arches destroying them all. Cheers of dragon vocal chords fill the skies with joy, as they look on while the hand of fire retreats back into river Styx. Silence around the earth, except for the fire burning on the ground where the frontline of the Diablo Arches used to be. Lylock looking on, pissed with rage as he accidently kills one of his royal guards swinging his fist to the side of him with disappointment.

The House of Diablo Arches gather on the top of the hill, thinking of another plan of attack. They were never expecting to go up against the power of a psychopompoi from the human underworld Tartarus.

Bledri smelling fear in his opponent, yells out orders for his Gatekeepers to start shooting tree-trunk sized arrow towards the hills. The arrows kill more of the Diablo Arches instantly with their size. The Gatekeepers pull back another set of titan size crossbows sending the arrows flying through the air. Each one of the arrows whistle through the air, taking out twenty Diablo Arches with every pull. Baron yells out to his father Lylock that they won't last much longer if they don't find a way inside the castle.

Stratford sitting in one of the royal rooms in Amelia's chamber back above the upper levels of Selwyn's Chancer. Is playing chess against himself when he senses that his Diablo Arches are failing him once more. He gets up and walks outside of the castle to the area where the Alynn dragon heart is beating below the glass floor. He ponders for a short second thinking of the perfect plan to get the Diablo Arches inside of the castle to the House of Cynfor.

"Ceri," Stratford whispers. If he informs her of the marriage of Tim and Princess Nia, she will become enraged from Amelia's has very own love potion and tracking potion she infected her with in Troia Nova. Stratford smiling from ear to ear with another devious plan. Looks over at Sylkin towards the purple crystal castle inside of the belly of the Alynn dragon. Stratford makes his body begin to disappear slowly but stops himself for he forget to feed Sylkin before he leaves. The last thing he needs is Sylkin breaking himself free from hunger and killing his wife and new kids. He magically appears another Tyrannosaurus for his pet eat. Sylkin pounces on the dinosaur shredding it to pieces like he always does.

Stratford almost forgetting, claps his hands in front of him making his snitches Verlock and Alfred appear in front of him.

"I should kill you both where you stand. How would you think, you can keep any secret from me," Stratford says. Smacking them both in the face with disrespect.

"We where going to tell you my lord, but....," Verlock mumbling. Stratford burns his right arm making Verlock scream with agony. His brother Alfred rushes down to the floor to aid his twin brother. Stratford does the same thing to Alfred but instead burning his right leg. Alfred screams out as his body rolls over Verlock in pain leaving this both sorry for every helping Tim at all.

"I should of killed you both. You are very lucky I need you. The Diablo

Arches have failed me once more in the Death of Ages. I might have to rethink their power in my world," Stratford says. Walking over to the Alynn heart, which is beating below the glass floor.

"Both of you will travel to where ever those newlyweds are, and inform me of their doing. Don't fail me again or I will make that pain last for an eternity," Stratford says. He claps his hands once, making the twin-wyvern gargoyles vanish in thin air back into the Death of Ages.

Before Stratford goes back into the depths of his parallel world. He looks up at the balcony of the Amelia's Chamber where he notices his wife Amelia standing. Holding one his newborn Cayne in her arms. Amelia's body double, the spirit Megan Lynelle is holding their daughter Amelia II. Stratford transports his athletic body through the air. Landing on the balcony next to them. Stratford's face lights up like a candle with a father's joy. Even throughout the madness down in the Death of Ages. He picks up his son Cayne from Amelia's arms. Holding him high in the air. Sylkin below roars with his animal instinct, happy for them as well. Megan Lynelle merges her spirit back into Amelia's body. Makes Amelia hold her daughter in her hand without moving. Amelia uses her magic to make the ancient piano play a sweet tune for their newborns. Both babies fall back to sleep in their parents arms. For the first time, Stratford has more chaos than ever in Selwyn's Chancer, but happy in his heart bearing heirs to the throne of his kingdom as well.

TIM HARTWELL: Open Your Heart Trilogy (Books 1-3)

When A Kingdom Falls

Rain begins to pour from the low-level Nimbostratus and stratocumulus clouds high above the Last Fairy Maze Forest. Rain drops hitting the leaves, natural melodies of water dripping off tree branches throughout the forest.

Mother Mary and Hynwyn Reese are riding Jupiter's horse down a path throughout the maze. Mary looks over to Hynwyn still wearing his armor. He stops in a section of the path before his ears pick up sounds from the right side of the forest. He raises his hands in the air letting Mary know that someone has following them. Hynwyn unsheathes a sword he was able to steal away from a Gatekeeper who back at the castle. Hynwyn unafraid of death, yells out into the forest, wanting this mysterious figure to reveal their identity.

"Show yourself, I can hear your footsteps. No need to pretend, we know you are following us," He says. A twig on the ground snaps inside of the darkness. Mother Mary and Hynwyn look fast, for they see the Fairy Watcher. Ceri has been following them, she as the watcher was able to hear them riding when they have first arrived. The Fairy Watcher begins to speak to them, Mary looks at Ceri's face poking through a key shape coat of arms mounted onto one of the trees.

"What are you doing in my precious realm, I am very surprised to hear the sounds of the mother of the son who carries the Galon in my presence," She says. Ceri sniffs the air, she can identify both of them even though she completely is blind.

"Ceri Gwynwell or should I say Zoe Beckham from Greenhill. I see you have been cursed to be the watcher of this dreadful forest," Mother Mary says. Sad for her, a few tears fall down her face in sadness. Especially since she is the last bloodline to the House of Gwynwell.

They continue to speak, when another sound brushes against the beautiful trees back to the right of the as the sky turns from dark orange to a midnight blue. Stratford has come to change the order of events. Stratford looks up towards the rain as it graces his face. He raises his right hand in the air raising his hand in the air magically makes the rain stop, but only surrounding the area where they all stand.

"I see both of you met the new Fairy Watcher, Oh Mary, I see your son growing up mighty fast in the Death of Ages. I have heard he is also the prince to the House of Cynfor by marriage of Princess Nia. You should be proud of him Ceri." Stratford says looking over towards Ceri's face. He walks into the clear path still thick mist. Gracefully dissolving in different parts of the forest. Ceri's face begins shed tears down her face, even though the trio cannot see her eyes. The love blood potion injected by Amelia has infected her train of thought. Enraged, Ceri makes the wind pick up all around the forest. Vines on the trees begin come alive, moving, stretching, throughout the forest. Some of the trees begin to grow even bigger from the roots bursting from the wet ground.

Ceri hearing those words of Tim marriage, thinks they are hidden in the castle of the House of Cynfor. Her mind is struck with revenge of confronting Princess Nia and Tim. She believes that Tim was supposed to give her love forever.

"I will kill them both, I will have my revenge. I will end the lives of every member of the House of Cynfor. If it's the last thing I do," Ceri says enraged. Mother Mary and Hynwyn try their best to explain, looking back noticing Stratford has disappeared. He left them in the wrath of the Fairy Watcher.

Knowing they could be killed instantly by the forest coming alive.

Ceri's face inside of the coat of arms disappears, leaving only the coat of arms on the tree trunk. She morphed into the four headed to the castle of Cynfor. Her plans, to bring the forest with her, taking down the unbreakable curtain wall which is exactly what Stratford wanted. His plan will not be complete, allowing the House of Diablo Arches to invade the castle all at once. The forest is making so much noise, each tree is stretching towards the castle. The path where Mother Mary and Hynwyn are standing is closing by the minute. They both head towards a tunnel which leads underground. It was a escape route for Princess Nia to leave the castle in case the day ever came for the House of Cynfor to save their race by sending her away.

"Mary, there is a tree with a blue heart that illuminates from it. We must find it immediately! This tunnel leads underground. It will take us back to the castle, follow me," Hynwyn says. The both ride their horses to a certain part of the forest. The wind continues to blow strong, while mist blocking their vision makes it hard for them to find. The rain pour even harder from above. Mary's red dress magically turns back from the red dress Stratford made for her back to her 21st century clothes she was wearing back at Tenby. As the continue riding, Hynwyn noticed blue streams of light, glowing coming from a section of the forest. Mary and Hynwyn ride their horses and notice a blue heart on a dark brown tree, with white spots. As they get close, they both can see a blue heart illuminating. Blinking on and off slowly as it fades in and out on the bark of the huge tree.

"This is it!" Hynwyn says as he walks over to the trees which are moving slowly. He takes his hand and presses it gently onto the tree with the right amount of pressure. A path of light appear below their feet. Outlining a large box, the size of an ordinary room in a home. Hynwyn notices behind them, tons of trees moving towards them. Large thumping sounds of the same beast that tried to kill Tim while he was in the forest is coming their way. The ground below sinks down to an angled driveway making a ramp that leads into a circle tunnel below the ground. Little do they know war is waiting for them as soon as they arrive back.

As they ride into the opening of the lowered path. Hynwyn turns around noticing a large dragon leaping towards them both trying to kill him. The mouth of the dragon is huge, but Hynwyn's long blade slides through the side of the mouth dragon. The dragon beast shoots a small amount of fire out of it's mouth. Hynwyn using his Scorpus claw shields himself from the dragon's fire. Without the beast knowledge, three large trees come from the side of the dragon. Tree branches and vines cocoon the entire dragon within seconds. Hynwyn on his horse shoots down into the tunnel behind Mother Mary as the ground begins to lift back. Sounds of the dragon in complete agony. The ground completely shuts off any light from above their heads but keeping them safe from the forest destroying everything above ground.

The moisture is thick down in the tunnel. Pitch black to be exact. Hynwyn searching for something to make a torch with. ***"Fymru nacht spell,"*** Mary whispers. Her mother Lily has taught her how to make fire using an old ancient spell from the House of Hartwell. Only females from the House can summon such power if they ever used the 1st Galon. A secret her son Tim never knew yet. Hynwyn looks at Mary with one of her arms covered in light-pink flame.

"Mother of God, how do you know such magic," Hynwyn asking Mary. "In time you will know more about the Galon, but for now we need to get out of this place. Which way do we go?" Mary replying back. The path they ride through is made from hard dirt. Reinforced with iron to hold it's shape over the ages.

"Somehow I truly believe Selwyn's Chancer is becoming

more alive even without Stratford's knowing," Mary says heading through the underground passage. They both can still hear the earth moving above. Mary thinks to herself about how Ceri has completely lost it, when they saw her earlier. A distant light peaks ahead from the tunnel from afar. The horse of Jupiter that Mary is riding is snorts, sensing danger in the tunnel. The horse senses can feel someone else in the tunnel.

A goblin named *Phylip Prysorwen* is waiting for them to come further in the tunnel. His favorite food is horses, even though he hasn't has one in a long time.

"Come my guests, come give

me what I want," Prysorwen says. He will not let them pass until they give up their horses. Prysorwen hates light. His body is the color green. Warts are covering his shoulder on his upper torso, but has smaller legs. Phylip Prysorwen can only walk with his arms with his hairy first that help him throughout the tunnel. The stench from his body smells like old milk. He never like water, or washing one bit. His hair used to be blond, but is almost dark brown-black from the dirt and fungus growing from it. Prysorwen has elf shaped ears and sharp teeth, many of them are missing or broken off from tooth decay. He doesn't wear a shirt, only black cargo pants that stop at his knees. His leather strap boots on his feet are so worn, his dirty toes stick from the front of them.

Prysorwen used to be part of the House of Diablo Arches, but after his body was deformed from sleeping with a witch in the outer region. He was locked up in the dungeon, then he was ordered to dig the tunnel and a small room area for him to remain there. His only purpose was to maintain the tunnel incase Princess Nia ever needed to escape.

Phylip Prysorwen moves by animal instinct. He continues to demand his new guest for their horses as he slides over to another part of the tunnel fixing and repair it right in front of them unexpectedly. Hynwyn look at Mary and raises his eyebrows. They both think Phylip Prysorwen is out of his mind from seclusion in the tunnel. They both continue to watch him move throughout the tunnel fixing different parts of the iron braces and locks. He leaves multiple different tools in different areas of the tunnel, due to his short memory span.

Prysorwen keeps a dirty tan cloth in his pocket, using it to squeeze the dirt from underneath his finger nails every time he finished a segment of the tunnel. Mary raises her hand which is still illuminated from the *Fymru nacht spell*. The light-pink fire annoys Prysorwen holding his hand in front of his eyes, blocking the fire illumination.

"Fire, fire, get away, fire, leave fire be, leave fire away," Prysorwen says with his high-pitch voice. He notices more once water leakage in another part of the tunnel beside him. Mother Mary taps Hynwyn on the shoulder pointing towards the side of Prysorwen pants. There is a scratched away House of Diablo Arches coat of arms which is almost faded away completely.

Mother Mary knowing they don't have much time. Tries to speed things along by informing Prysorwen that they need to pass. Prysorwen stubborn in his own way, since the only food down there are the rats they manage to find their way from the castle into the tunnel passageway.

"No pass, give me those horse, I will let you pass then. Only if horses I keep." Prysorwen says. He demands them to give him something that he doesn't even own. Mary not feeling his offer, makes a proposition of her own.

"Look you, we need to pass now. Why do you keep blocking us from going on our way," She says. Phylip Prysorwen ignoring them, continues working on the tunnel as if he didn't hear what she said. Even though he did. "Only Princess Nia tell me what to do. Only Princess Nia allowed to travel through tunnel. No one allowed to travel through tunnel, only Princess Nia. Prysorwen says with his sporadic way of speaking. Jupiter's horse instincts come into play, both horses eyes begin to charge with electricity as if they are about to kill him. Prysorwen is frightened by the horses eyes, his taste buds go from hungry to not hungry at all. He begins to change his mind, deciding to let his guest pass. Mary liking the horses taken charge, she begins to pet the side of the horse thanking him for helping them. Prysorwen jumps back to the side of the tunnel when they go by. Prysorwen accidently breaks one of the brackets to one a long metal beam holding part of the tunnel together. Water splashes all over him, which make him paranoid, his instincts believes that he will be punished for not fixing the brackets. He jumps up to his feet with his clothes soaken wet. Attending to any part of the broken bracket that needs fixing. Mary and Hynwyn pass by leaving Phylip Prysorwen to tend what he has broken. Mother Mary and Hynwyn Reese continue down the path laughing at what they just encountered. They never met such a foolish and crazy goblin-type creature in their life before.

Both of them finally make it to the end of the tunnel. Leading to a circular iron door with twenty-three locks on it. Mother Mary looks over towards Hynwyn with her eyes wide. "So how do we plan on getting in, there are so many locks?" Mary says. Hynwyn jumps off his horse walking over to the doorway. He examines each lock carefully. Using his Scorpus claw, he snaps the first one with ease. Mary looks over toward him with amazement. She doesn't have magic strong enough to break Cynforian metal.

"I don't think I ever would of thought of that first." Mary smiling. Hynwyn continues to break each one of the huge locks. Each one has the House of Cynfor senate coat of arms on them, since it was their idea for the tunnel for Princess Nia's safety.

"On the other side of the wall, there should be a hidden room leading underneath the main bailey near the main building of the castle. We will have to run down inside the *Snowyn chamber,* gather all of the supplies we can from one of the utility rooms. There is only once place we can survive in the outer regions of the Death of Ages. Until we can find a safer route back up to the higher regions of Selwyn's Chancer," Hynwyn says. He breaks the last lock on the circular iron doorway. With his human had he waves for Mary to stand back as he used his Scorpus Claw to pry open the doorway.

Unexpectedly, smoke begins to come stream into the tunnel catching Mary's attention right away. She quickly points down at Hynwyn's feet. The pressure blows the door completely off the large metal hinges to the door.

"BOOOM!"

The door slams past them, almost killing them both as they duck down. Mother Mary and Hynwyn get back on their horses walking though the destruction. Hynwyn jumps off his horse when inside noticing the *Snowyn chamber* is not full of ice. The entire place is burning on fire in certain spots. Everything is completely destroyed. Black smoke fills the chamber as Mary and Hynwyn look at the aftermath. Both of them are wondering what happened, but they can only think of one answer. The Diablo Arches. All of the dead spirits are screaming for to let free, Their cells are burnt to a crisp while the prisoners inside are unharmed.

    Mary uses her magical **Wyntearia**

spell. Her lips blows wind throughout the *Snowyn chamber,* extinguishing the fire for them to ride through. Hynwyn jumps back on Jupiter's horse, heading outside to safely. "How did they get in here?" Mary says to Hynwyn as he shrugs his shoulders, but thinking the Fairy Watcher must of knocked down one of the curtain walls for the Diablo Arches to raid the castle grounds. "Even though the House of Cynfor where smarter and larger by size. It looks like they have been completely wiped out," Hynwyn says. Mother Mary turns around not hearing the horses, they have turned themselves into small Emosiwn Melyn diamond chess pieces on the ground. She picks them up, tucking them into her back pocket of her blue jeans.

"Someone purposely destroyed the *Snowyn Chamber*," he says. While the continue riding down another huge hallway leading to the outer doors of the dungeon. Facing the west Gates of Death in the mist of the action, Hynwyn asks Mary a question he's been thinking. He looks over towards her with her back on the stone wall looking outside into the main bailey which is covered in forest. "It looks like Ceri has made her way in," she says. Bodies of dead Cynfor dragons from all ranks are laying everywhere. Hynwyn knows something is very wrong with this picture.

"How are you able to breath the air of the Death of Ages, where you given the Gwenwyna potion like I was by Darron and Darryn?" Hynwyn says on subject. Even speaking their name makes his blood boil from betrayal.

"I am not sure, all I remember I was painting in my room back in Wales. The next thing I know, I feel a hard thump on the back of my head. After that, I remember seeing my feet drag against the floor of this castle. Carried by the Gatekeepers to the Carantoc Gladiator games to meet Bledri and Tomes," She explains. "Only the House of Scorpus has the capability to send living humans from the reality world," She continues. "I see," Hynwyn replies.

Out of the corner of their eyes, they notice multiple shadows appearing beneath an archway through the stone wall from the lower bailey. They both hear voices that begin to speak.

"Remove all of the dead bodies and kill the rest of the wounded," Lylock says.

"That is the voice Lylock," Hynwyn whispers over Mary. They are inspecting the damage making sure the area is secure. Mary and Hynwyn jump back to hide out of their site while multiple Diablo Arches on their black horses riding through the main bailey. Some of them are pulling dead bodies into the center to burn in the pyre they made. Baron Milwr walks from behind his father Lylock with a pleased grin on his face. Finally conquering the land that has been ruled by the House of Cynfor for ages. The forest has completely knocked down the Gates of Death, but hasn't grown anywhere else in the castle. Mary and Hynwyn continue to watch the Diablo Arches with their burning arrow stretched towards Bledri and Tomes who are shackled by their necks and feet. They are badly beatened with cuts. Except for two Cynfor dragons who are walking with the House of Diablo Arches, unharmed.

"They are Fyanicrum, Jupira, Derilyn, and Geulia. Third in-line to the throne. They must of betrayed

Bledri and Tomes. Everyone knew they both wanted the hand of marriage from Princess Nia. I guess this is their revenge," Hynwyn whispering over to Mary. Fyanicrum takes his large foot and kicks the face of Bledri. Making their entire body fall back to their side on the ground.

"Who is your leader now?" Fyanicrum says. His lionface Jupira grins while they cause pain to their prior rules. They are wearing huge necklaces of pink and yellow Emosiwn Melyn diamonds coronets which keep them safe around Baron Milwr. Lylock walks over to the side of the fallen kings with his hands on his sides. He points towards Fyanicrum to execute their rulers in good faith. For sparing their lives, they will be allowed to live if they show this special measure of good faith.

Fyanicrum and Jupira walk over to Bledri and Tomes with their large blades in one hand. Fyanicrum looks down at the face of Bledri with teeth missing and blood coughing out of his mouth. He raises his large blade in the air shining off the morning sun. His sword slices though Bledri and Tomes heads at once sending their body rolling over to the wall. Fyanicrum and Jupira walk over picking their heads up like trophies into the air.

"You see my lord, we mean business," Fyanicrum says with huge smile on his face. Jupira looks over to his dragon head on his body and laughs. When they turn around, Lylock and Baron Milwr aren't looking at them as allies anymore. They are disgraced they could do such a thing. No honor. It was a test for Lylock. Either way, he was going to be kill them. Lylock wanted to see for himself the untrustworthy race they have become.

"So I guess this means you are like Darron and Darryn, trade your own king in eh?" Baron says. Fyanicrum and Jupira, Derilyn, and Geulia haven't noticed that vines from the forest are about to grab them from behind. In a instant, the vines drag them back towards the curtain wall. Pulling their bodies up the wall as the dangle in the air. Swinging left to right like a vintage clock from side to side. Mother Mary and Hynwyn look on with amazement. A lightning strike comes from the sky, shooting down like a comet smashing into the ground with dirt and debris flying all over the place. It's Stratford, he has comes to check up on the progress of their raid into the castle. Stratford made sure to wear his pink and yellow Emosiwn Melyn diamond coronet around his neck. He wanted to say a few words to the last of the last royal Cynforians.

"Did you really think we would keep you alive, you aren't House of Diablo Arches material, both of you are too big in height anyway,"

Stratford taunting the Cynfor dragons. Without looking back, Stratford points backwards to Baron Milwr to come closer. He looks towards the opening through the damages Gates of Death which leads down a narrow mid-size path of the destroyed Last Fairy Maze Forest. Ceri, he Fairy Watcher appears on one of the large trees that is slumped inside of the main bailey. "If it isn't the trustworthy fairy to come check up on us," Stratford says to Ceri. "I have destroyed the curtain wall like you asked master," She says. Fyanicrum and Jupira hanging upside down, knowing their lives are going to end before they know it. "Baron, use your voice of destruction. Please end their miserable lives. They bore me." Stratford says yawning with sarcasm.

Baron Milwr walks in front of Fyanicrum and Jupira who are begging for their lives. He yanks the coronets from around their necks from both of the traitors. Mary pulls out the horse chess pieces from her back pocket. Giving one of them to Hynwyn to hold near their ears for if they don't, they would die from Baron Milwr's life killing voice.

Baron stands ready. Stratford walks up to Fyanicrum, Jupira, Derilyn, and Geulia asking one last question before he lets Baron kill them.

"Where is the location of this world you have hidden from my senses, where Princess Nia and Tim? Tell me now!" Stratford demanding answers. "You should of asked before you tricked up!" Fyanicrum says spitting in Stratford's face. Knowing their lives are ended anyway, they refuse to talk as they dangle upside down on the curtain wall. Stratford smacks the hell out of all of them, then waves his hand towards Baron to end their lives immediately.

"**ROARRRRRRRR!!!!!!!!!!!!!**"

Baron screams out which deadly octaves smashing their bodies against the stone wall like Welsh bread. "Those traitors, now it's up to you to find Princess Nia and Tim, I have bailed you out the last time, you don't want to see yourselves like them do you?" Stratford making death threats towards the House of Diablo Arches.

One of the Diablo Arches in command brings a scroll to Lylock who hands it immediately to Stratford. "Is this the scroll of Charun, he looks down at the Welsh dactylic hexameter writing scroll, noticing the first wish has a burned line through it. Indicating it has already been used.

"Two wishes are left? This might come to some use, when I have time to restore order in the Death of Ages." Stratford whispering to himself. He orders Lylock and Baron Milwr to head towards the outer regions to begin mining the Emosiwn Melyn Diamonds once more. Stratford vanishes in thin air, while the House of Diablo Arches head towards the outer regions leaving only a few Diablo Arches to watch the grounds.

Mary and Hynwyn plans have now changed. The Death of Ages are now completely controlled by House of Diablo Arches. Hynwyn knows there is only one way to end this tragedy. "There is only a few more royal houses in the Selwyn's Chancer who have chosen to live in the outer regions of the Death of Ages. One of them are the *House of Vonixrians* who control the train of souls that arrive to the Gates of Death each year. We have to follow the tracks to their region," He says. Both of them run back up to the spiral staircase inside the spiral turrent for a few loose supplies, including Hynwyn own blade and battle axe. They sneak through the hallways all they through abandoned hallways through the colosseum. When they reach outside of the castle, where the river Styx and the Vonixrians train tracks meet.

Mary pulls the horse chess pieces from her pockets tosses them onto the ground. In a flash, Jupiter hoses grow back up to normal size. They ride away without alarming the Diablo Arches who remained back at the castle.

"We will have to make it to the never-ending **Cliff of Wmfre.** We can summon a Trydan dragon to fly over the **Sky of Wymfreya** to the mountains of the fallen wizards from Windsor. This might be the only way they can get to defeat the Diablo Arches and save Princess Nia and Tim." Hynwyn says. Knowing the newlyweds are unaware of what happened to her race. Hynwyn Reese and Mother Mary ride through to the far ends of the outer regions toward the *Cliff of Wmfre*. Mary worries for her only son.

As day turns into night, Hynwyn can hear howls from ancient wolves who thrive around the area.

"Not even the House of Vonixrians would go to the cliffs. They fear the wizards from Berkshire, England. They use to live under the

Windsor Bridge, before they where doomed to the Death of Ages for using their magic," Hynwyn says. Jupiter's horses snort many times near some of the trees ahead of them. The horses move their heads from left and right sensing movement above in the trees. Dawn over the sky, in a fast way across the horizon.

Light shines through the forest revealing a tall female figure sitting on a large brand in the trees above. Hynwyn ready for defend himself and Mary notice that the huge woman is Goddess Venus. She has come to inform them what the future has in stored for them, for they must be prepared to fight for their ultimate survival if they continue towards the never-ending *Cliff of Wmfre*.

TIM HARTWELL: Open Your Heart Trilogy (Books 1-3)

The Bluebells Forest

In a sacred and unknown part of the Death of Ages lies the Bluebells forest. Some of the most beautiful trees surrounding Cynfornia. The Bluebells flowers sway in the with their Hyacinthoides non-scripta. They are bulbous perennial plants that make the forest seem like Gods took a little extra time to make them. Cynfornia is perfect place to raise an heir of the House of Cynfor in Princess Nia's Mind. The white carriage rolls through the forest, down a dirt parallel road which leads to an abandoned castle built just for Princess Nia and her newlywed husband Tim Hartwell. When they birth a child a magical army of Cynfornia will appear from behind a waterfall of the castle to protect the new kingdom of Cynfornia.

    Tim looks around, falling in love with what he sees. Princess Nia holds Tim's hand. The white carriage breaks out of the forest into the circular driveway. On the right-hand side of the castle. They can hear the waterfall behind the castle, which is filled with enough fish for them to eat forever. The forest surrounding them are filled with plenty of animals for them to hunt. The Bluebells forest location was built specifically for this moment. It has been abandoned for centuries, waiting for Princess Nia who never ages until she is married. Once she exchanges her vows Princess Nia will finally be able to grow older with the love of her life. Her age will match her Tim at eleven and a half years old. She is more happy than ever to be able to become a woman.

    The carriage stops in front of the **Castle of Cynfornia**. The door open up allowing Tim to step out. He turns around and holding his beautiful wife's hand. Her long bridal dress slides behind her as they look around, feeling the warmth from the sky above. Listening to the birds sing in the warm fall wind.

By the end of next spring, both of them will spend their 12th birthday together for the very first time. Tim wants to give her a quick kiss on the cheek. So she wraps a lock of her hair behind her ear so Tim can kiss her sweet skin. His lips touch her cheeks as soft as can be. She wraps her arms around Tim holding him tight, then proceed up the steps to enter the *Castle of Cynfornia* for the very first time. Walking up the steps, they both notice how the steps are white marble with not one dirt stain on them, protected by the magic her grandfather Miniver and Cynhafar had blessed her with.

They continue up the steps, when two lovely white doves fly right in front of them, making Nia smile from ear to ear. Her blonde hair is shining from the sun. Her blue eyes sparkle with every twist of her face. Somehow, music from a harp box playing inside of the castle catching their attention. Both of them run inside into the foyer noticing a stairwell which leads up both sides of the large inner foyer. A fountain of water is in the middle statue of Goddess Venus and her helpers in the middle. The helpers are holding vases that pour water into the fountain. The body of Goddess Venus lays in the center with the appearance of taking a bath, a true symbol of mythology right in front of them.

The melody is music is actually not coming from a music box. The beautiful sound is coming from the large pink and yellow Emosiwn Melyn Diamond Chandelier above them. Making the sweetest melodies of joy for them to hear.

"Cynfornia is more magical than I've ever dreamed, my beautiful husband," Princess Nia says. Tim leads into the fireplace cloister, where a large fire is burning for them to enjoy.

The cloister overlooks tall windows overlooking the middle ward below them. The ward has private apartments with completely finished rooms for them to raise kids in when they come of age.

The private apartments is connected to a gateway that leads to the *White Tower*. A hoist leads all the way up the tower with height that is eleven meters shorter than the Elizabeth Tower in London, overlooking the horizon for as far as they can see in the Death of Ages. At this very moment, both Princess Nia and Tim Hartwell are worry free about young lives.

Night falls around the Bluebells forest with a large amount of altocumulus clouds that are covering the sky, but leaving just enough light for the full moon to shine into the Royal Deanery. They both enjoy their first meal in their new castle. Princess Nia is sitting right next to Tim so she can feel the warmth of his skin. She knows they can't have any intimacy but she for sure wants to feel his body warmth next to hers.

Tim cuts some more of the deer meat from the fresh kill he hunted while in the forest. He used a bow and arrow from the weaponry ward on the first floor of the apartments. The bell in the *White Tower* is made is a exact replica from bell the Cynforian chapel. It rings eleven times marking their age. After that, it will only ring once a year on their birthday. Both of them rush to their master bedroom for the very first time. The notice the dishes have magically clean themselves and parked back into the cabinets in the kitchen area of the Royal Deanery. Walking down the halls, they both laugh and giggle making their way back into their master bedroom private apartment. Both of them decide the castle is too big to look tonight, from such a long journey through to the Bluebells forest.

Once Tim opens the master bedroom, he notices the Shield of Aeneas leaning against the bed with the Book of Hartwell resting on top of his messenger bag on their bed. A white canopy with linen drapes dangling from the top of the bed dance with the slight wind from the windows. Princess Nia walks over to her personal closet filled with luxurious clothes. Each section is color coated and including fancy heels in different sizes for when she grows older. Princess Nia puts both of her hands on her face for this is everything she could of ever dream of.

"Is all this for me?" Princess Nia whispers with joy. She is more excited than she has ever. Luxurious jewelry begins to float inside of her closet right in front of her. All types of beautiful pendants, charms, necklaces, rings, and gold to silver. Even Cynforian Silhouette pieces that have been carved in the middle of some of them.

Tim is standing behind her while she enjoys every bit of her new life, including himself. Princess Nia turns around and faces Tim loving the life she has always dreamed of. The power of the ***"Love of Venus,"*** has even forgiven Tim for what he has done to her father Miniver and Cynhafar. They knew that their sons Bledri and Tomes would never of kept their promise if they day ever came. Tim looks directly in her eyes wiping her tears away. He kisses her on her cheek, then sits down watching her try on some of the clothes before it gets too late. Her body begins swirling around trying on everything that she possibly can. Tim goes over to his closet and sees royal clothing that ranges from almost a thousand years to the present in British and or Welsh culture. He is now a Prince of Cynfor, also the carrier of the magical Galon of Wales.

Midnight approaches, both of them jump into bed in their night clothes. A full moon in perfect view out the window from their royal bedroom as they watch together until they fall asleep.

Night flows into dawn, turning into morning twilight. God's rays flow through the entire room in the morning. Tim wakes up first noticing that breakfast has magically appears in their room. His favorite Welsh bacon to laver bread, hot tea, eggs and some crystal wine glasses filled with water, and juice for them to drink. "Good morning honey, should we visit the waterfall today?" Tim says. Princess Nia is just getting up, putting the slippers on beneath her feet. She walks over to the breakfast table next to her husband smiling at each other. The relax in the room not even worried on bit. She feels excited for Tim to do exactly what he wants to do. Both of them walks across the walk into the showers where natural flowing water goes through the castle straight from the waterfall. Both of them get ready and they head outside to the waterfall to hear the sounds of nature and to see what else this magical kingdom has to offer.

Where the Bluebells forest connects to the waterfall, they notice the same white unicorn coming out of the forest drinking some of the water. Unafraid of them. Tim wraps his arm around Nia as they just lay under the sun for hours. Tim brought a picnic basket from the castle filled with fruits and vegetables for them to snack on. Princess Nia grabs some of the strawberries and feeds her husband some of them. Then, the white unicorn comes right over to them, for it wants some of the sweet fruit and lettuce to eat. Tim gives Nia some of the lettuce holds it directly in her palm for the unicorn to eat. The beautiful white unicorn at first steps back, then, steps forward eating from her hand. Nia looks back at Tim with a golden smile as the unicorns begs for some of the fruit in the basket as well. "I guess he is pretty hungry," Tim says. Nia leans down and looks underneath the horse for a second. "It looks like it a girl from here," She says laughing. The unicorn runs off, back into the Bluebells forest. "I wonder how the unicorn found us?" Tim says curiously.

"All living things in this forest can breath the air, but that horse is the last magical unicorn on earth and in Selwyn's Chancer," She says. Tim gets up and jumps into the water and begins to swim in the cool water. Princess Nia jumps into the water after him as they wrestle a bit, having fun underneath the shining weather, with a Single-cell Cumulonimbus capillatus incus cloud in the sky.

The magical power of the Galon inside of Tim, and the **"Voice of Venus"** inside of Princess Nia together, has made both of their emotions wild for each other. Tim looks into her eyes, never wanting to see any other woman in his life. For it's only the second day in Cynfornia, and both of them have almost completely forgot about what they left behind them.

A few days pass, the sky goes from blue to orange while lightning strikes in the air while they where enjoying another day relaxing at the waterfall. Rain begins to pour so they both head back to he castle for the rest of the day. Both of them dry off and head down to the library. There are books that reach high into the ceiling wit a ladder to reach the highest ones.

Princess Nia picks out a few that she likes, some of them are about becoming a mother and nursing children. Others are about woman responsibilities when she starts to ovulate. Both of them are side by side reading for a few hours near the fireplace. The rains sounds pouring on top of the castle are somewhat relaxing. Tim looks over at her and puts his fingers through her hair. He holds her around the waist for he have never felt such love for someone they way he does for. Tim is beginning to remember how is father left his family at such an early age. In his heart he can feel that he wants to be the best father he can be. Princess Nia still reading stops, and begins to speak.

"Do you love me honey, for I love you, more than life, I hope you always remember that," She says. Tim kisses her on her cheek and walks over to the fire, tossing another log in the fire, even though he doesn't have to. He whispers his *Firewyn spell* igniting the light-blue flame around his arms. Princess Nia looks back at him with her eyes wide wondering what he is doing.

"Humans to be able to control

fire, who would of ever thought." Tim says. Princess Nia looks at him staring at his arms while he looks over to the fireplace. "My love, let's make sure we keep things fresh while together. I never want you to feel that you don't want to be around me," She says. Princess Nia goes to reach for his hand that are still on fire. Tim quickly says *"Firewyn"* distinguishing the fire wrapped around hands and wrist. "Honey you almost burned yourself, be careful," Tim says. "I was just playing around, I knew you would put the flame out," She says as the day begins to wind down into late afternoon. For the rest of the night, they place chess together, silently falling asleep.

For the next few months, Tim and Nia spend every morning and afternoon going outside carving each other out of marble. Both of them trying the best that they can, for Nia knows she can use her magic to straighten things out. As more days go by leading into Halloween, they both play trick or treat with each other and baking candy with each other.

The night before Christmas while Nia is sleeping. Tim goes out in the forest and plucks lots of pink roses from the forest forming a bouquet for his lovely wife. When she wakes up Christmas morning he has many gifts wrapped for her. Together, the decorated the large Christmas tree in the library with all sorts of decorations. Princess Nia used her magic power lift a huge pine tree from the forest bringing it right into the library. When they are ready to open each other presents, Nia hands him his first present. Tim opens it up and notices that she has made a necklace for him with a picture of her engraved on the metal. The necklace has thirty separate three-carat Emosiwn Melyn Diamond going around a golden necklace that she made herself. Tim is ready to show her the bouquet he designed for her in the shape of a heart. She looks at it and gets really emotional. One this very day, they are more happy then ever spending their first Christmas together.

On New Years, they both sit in

the *White Tower*. Tim uses his *Firewyn spell* to shoot down towards fireworks on the circular driveway. They look out the *White Tower*, fireworks go off for about an hour as they hold each their hands, watching the fireworks explode in all sorts of shapes in the sky. The very last one, Princess Nia waves her hand in the air which makes it spell out "I love you," in the night sky.

The first day of the new year, snow falls from the sky. Tim and Nia spend so much times together during the winter making snowmen and snow angels in the snow.

Later that day, they both notice the white unicorn coming out of the snow forest to play with them for a bit. Both of them race around as the unicorn hangs around for a bit, then dashing back off into the Bluebells forest covered in snow.

In February, Valentine's Day rolls around and Tim tries his best to make sure this is the best day she has ever had. When Princess Nia wakes up, she notices there are rose petals that lead out of the room, down the hallway, through the gateway into the front of the castle. The rose petals are directed towards the right as she follows them leading to the back of the castle facing the waterfall. Tim has set up a fire outside with a table that has hot cocoa and cookies for her to eat. He cut pieces of paper into a homemade letter.

"Go ahead open it," Tim says. She sits down with anticipation not sure what's inside of the letter. She opens the letter slowly to find a poem written by Tim.

Nia,

On this very day,
I love you more than ever.
Forever I will stay by
your side now Kiss me baby!

Your love,
TIM

She jump out of her seat pouncing on Tim as he falls back into his chair. Her hair dangles down. She uses her right hand pulling back her hair from dangling in Tim's face. She gives Tim one of the longest sentimental kisses on the lips since they been there. Nia loves is growing for Tim. She know their 12th birthday will be coming up very soon in April.

"Can you believe our birthdays are almost here, we will be twelve years old finally," She says. Princess Nia begins to kiss Tim aggressively, knowing she is not supposed to, for she has never kissed a boy until she married him. They both get up knowing they must follow the order of marriage exactly as planned and not a day sooner. Both of them enjoy their hot cocoa and laver bread as they watch the waterfall still flowing into the lake which is frozen.

"Thank you for giving me such a wonderful first Valentine's Day. You don't even know how many times Fyanicrum and Jupira, or Derilyn and Guelia tried to give me flowers and gifts on Valentine's Day, but I would never except them. They weren't worthy of my love. Do you believe everything happens for a reason?" She asks, for she is dying to know what he thinks about life and coincidences. "I believe everything happens for a reason. I mean, I would of never dreamed of living a life in a magical land like

Cynfornia. Being married at eleven years of age to the most beautiful woman in the world. So the answer to your question? Yes, I believe everything happens for a reason. I have met some of the most legendary people in such a small time frame, from Goddess Diana, Brutus of Troy and Venus, but..." Tim says stopping abruptly to tell her about something which has been bothering him.

"There is another girl from my school back where I comes from. She really liked me but now she is lost forever," He says. Nia kisses him, putting her finger over his mouth. She knows it's hard for him. The rest of the night they continue to hold each other while they sit in front of the fireplace all night back in the castle. She desperately wants to make things easy on him. Both of them thinking about the next five years in Cynfornia.

During the night, Tim wakes up and hears voices from all the way down i the foyer to the front of the castle. He gets out of bed while Princess Nia is still sleep. Walking downstairs he notices there is a large painting on the side of the wall which wasn't there when they first arrived.

Tim looks at the painting above him noticing a picture of the Crystal Dynasty that Brutus of Troy was mentioning during his training. There are eight people in the oil painting in alphabetical order. Aeneas of Troy, Brutus's son Albanactus, the first roman emperor Augustus, Brutus of Troy, the might Ceaser of Rome, Emperor Claudius, Brutus' younger son Kamber, and Paris of Troy. Tim Hartwell looks at the picture totally amazed for it seems they where standing side by side while the painter illustrates their royal stances. Tim towards the bottom right hand corver of the painting to see the name Federico Barocci signed in a golden ink. "How can this be?" Tim ponders to himself as yawning from exhaustion. At this very moment, he knows the Goddesses Venus, and Diana has something to do with this. Not thinking anymore about it, he runs back upstairs to more sleep and let destiny run its magical course.

Back on the other side of the Death of Ages, Hynwyn Reese and Mary are still standing in front of Goddess Venus. Both of them are wonderful what she is about to say. Venus jumps down from off the long tree branch above them. When she land, due to her height, the ground rumbles a bit. Venus turns around, where some of the deer which live in the forest can feel her presence.

She looks at one of them and pets the fur on the side of one of the female deer. Mother Mary more anxious than ever, begins to speak about why she is there. Before she can utter a few words, Venus puts her hand in the air and points towards the moon in the sky. When Hynwyn and Mary look up, they notice the moon getting closer and closer to them. The bright sphere in the sky, passes through a Cumulus arcus roll cloud from above. The moon's body pushes through the cloud which leads into another set of Cumulonimbus calvus clouds after that. With their eyes still looking up, the moon as it descends towards their location begins to shrink in shape.

The more the moon gets closer, the more the moon take shape of a woman. As moon rubs through the top of the trees, the body of the moon is in full shape of woman who illuminating through the trees. The glowing woman glides down the branches and lands right next to Venus. The moon has taken shape of Goddess Diana. She is wearing a beautiful white, dress, while Venus has a linen light-purple dress on. Both of them are wearing beautiful sheer scarfs looking like twins standing next to each other.

Hello you two, I see you are wanting to head towards the never ending cliffs,: Diana says. There is only a small problem with you wanting to travel there," Diana speaking as she takes her left hand, taking the illumination from her body. She uses her fingers to throw magical dust in the air, that travels through the branches and headed back up into the sky. As the dust goes through the Cumulonimbus calvus cloud, a large lightning burst through its mist. The magical dust continues to head upwards in the atmosphere and takes shape of a ring. The rings begins to fill itself in the sky until it completely full looking like a crescent moon.

Hynwyn and Mother Mary look on waiting for them to speak their peace. Goddess Venus and Diana hold each others hands and transports them to the Bluebells forest in Cynfornia, there is something they must see. All of their bodies transport to the circular driveway to the Castle of Cynfornia. Hynwyn and Mary look around at this magical world. Mary notices the air smells a bit different from the Death of Ages. A million times fresher.

"I'm not going to take you inside and disturb what must be, I have brought you here to show you that, this is the future. Without Cynfornia, there will be no future to the people in Selwyn's Chancer. I wanted to show you, that I helped Tim get here Mary, as I did for my son Aeneas to Rome. Imagine if he never reached Latium, where would the world be then?" Diana says.

"I don't think anyone on earth can even muster an answer,"Mother Mary replies.

"I thank you for helping my son, but do you think it was not right for you to interfere with Princess Nia to fall in love with him?" She says. Venus looks at them, and taps Goddess Diana on the shoulder, for no human was ever bold enough to judge her on her motives. Goddess Diana claps her hands sending them to the land of Llyn Cwellyn just before midnight.

All of them are looking at the reservoir moving below them. As the moon reaches between Mynydd Mawr and Snowdon, Charun flows his boat into the water. He rides up to them at a slow pace. Venus looks at Charun and tosses him five ancient coins with Ceaser's face on it. Charun sticking his hand out, tosses the coins in his lower deck. He then turns around and points towards the castle to the House of Scorpus behind him.

"We aren't going there, I just wanted to show you the world, Brutus of Troy found, when he traveled to these lands. There are many parallel worlds on Earth, Some have been found, some have not.

"Hold on, didn't Stratford make Selwyn's Chancer?" Hynwyn says.

"Yes, of course, but little did he know, Brutus of Troy would find a royal House of Scorpus who have the capability to reach the Death of Ages. I hope you see, the train of events unfolding in Selwyn's Chancer. For you son, Tim, must not escape the Death of Ages as of yet," Diana says.

"What about our families Book of Hartwell? I am sure Stratford has something up his sleeve to stop him from getting out," Mother Mary says, brushing her hair back into a ponytail with her hands. That was before, Tim married Princess Nia. Now there is a new prophecy, he will have to defend, or the reality worlds you live in Tenby, will be no more. Stratford's ultimate goal will be to merge both world and destroy making Earth his world." Venus says, as the Planet Jupiter flies into the sky, slowing down near the moon in the sky. Venus points to Mercury arriving around the same time.

"Something is up, the planets are listening. The universe is wanting to know exactly what is going on Mother Earth. We must leave now!" Diana and Venus speaking in unison, sending Mary and Hynwyn back to the Death of Ages outer region. Both of the notice, dawn is breaking over the horizon.

The only difference, Venus and Diana have helped them out, by transporting them to the Cliff of Wmfre, Both of them are astonished by the clouds formations ahead of them. Cirrus floccus, Cirrus radiatus, Cirrus spissatus undulatus, cirrocumulus stratiformis, Cirrus fibratus radiatus clouds are everywhere.

Hynwyn points towards a Altocumulus lenticularis duplicatus clouds which is very far away from the cliff. This must be the Sky of Wymfreya over there. The Wizards of Windsor live there,. Hynwyn using his human hand, pulls out a Scorpus conical horn to summon a Trydan dragon to fly there. With it's small size, her has implanted it within his claw. No one knew he ever had it on him at the castle of the House of Scorpus. "Are you ready to fly?" Hynwyn says, blowing the horn which has such a distinct sound.

"Only the lungs on a Scorpus scorpion can use this instrument." He says, as they look above, noticing the clouds are moving, pushing together like cotton candy. Hynwyn informs Mary, this particular Trydan doesn't stop moving. When the wing gets closer to the edge, they will have to jump for it.

The head of the Trydan dragon makes a fallstreak hole in the altocumulus stratiformis translucidus lacunosus cloud above. Gliding down towards the cliff, Hynwyn and Mother Mary hold hand, jumping off the Cliff of Wmfre into the depths of the Stratocumulus castellanus cumulogenitus cloud. The can't see a thing as the glide over the Cliff of Wmfre. Only by hope from the gusts of wind. Shall they make a safe landing on the wings of an ancient Trydan dragon.

Y Diwedd
(The End)

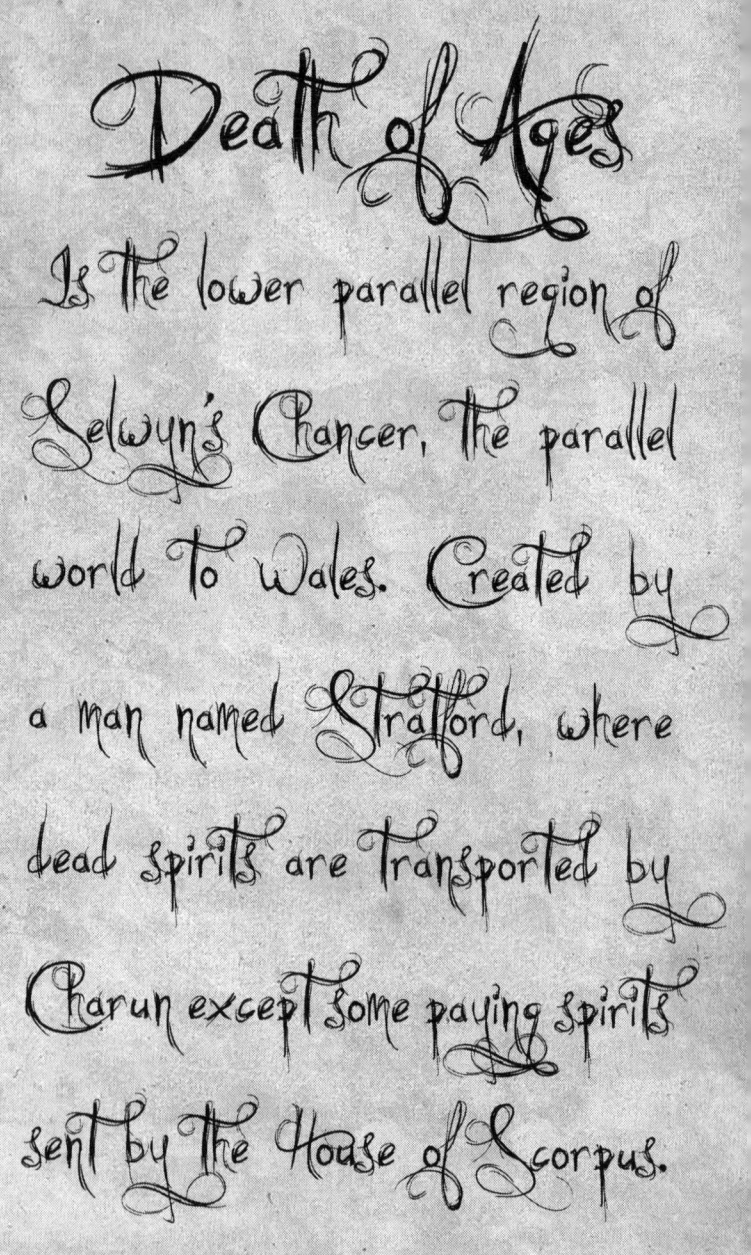

TIM HARTWELL: Open Your Heart Trilogy (Books 1-3)

Death of Ages

Is the lower parallel region of Selwyn's Chancer, the parallel world to Wales. Created by a man named Stratford, where dead spirits are transported by Charun except some paying spirits sent by the House of Scorpus.

Emosiwn Outer Region

Under the earth of mountain Mynydd Mawr lies the Death of Ages. The new rulers to the House of Cynfor, Bledri and Tomes, control the mines to the most precious mineral in Stratford's Selwyn's Chancer, parallel world to Wales. The pink & yellow Emosiwn Melyn diamonds were previously controlled by the ruthless House of Diablo Arches.

Death of Ages

Location: underneath Snowdon
Nant y Betws, Gwynedd, North Wales

TIM HARTWELL: Open Your Heart Trilogy (Books 1-3)

Goddess Diana

Brutus of Troy TIM

Castle to the House of Scorpus

HALL OF JUDGEMENT

CHAMBER
OF GWENWYNA

House of Scorpus

LLYN CWELLYN RESERVOIR

733

TIM HARTWELL: Open Your Heart Trilogy (Books 1-3)

MYNYDD MAWR

SNOWDON MASSIF

ONLY AT TWILIGHT, WILL THE CASTLE OF THE HOUSE OF SCORPUS APPEAR ON THE HORIZON BETWEEN THE RESERVOIR OF LLYN CWELLYN AND THE MOUNTAIN OF MYNYDD MAWR.

- BRUTUS OF TROY

Llyn Cwellyn

LOCATION: NANT Y BETWS, GWYNEDD, NORTH WALES

Stratford

TIM HARTWELL: Open Your Heart Trilogy (Books 1-3)

Coat of Hartwell

(Worn by The House of Hartwell)

736

TIM HARTWELL: Open Your Heart Trilogy (Books 1-3)

Coat of Gwynwell

(Worn by The House of Gwynwell)

Seven Wonders of Wales

SNOWDON
PISTYLL RHAEADR
GRESFORD BELLS
ST. GILES' CHURCH
OVERTON YEW TREES
LLANGOLLEN BRIDGE
ST. WINEFRIDE'S WELL

TIM HARTWELL: Open Your Heart Trilogy (Books 1-3)

Arma

virumque

cano

(I sing of arms and of man - The Aeneid)

739

TIM HARTWELL: Open Your Heart Trilogy (Books 1-3)

Cymru am byth

Welch: Wales forever

740

Made in the USA
Columbia, SC
27 November 2023